For Ella — I hope you enjoy this gentle love story!

Best wishes,

Christine

Kindred Spirits

D1743903

Christine Hornsby was born in North Yorkshire, England and spent her early childhood in the Far East and Buckinghamshire. She was educated in a convent. Deciding on a career in teaching, Christine moved to South Yorkshire training at Scawsby College and then teaching English at a local Secondary school. Still living in South Yorkshire Christine now spends her time swimming, perfecting her French, reading and, of course, writing novels.

Kindred Spirits is her third novel.

Also by Christine Hornsby

Lightning Strike

Man out of Jail

Kindred Spirits

Christine Hornsby

2014

Copyright © 2014 by Christine Hornsby

All rights reserved. This book or any portion thereof may not be reproduced or used in any manner whatsoever without the express written permission of the publisher except for the use of brief quotations in a book review or scholarly journal.

First Published: 2014

ISBN 978-1-291-99673-9

Hornsby Publishing
55 Broughton Road, Bessecarr
Doncaster, South Yorkshire. DN4 7HE

www.christinehornsby.co.uk

Also available on Kindle via Amazon.

Dedication

For my four children: Karl, Debbie, Ashley and Desmond.

Acknowledgements

Thanks to my son Karl and Paul Farley for their technical support and to Terry Chipp for his artistic representation of the novel.

Meet me, my love, meet me, my love
By the low branching juniper tree
O I will meet you there, my love
If no harm comes to me.

Wilfred Watson

Chapter 1

Bethany was about to shower when she heard the dull thud. It occurred to her that their neighbour, Mrs. 'The Snooper' Crooks was giving her Turkish rug a good hiding. Every month, without fail, she'd hang it over the washing line and assault it with the rigor of a sumo wrestler. 'This must be the time,' she thought, stepping into the bath and adjusting the shower head. It was archaic. Its corroding jets dribbled and spat capriciously. 'A bit like my mood swings these days. Mum's right about those!' she thought, snatching her towelling robe off the hook. Then, turbaning her long, red hair she peered into her dressing table mirror. Spots! "Great...just what I **don't** need!" When her toner found its mark, she flinched. That's when, in the mirror's reflection, she saw it -

"Oh, my God!" Bethany's hand moved to her mouth, her chest constricting...She swooned, closing her eyes against the ghostly image on the window, as if by doing so it would be wiped from her mind forever, stop her heart racing and ease the stab of pain that left her gasping. But seeing was believing, wasn't it? There would be an explanation, wouldn't there? Everything was real; everything could be explained. It was scientific. Bethany gripped the edges of her dressing table, her knuckles white as her face. She tried not to think of its last agony. 'But I have to look. I have to!' Drawing in a deep breath she opened her eyes and abandoned herself to the imprint of the bird's outstretched wings and their feathery pattern. Perfect symmetry. The image seemed to stand out in 3D. Its crown and beak were there too, details that came to her like a haunting. "Please don't let it be one of my seagulls!" Then, obeying a call that came like a whisper she moved across to the window. Drawn to the empty sockets where its eyes should have been, she reached out to touch the image but shrank away as if a nerve had suddenly been exposed. Bethany cringed. The unworldly spectre was clouding her reasoning. In an instant she had become a fugitive. But to what? To whom? Her disabled will tried for a come-back...

'This is ridiculous,' she told herself. 'It's only like a finger print...an outline of a seagull, that's all...' but she stepped back, knowing somehow that it was more, more than a vague tracery. The image had an identity...a previous existence and, though mute, in some strange way it seemed to speak to her so that she found herself wanting to understand and embrace its very essence. Bethany's need for human contact was suddenly overwhelming.

"Mum! Mum!"

"What...what is it?" her mother shouted, "I'm busy, Bethany."

"Mum! Come up, quick...quickly!"

"I just hope you haven't got me up here on a wild goose chase!" her mother said when, out of breath from rushing upstairs, she lent against the door jamb. "Whatever's the matter?"

"Look, mum, look!"

"Oh, is that all?" she said, pushing the loose strands of grey hair behind her ears. "You had me worried sick for a moment. It happens. They see the reflection of the outdoors in the window. It's just one of those things."

"Will it be dead?"

"Probably. But try not to take on so. I know you. Get dressed and we'll have a look."

'But look at what exactly?' Bethany thought. 'How can you see something that's almost unreal, a transitory something that weaves in and out of your conscious mind.'

The seagull was lying on the crazy paving beneath her bedroom window. Its legs were drawn up with its white, under feathers fluffing up in the breeze. Bethany picked it up. "I shouldn't! They carry diseases," her mother warned.

Cradling it in her hand she stroked the back of its head. "Not this one...and... oh, Mum! Its heart's still beating."

"I know, but it won't survive. They never do. It's the shock. Look." A speck of blood had congealed at the side of its beak. "The poor thing. It'll have broken its neck. Here," she said, reaching into the back porch for a plastic bag, "best put it in the dustbin."

"No way. it's still alive!"

"Yes, but not for long. Besides, you don't want the cats to get at it. There'll be feathers everywhere."

"God, mum! Nooo! How can you be like that! I'll leave it under the rhododendron bush; it'll be hidden there. It might have a chance...and it could be one of mine, you know..." she said with an anguished look that left Mrs. Mallinson sighing and tutting her way downstairs. "Yes, Bethany, all right, but I do wish you wouldn't get so upset."

Bethany had lived with seagulls all her life. Until now, there had never been anything mysterious about them. She had listened to them squabbling above the roof tops like naughty children, seen them riding the thermals and wondered how they managed to just hang there, so silent, so majestic. Dipping, they would surf roll, their wing tips catching the sunlight: distant sightings. Closer still, she'd see them strutting on the sea wall, unconcerned and happy it seemed to share their space with the tourists. More disturbing of course were the surprise attacks. With a banshee screech they might wing in out of nowhere and snatch the bag of chips out of your hand so that it would be a while before your beating heart settled.

Just last week a pair had decided to roost on her bedroom window sill. Shuffling about, they had jostled for a sure footing until, settled at last, they had begun to preen one another's feathers. She had never seen them so intimately. Well, now she definitely needed to see if both of them turned up again. Taking the stairs two at a time Bethany raced back to her bedroom. She wouldn't have long to wait. The sun was well down. Her mother thought she was crackers of course. 'Well, so what, how could she possibly understand? 'I mean,' Bethany thought, 'who would- and when did her mum ever, anyway!'

Looking for a distraction she tried writing her diary; it didn't work. The light was fading but her eyes were forever drawn to the image. Then came the sharp sting of sadness. She tried putting on the CD her best friend, Ron, had lent her but the words and the music wouldn't take away the uneasy restlessness that swept over her like an unwelcome memory.

"For goodness sake Bethany! Come on down; you can't wait up there all night!" her mother shouted. "Besides, you're not the sort to lie around moping!" True! Being grounded for whatever house rule she might have broken or being cooped up on a foul day was a nightmare. Mooching had never been her style. Some of the other kids seemed to feel comfortable with it though, apparently happy to hang around and chat about this and that: music, clubbing and each other mostly, and of course the dating game. But this was different; this was... well, she just had to wait and see if both seagulls turned up.

"I won't be long." Bethany sank back against her pillows, warmed by the duvet molding to her body. Then, just as she was about to turn on her bedside light, a shadow fell across her window. In a flurry and a cloud of dust a seagull burst onto the sill. Side-stepping to and fro, it finally settled, staring out into the fast fading light. Bethany shivered, wrapping her arms around herself against the cold that suddenly embraced her. And still she waited. Only when the lone seagull began to peck at the window and look at her with its yellow, penetrating eyes, eyes deep with longing, did she accept that her seagull had lost its mate.

'So it's dead. Dead. Dead!' she told herself. But the ghostly image on the window stayed with her. All through the night she tossed and turned; all through the night she wondered why, why such a small death should invade her every thought leaving her restless and unsatisfied.

Chapter 2

Bethany loved the sunshine but just now, in class the next day, it was too strong, too intrusive. Besides, it was sure to bring out her freckles. Swivelling around in her seat, she shielded her eyes like a sailor adrift on the high seas. For a moment the classroom became a dark place of shadowy forms, their silhouettes fuzzy with purple edging. Half asleep after her disturbed night, she yawned and wondered what excuse Ron would have for being late this time. Bethany needed to talk so where was her best friend? Probably in the girl's loo, frantically dragging on the ciggy that had to last till break! Then, like a Fairy Godmother in a mist, she drifted in.

"Swagger bragger's on his way," she said, sliding into the chair beside Bethany.

"About time, and you certainly took yours. Where have you been?" Bethany grimaced. "As if I didn't know!"

"Hm. Anyway, Miss Goody two shoes, what's up? You look like thunder." Bethany rolled her eyes. "Could it be I just needed a friend…you know, one of those people who are always around…to listen maybe!"

"Well, I'm here now and what's with all the sarcasm? Go on then," she insisted," what's up…what?" but the door opened. 'Swagger bragger' made his grand entry.

"All right people," Mr. Dunleavy said, "let's be having you!"

"In your dreams! Ouch!" Ron's elbow had hit home. The teacher's voice carried. Held by his engaging blue eyes, the girls' chatter stopped 'How could I have ever had a crush on him?' she thought. 'He's gross. He's jargonized!' Turning to the front she opened her Debating Society note book.

"You'll love this one, Bethany!" he said, facing the white board. Bethany stuck out her tongue. Daniel Foster, sitting across from her, smiled and shook his head like a disapproving headmaster. 'Another schmuck!' she thought. Flushing and feigning interest, she cupped her chin in her right hand.

Vivisection!

The word jumped out at her. Her heart raced.

"So who's going to be brave enough to take Bethany on?" Bethany scowled. Being singled out was not cool but huffing and puffing would only encourage the rest of them to complain. Still, she couldn't help herself!

"Yeah but why me? Why pick on me, Sir?"

"Because you'll get us all off to a good start. Come on now, Bethany! No one's more passionate about it than you."

Sighing, she gave the teacher her best, 'Thanks a lot!' look.

"Well," she said with a begrudging pout, "nobody in their right mind can possibly go along with it. For a start, it's cruel - *really* cruel!"

"But necessary, *really* necessary!" Daniel's parody brought a titter from the class. Relaxing into his seat he looked her straight in the eye. Bethany wanted to stare him out, but couldn't. Instead, she turned to Ron. "The arrogant sod," she mouthed behind a well positioned hand.

"All I know is," Daniel continued, "you wouldn't be so keen to get on your crusading high horse if a family member was dying for the want of animal research! Take tuberculosis, the new strain -!"

"Is that right?" she snapped. "Then you can tell your so-called heroes on the football pitch to stop spitting for a start. It's not rocket science!"

"All right you two, that's enough! This isn't personal, you know. You're beginning to sound like an old married couple!"

"Yeah...yeah," the others chorused. Bethany was not impressed. Daniel Foster had been winding her up since Junior School. He was a pain, and definitely a schmuck! Incensed, she blundered in. "Yeah yeah, nothing, Sir! And in any case, not all old married couples bicker. That's warped. It's a cliché and it's got whiskers on it!" Mr. Dunleavy's indulgent, watered down smile

6

annoyed her even more. 'How dare he patronise me and, anyway, what did any of them know!' she thought.

Later, lost in the swell of pupils teeming toward the stairwell the two girls headed for the dining hall, the poor man's Macdonald's.

"Save me a place, Beth. I must...you know," Ron said, indicating the girl's loos with a flick of her head. "Then you can tell me what's bugging you!"

Bethany raised her eyebrows. "Hm...no probs," And maybe there wouldn't be, just as long as she could tie her down long enough. Ron was a different kind of girl, a mismatch really but the best friend Bethany ever had. Veronica, Vron, Ron. That was the way her name had evolved. Ever since top infants when they'd revised tapping out sounds she'd been 2nd syllable Ron. Bethany watched her disappearing into a bubbling sea of heads: black to brown; fair to blonde; auburn to mousy; short to long; thin to thick; straight to curly, all bobbing and flowing till the sea threatened to engulf her.

Bethany grinned. Ron was back, popping up like a periscope on the wavy surface of an ocean. Then, using her size 14 on a good day (now going on 16) she waded through, her hefty shoulder and sharp elbow leading the way.

"Hey! Get lost, Ron!"

"Give over!"

"What the hell! Give over, Big Ron!" But Ron would have her way!

In no time at all they were in the main dining area with its faded Easter Bonnet display. Shrivelled balloons not worth the popping hung from the ceiling; blown up empty crisp packets would make more noise. Everything had a tired, 'I've been here far too long' look and most of the teachers were het up, their mouths pursed in concentration. Ron nodded in the direction of the staff trying to bring order back to the dinner queue. "They're stressed. I'd like a quid for every time they've chosen not to notice someone chewing in class, even the boffins get away with it these days. And theat", she whispered in her best 'plum-in-the-mouth' accent "is further proof of how standards are falling, which was precisely the cornerstone of today's assembly," she added in a grave imitation of the Year Tutor.

"You're not wrong, Ron! And theat," Beth countered with a clever-dick grin as her face, "is a perfect example of assonance!"

"Sure it is!"

"It is! And you're meant to be impressed! Assonance is when- oh never mind! What's the point! You're in danger of turning into a pleb, you know that! Anyway, what's he gawping at?"

Annoyed at the sudden change of subject Ron swung round. She scanned the scene. "Who, Smithard?" she snapped.

"Don't turn round!" Bethany said clutching her arm. "And don't stare! He's a right weirdo, always was! But nooo! Not him!"

"OK so how else am I supposed to know who you're talking about if I don't turn round and you won't tell me- nutter!" Ron raised her eyes heavenwards and paused, as if divine intervention might be lurking somewhere amongst the faded balloons.

"God! You're touchy these days, Ron! Are you due on or something?"

"You can talk!"

Bethany ignored her withering look. "Come on. We can sit- oh God! Quick, grab those two places. I'm not sitting next to that geek."

"Who? Daniel Foster?"

"Ah! At last! The penny's dropped. Yeah, he's arrogant and stupid! Ugh! I don't know which I hate more, this or him," she said, shoving aside the slice of gateau all perfectly layered and sandwiched with ersatz cream.

"Well, he's a bit gassed up, yeah maybe, but Beth," Ron added, this time imitating the haughty tones of the sex education teacher - "just give the old hormones a chance, my dear and get that eaten, anorexia won't suit you! You weren't made to be the reedy cat-walk type. I mean, not with those boobs!" Beth's back hander was well aimed. Ron ducked, her smirk cancelling out any hurt Bethany might have felt.

"Tell me about it," she said. And just think, if I'd been born a hundred or so years ago, and Chinese, I'd have had them bound and flattened."

"Yep, and your feet. Then we'd really have seen some weird foot work on the basketball pitch!"

"Anyway, I wouldn't be seen dead with the moron. He's stuck up! I mean, sounding off like that. And actually trying to justify experimenting on animals! He gave 'swagger bragger ' a run for his money though. I'll give him that!"

"There you go then. You both like to spout and wind Swagger bragger up so that's two things you've got in common! So give him a whirl, girl!" Veronica grinned, pleased and surprised with her own unrehearsed use of assonance. In a show of peacock pride she shook her head. "Yeah! Who's your daddy!" she said, giving Bethany a high five.

"Yeah yeah!" Bethany sang with a grudging acceptance. "But me, go out with a geek like that? Not likely! Anyway, let's change the subject. How about going bowling this week. That's if -" Bethany paused, an image of her mother's disapproving look clouding her thoughts "that's if, well, you know my mum."

"OK. So come on, apart from loathing The Schmuck, having a eureka moment about your crush on swagger bragger and resenting an over protective mother, what's up?" Taken aback by the blunt and sudden question, Bethany winced. Where could she begin? After all the stupid banter and Ron being so up-beat about everything, it didn't seem to be the right time, nor to her surprise the right person to confide in. It had to be someone, someone who could...but Ron would probably only laugh anyway. Visionaries and dreamers, people like that weren't really her thing. 'And I mean,' Bethany thought, 'how could I even begin to explain about the seagull, well my seagull that might not be a seagull at all, more like somebody masquerading as one.'

"Well?" Ron waited for the glazed and distant look on her friend's face to fall away.

"It's OK. It'll keep," Bethany said when the bell rang for the afternoon sessions. No way could she expect Ron to understand that when her seagull looked at her with such probing eyes...it...it was weird...or that the imprint of the dead seagull was stalking her mind and that maybe it was trying to communicate something to her...something, yes...but what?

"Yeah. OK. See you then," Ron said, slapping Bethany's upturned hand.

Chapter 3

School over, Bethany settled into a window seat on the Abbotsby-Penhill rattle trap. It was slow and rickety but she couldn't have cared less if a man with a red flag had been walking in front; now she could look out over her beloved moors. The huge expanse of heather would soon erupt into a purple sea. In a few weeks she'd be on holiday, able to cycle every which way and explore the tiny inlets, the haunts of smugglers, the land and seascapes that inspired poets and artists. Freedom!' Bethany thought. 'No more school, no more bells telling me where to be and when and for how long. No more Daniel Fosters on my back!'

The squeal of reluctant brakes jostled her preoccupation to one side. It was just as well. She'd been that absorbed, the chances were she'd have missed her stop. Then she'd have had some explaining to do.

"Tarra love!" The bus driver's cheerful tone brought a smile to her face. She'd known and liked him since the day she'd made her first trip on her own. She had been just eight, a little girl making her own way to see her Aunty Barbara in Abbotsby. Her nervousness must have shown. Seeing her close to tears he'd whispered, "Eee, you're not going to blub are yer, lass? Listen 'ere. It don't seem that long since I fost saw thee sitting on yer mam's lap sucking yer dummy-tit like there were no tomorrer and 'ere you are, all grown, meckin t' journey on your todd. It's nowt like auld days; me mam ad 'ave bassaked me backside if I'd gone on t' bus bi messen. You aren't 'arf a clever lass."

It was a good memory. "Thanks, Joe!" she said and headed off down the steep hill to the bay.

"Hi, mum!"

"Now then." Mrs. Mallinson shuffled off the settee, her cup of hot tea rattling in the saucer. Bethany dropped her bag on the floor and moved to take it from her.

"It's OK, I can manage," she said.

"The problem wouldn't be there if you changed the habit of a lifetime and used a mug instead. Everybody uses mugs these days, mum!"

"Hm, but I'm not everybody, Bethany. And of all people, who are you to recommend wholesale conformity!"

Bethany grinned.

"At least you have the good grace to admit it! Anyway, what sort of day have you had? You're home early for a change!" her mother said, taking the starched white cloth from the sideboard drawer. In one dexterous move the pristine cloud of cotton floated down onto the table.

"I know. Just wanted to be home I suppose."

"Well, did you ever!" her mother said with an unconvincing glance.

"Honestly, mum. Besides, we've been given another English project. It'll take forever but we can do it in pairs. Probably Ron and me. And you can help this time, mum," Bethany said as she began to lay the table.

"Me?"

"Yeah. The teacher wants us to do a sort of biography but not just an account of somebody's life."

Mrs. Mallinson looked up, a suspicious frown forming. "Whose then?"

"Well, that's where you come in. It has to start with a memento. Something special, something old that tells a story."

"Gracious, Bethany. I don't know...really I don't," her mother said, looking around the tiny sitting-cum-dining room.

"It could be a postcard, a diary extract, even a story told through the years- anything. We've got to try and bring a bit of history into it if we can. I'll enjoy the research."

"It's beginning to sound a bit intrusive to me. You can't go delving into folk's backgrounds. I don't think she should ask you to do that. It's not right!"

"Oh come on, mum. It'll be OK."

"That's your opinion, young lady," she said "and just for the record, I suppose I'm entitled to one as well?" Then, sniffing on her disapproval she drew a line under the argument.

"So what about my project, mum?" Bethany said after she'd helped with the dishes and ironed a school shirt for the morning. She hated herself for the manipulative way she sometimes treated her mother. 'Why do I have to be a little creep, peeling spuds, doing the pots? Why can't we just be friends and get on like everyone else!' she thought.

"Come on; let's look in the cabinet," Bethany said trying to tone down her enthusiasm.

"You won't find much in there. Besides I'm not having you writing about anyone in our family." Her mother's tone was antagonistic, defensive.

"Hang on, mum! Not you or dad. Someone from the past. Like I said, the teacher wants us to use a family memento to set us off."

"Well we haven't got anything like -"

"Oh yes we have mum!" Bethany was pushing it. "Look, this is great," she said, gently guiding her mother to the late eighteenth century glass cabinet. "Lovely isn't it?" she said running her fingers across its gold lacquered trim and Chinese motifs.

"It is." For a moment her mother was lost in thought..."We bought it in the auction room. Your father and I, when we were first married. Your dad thought it would be a good investment but I just liked it."

"Put the light on, mum!"

"There's nothing in there that's even faintly biographical, Bethany."

"Yes there is. Look, what's that?" she said, pointing to the round, silver case that seemed to wink at her.

"That was your great grandmother's pocket watch."

"Well, there you go then! Who gave it to her anyway? Was it a roving gypsy boy who nearly stole her heart away from my great grandfather? And did she wear it close to her heart, setting it forever at the exact time the saucy fellow was sent on his way, never to be seen or heard of again!"

"No of course not! Her father gave it to her on her twenty first birthday."

"Hm…pretty boring. Still, you've never told me anything about her. What was she called?"

Mrs. Mallinson paused. "Bess. I was just a little girl when she died. Can't remember much about her. I know she helped to make ends meet by mending the fishermen's nets. Mother said she used to sit on the stone step surrounded by an enormous mound of webbed hemp. The needle used to go fifty to the dozen flashing in the sunlight and the kids used to gather round and help her unravel it. She'd tell them a yarn then and right at the best bit she'd stop, put down her hook, reach out behind her and bring out this colander full of winkles. She always used to have pins at the ready, at least ten of them neatly pinned to her apron bib. By they were good! Even I remember those."

"Mum, they're awful! The look of them and they pong!"

"Get away! With a bit of vinegar they go down a treat!"

Bethany wrinkled her nose. "What's that then?" she said, turning to the cabinet again.

"It's a beaded pocket. It should hang on the wall really. Women did nothing else but needlework in those days. Pillow slips, tablecloths, serviettes, everything, usually with monograms. Even the silverware was engraved, if they were well off enough that is. Our family never had that kind of money though."

"What about that then?" Bethany said, pointing to what looked like a miniature beer barrel.

"Oh that! It's nothing, nothing at all, just another cheap jack memento."

Bethany peered at it more closely. "I've never really looked at the engravings. Get the key mum, let's have a look!"

"You don't need to get things out!"

"I do, mum. I'm interested."

"Tst! I just wish your teacher would give you a proper essay to do," she said taking the key from underneath the vase that stood close by.

"Like what? The day in the life of something or other? Oh mum, get real!"

"Get real?" Mrs. Mallinson rolled her eyes. "But -"

"No buts!" Bethany reached for the key. "Come on, mum; you want my project to be the best, don't you?" she said with a conspiratorial grin.

"That's not fair, Bethany. I just don't want you prying into the past. It's not right and I don't like it!"

"It's history, mum! Just history. These people are dead and buried. They're not going to be hurt by a bit of delving."

"Well, I don't know. I just don't like it," her mother said, handing over the barrel. Bethany turned it over and over trying to loosen the top. "Does it open?"

"Go careful with it!" her mother snapped. "No, it's just a carved barrel. Give it here. You won't be satisfied till you've broken it!"

"Stop fussing, mum!" Bethany hugged it to her chest. "Look, everything seems to have something to do with the sea," she said, rubbing her thumb across the engravings - "and there's some sort of monogram but the letters are entwined and decorated. Yes, this'll do. It'll be great. So who did it belong to?"

"Oh I don't know! These things seem to have been with us for ever, just handed down, that's all. Since it was special to your grandma, I thought I'd better keep it."

"So you have a hoarder's instinct as well, mum?" Bethany grinned. "And to think how you go on at me!"

"Get away...now come on, put it back!" her mother said reaching for it.

"But mum this is exactly the sort of thing I need." Remembering what her dad used to say about possession being nine tenths of the law, Bethany held it to her chest. A teasing smile crossed her face. "Oh come on, mum. It's great and it'd be fun finding out about it."

"Don't be silly!" she said, reaching out for it again. "Besides, for a start, I'm not having it out of the house!"

"Not take it out? Why ever not?"

"Because it's an heirloom...and because it belongs in the cabinet. Give it here now!" Bending to the edge on her mother's voice, Bethany breathed a deep sigh and handed it over.

"But mum -"

"No buts! You can sketch or photograph it, but its not going out of this house!" In that instant all the friendly feelings she had had towards her mother disappeared. The old resentments resurfaced. The barriers were up. The statement had been made. There would be no discussion. There wasn't even going to be an agenda.

Chapter 4

Slinging her bag over her shoulder Bethany flounced up to her room.

"God, my mother's hard work," she said, slipping off her school skirt and abandoning her shirt and tie. Then, deciding she was a first rate jerk for talking to herself she collapsed on the bed. Hugging, biting and growling into the pillow she finally relaxed with a sigh that could have dried a line of washing on a still, winter's day.

But the framed snap shot on the wall drew her in. It was a happy picture. Her father's arm was wrapped around her mother's shoulder in a loose, friendly but protective kind of way. They were smiling at one another. Drawn to it, Bethany scrambled off the bed, donned her over-sized 'Save the Calves' T shirt, fiddled her long, red hair into a loose plait, switched on her CD player and took the frame down. Then, settling into the cushioned window seat, she drew her knees up to her chin, pulling the calves' legs well down over her own.

She had often glanced at the photo but this time she looked at it, really looked. They had been standing in front of the rhododendron bush by the garden gate. The blooms were past their best and petals lay scattered on the lawn. It must have been a day in June or July. A windy day judging by the fly-away strands of her mother's hair and the way her father's shirt seemed to billow out. But what really caught Bethany's interest was the loving look passing between them. A knowing, secret glance as if they knew and shared something others didn't. Again Bethany sighed. A pang of guilt surged through her. Reaching across to her bedside table, she swapped the photo for her diary –'the one thing that keeps me sane,' she thought. It was great, a ritual Christmas present from Ron, bound this year in a soft shade of blue suede and it had a key.

Dear diary,

'What a day! I mean that Daniel Foster. He thinks he's so cool. The reality is, he's a geek. A reincarnated Einstein is who he thinks he might be but listen up, diary; I think he was spawned by something that crawled out of a swamp. Well, one thing's for sure, he'll never get the better of me. Not even with the help of 'swagger bragger.' Remembering how she used to favour Mr. Dunleavy's take on politics, she shuddered. *Heck, talk about subtle indoctrination. But today was something else. I think he privately enjoyed watching me and the Geek having a go at each other. Still, whilst I was indulging in the greatest sulk of the century, Geek did keep him on his toes; I'll say that for him. So OK, let's be generous – a spawned geek with half a brain! As for mum, what is the matter with her? I know she misses dad. I do...but then, this isn't all about me or is it? Am I such a clumsy, insensitive prat that I jump headlong into things, wanting everything...like...like yesterday. But come on. She's my mum! I shouldn't have to walk about on tip toes all the time.* Picking up the photo again Bethany smoothed her thumb across her mum's face. *They sure looked good together, diary. And I suppose since dad died I've had five years of growing up and forgetting but mum's been without her best friend. Maybe that's why she's sad and mardy sometimes. But why be difficult about a stupid barrel! So it's precious- an heirloom, yes OK, I get it but not letting me have access to it is ridiculous! Then, oh my God, the bowling! Why did I even mention it? You would think I'd told her I was going on a trek through a virgin rainforest with that heavy breathing weirdo, Smithard, lurking beneath the canopy. Grrrr!*

"Oh well, after all, tomorrow is another day!" she said, remembering the Literary quiz they'd had at school about the well known first and last lines of novels.

Resting her head against the wall she looked out across the red roof tops and out to sea. "Oh!" Bethany flinched. The seagull had homed in. Settling on the window ledge it side-stepped and shuffled about, peering in, its long beak tapping at its own reflection. "I've been adopted!" she had told her mother. "I saw it in its eyes! It's weighing me up, wondering if I'll make a replacement soul mate!"

"Nonsense!" Her mother's reaction, ever negative, had annoyed Bethany. "Anyway, mind you keep your window shut, and don't even think of giving it tit-bits, it'll have your finger off!"

Shifting her position ever so slightly she watched the bird settle, watched it probe and ruffle its feathers till the escaping down chased the breeze like cabbage white butterflies. Bethany's sigh was anything but a contented one. *Another thing, diary, mum's forever going on about me being out of step with the world. She's right though. One minute my head's a hornet's nest buzzing with ideas and questions, and the next, a place of mystery, a place inhabited by imposters. One anyway. I can't pin-point the first time I sensed it, only that it was overwhelming. It sort of disturbed me, just like the seagull impression had. What's going on, diary? Why do I have this uneasy feeling of expectancy?* Even now Bethany's eyes were drawn to the window. Even though the bird's image had faded, something was still there and it was disturbing. Behind a vapory mist an amoebic-like form drifted in and out of her mental space like a torment. Bethany shuddered. *But who can I tell? What should I say? Whoever! Whenever! They'll only think I'm crackers. Imagine it, diary: "Bethany Mallinson's losing her marbles, you know, the light's on but there's no one in...she's definitely going psycho, big time. Maybe it's the prelim to her Gothic stage." Well anyway, one thing's for sure. I'd best not leave you lying around anymore!*

Chapter 5

Bethany clicked her fingers to the beat of the pop music blaring out of the bowling alley. "I've been looking forward to this," she said. Ron gave her a sideways glance.

"Does your mum know?"

"'course! Would I lie to my mother?" Trying to be equivocal, Ron wagged her head. "Um…if push comes to shove, yes, you might!"

"Well I didn't. Said I was meeting you. What is it with you two anyway? How come she thinks the sun shines out of your -"

"Yeah, all right. Let's leave my bum out of it!" Veronica grinned. "It's about time you rejoined the human race, that's all. I mean, we mortals like to enjoy ourselves; it's what makes us connect!"

"I know." Bethany pushed through the doors and made for the check-in desk.

"So what's up?" Ron asked as she fiddled around in her purse. Again Bethany flinched, alert once more to something lurking behind veils of mist, of a seagull drifting in and out of her mind like some sort of go-between and of a stupid barrel she felt compelled to investigate.

"Mum I suppose. She's difficult, that's all, and -" Bethany paused, coloured up and turned away. She'd caught Daniel Foster's eye. It was a split second thing but a moment when, with her defences down, she had acknowledged his half smile.

"And -," Ron prompted. "Hello! Is there anybody at home?" she said with a nudge and a bucketful of sarcasm.

"Yeah, sorry!"

"See what I mean! Come down to earth! So go on. Why is your mum giving you a hard time?"

"Yer, right. It's the English project. We've got this miniature barrel. It's carved. It's great and it has a monogram. I thought it would be fun finding out more about it."

"So what's the problem?"

"Search me. She doesn't even want it taken out of the house."

"So you had a ding dong!" Ron rolled her eyes, disbelief written on her face.

"Sort of. I just think she's being totally unreasonable. I mean, where's the harm?"

"Is it precious…an heirloom? Maybe that's why she's funny about it." Bethany tutted. "I might have known you'd see things from her point of view. You always do!"

"Oh come on! I'm just trying to figure out why she won't budge. There has to be a reason."

"Yes, well, apart from that, she's annoyed. She thinks Mrs. Bennett's out of order giving us a project that meddles in the past and that it's intruding into our private lives."

"Could be," Ron said, checking her ticket, "and don't carp on again about me taking her side. My gran would have said the same. It's a generation thing. Hey look, our lane isn't ready yet. Let's grab a coke. Besides," she said, returning to the subject "my guess is you'll have gone at it like a bull at a gate, as usual!"

Bethany poked her tongue out and grimaced.

"You're going to have to stop doing that, you know. It's becoming a habit." Bethany turned to see Daniel Foster glaring at her.

"I know," she said - "as of now."

Daniel's concentration was at an all time low. Minutes after he and Trev arrived at the bowling alley he saw Bethany. Their eyes had locked, just for an instant. He'd smiled. It was instinctive and he could have sworn she'd smiled back. He could have put his last quid on it. Then he'd remembered...

Yesterday in the school dining room he'd been scanning the hall for a couple of seats. He'd brushed past her and that long, untamed, auburn hair, hair that caught the light and...Balancing the tray had been a nightmare. His soup slopped and spilled over. As for the bread roll, well, that took off on a galactic mission of its own, landed and bounced off her table.

"Sorry," he'd pleaded, but over lunch Bethany wouldn't stop glaring at him. So when the peas he'd so carefully manoeuvred on to his fork and almost into his mouth, fell, scattering like a broken string of sea-green pearls, he'd flushed with humiliation.

Now, seeing her again he really wanted out. Somehow the bowling alley had never seemed so claustrophobic, to the point where he wondered what the attraction for bowling had ever been. The sounds that usually excited and geared him up for the contest, annoyed him. The dull rumble of the balls on the wooden lanes and the rising thunder of them hitting the gutters was jarring his nerves. Then came the chock of the ball careering into the pins, the rattle of them falling and then, the re-emergence of the triangle completing the cycle. 'Neat...a knackered, milkman's fantasy,' he'd thought.

"Hallelujah! Yes!" Fists clenched, arms raised, Trev savoured his win. "What's up, mate? You haven't even had a sniff of a strike in three games! Thought you were supposed to have an eye for the king pin. Losing your touch, that's what! Ah well, even you can't be top dog forever! Look, just one more game!" he chortled, "Give you a chance to make a come-back, then when I win, I'll let you buy me a beer!" Trevor waited for a response. Daniel could never resist a challenge.

"No. Look, Trev, I'm off," Daniel said, burying the tips of his fingers deep into his thick, black hair "but don't kid yourself into believing you can best me! Try an arm lock; you're not bad at that!"

Trevor grinned. "Understatement mate! Whenever you're up for it though!"

"You're on, but bowls? Forget it! It's all in the eye and body coordination and the controlled swing of the arm," Daniel said, giving a demonstration. "Get that right and it might be worth having another go at me!" Trev caught the gloating glint in Daniel's eye. "Another time then, OK?"

"You can count on it, but you're making a BIG mistake," Trev said, eyeing up the group of girls who had just sauntered in.

"Not me. I've had them up to here!" he said, flicking his head in the direction of Bethany and the snack bar.

"Good God, you're not still obsessed with her!"

"Obsessed! You've got to be joking...anyway who does she think she is, she and that Veronica. They're a couple of soap-opera wannabes if you ask me." Trev stared at his long time friend, inspiration coming to him in a blinding flash.

"Ah! I get it; you've got the hots for her, haven't yer mate?"

"Yeah, sure!"

"Awe, come off it, Dan. She's OK. A bit politically correct maybe especially when she's spouting all that crap about -"

"Bleating you mean -" Daniel stopped short. Somehow it didn't seem right to criticise her anymore.

"Your problem is you don't appreciate a catch when you see one."

"You make a play for her then, but you wouldn't last long, mate. You'd have to stop all that metaphorical stuff for a start."

"What d'yer mean?"

"All that talk about fishing and reeling the women in. Just like my dad come to think of it! She'd love that!"

"Well at least I'd have a go. You need to shape up!"

"Yeah, yeah. Anyway, I'm off. I'll see you around!"

"You arrogant sod!" Trevor mouthed, but as Daniel headed for the check-out he only grinned, and gave him a thumbs up sign.

He'd felt a bit mean leaving Trev without so much as an explanation. Still, he was glad to get out into the fresh air. Rubbing his shoulders against the keen wind he made for the cycle stand, undid the safety lock on his bike and lifted the front wheel out of its wooden support. It was a high, vertical and dramatic move from one who, deep down, hated flamboyance. All the same it reflected his current mood, a growing frustration with himself and an unfair instinct for taking it out on others. Still, the homing instinct was in him. Clasping the handle bars and pushing hard down on the peddles, he set off.

In the drive, his father's Mercedes gleamed; it was his pride, his trophy. Daniel took care not to scratch it as he pitched the bike against the wall. His father was in the lounge. Daniel could see him through the conservatory window inspecting a bottle of wine. The relaxed tones of the cricket commentator drifted through. Great. At least his father was absorbed. Daniel weighed up his next move. If only some gorgeous blonde would do a streak on the pitch or something. That would be one hell of a distraction! Some chance! Still, with a bit of luck the steel bands would begin to play. That would do the trick! He'd rant and rave, bluntly refusing to accept that a quiet pitch surrounded by sturdy British oaks was a thing of the past. As usual his mother was in the kitchen. It was her preferred domain.

"Nice one!" he said, helping himself to a home made bun.

"Hey!" she said, ringing her floured hands in mock annoyance. Grinning, Daniel sidled by. "I'm just off for a shower." Too late. His father's frame filled the doorway.

"Now then Danny Boy!" Daniel cringed. Why couldn't his father call him Dan like everybody else?

"Hi Dad."

"Fancy a gander at the cricket? Johnson's just hit a six...98 not out. Let's see if he can bag a century!"

"Yeah well, not at the moment, dad. I need a shower! I'm stinking!"

"Aw, come on, it's an historic moment, son!" His mother's antennae, second only to Jodrell Bank, were activated.

"For goodness sake, Miles, let the lad be. He's probably got something on his mind, a girl maybe," she said, raising an eye brow.

"Ah well, that's different!" His father pressed the record button. "So what's up, son?" Daniel turned away, his hands sinking deep into his pockets. Really he just wanted time out and gave his mum a 'thanks for nothing' look.

"I don't want to go into it dad, OK?"

"Fair enough, but something's got your goat. Your mother tells me you've been mooning about for a day or so. Still, if you'd rather -"

Remembering the times he'd complained that his father was always on some business trip and rarely had time for him, Daniel sighed. "OK, there's this girl, right? All through Junior school she's been a pain in everyone's butt! Talk about bossy and now..." Daniel paused, unsure of how to tell them about Bethany's brash confidence and the way she tried to undermine him with her put down glances and whispered asides.

"And now?"

"The same. She's got attitude, I suppose."

"More so than you, you mean!" his father interjected with a grin.

"You bet!"

"What about?"

"Oh, livestock in transit, veal, Amnesty International, nuclear energy, and you so much as hint at something sexist and she's off, sitting on her high horse driving us all crazy!"

"Sounds like a nice girl!" Daniel glared at his father.

"Now there's a conversation stopper, Miles!" his mother said, pouring herself a glass of wine.

"OK. So what's the attraction, son?"

"I'm not...I dunno," he stuttered, "there's just something about her. Maybe it's the challenge but it would take a bomb to motivate me in her direction." Disgusted with himself for inviting the put down he knew would come, he turned away.

"Well, what's the matter with you, boy! At your age I was scoring with the women every which way! Come on, son. Get a life!" His mother shifted uncomfortably.

"Take no notice of your father, Dan. Believe me it's all wishful thinking," she said, a defensive smirk on her face. "Besides, with all that experience, wouldn't I be wandering around with a silly grin on my face!"

Daniel smiled. "You're not kidding, mum!" he said with a conspiring grin. Beaten, his father shrugged his shoulders, picked up his wine and wandered back into the conservatory.

"Well, Daniel! It sounds like a case of two strange bees in a beehive to me."

"Got it in one mum; that's exactly it, two very strange bees in a beehive!"

Chapter 6

At school during afternoon break, news of a beached whale broke. At first it was only rumoured, then whispered until, finding its own momentum, it infiltrated every thought and emotion. And though it came like an unwelcome guest, all were agog to see it, so that when the final bell rang, every classroom door along the Humanities corridor and beyond seemed to open together. The rush developed spontaneously, a natural synchronisation of chattering pupils excited by the prospect of the unknown. "Another dangerous phenomenon," commented Mrs. Wilks as she stacked her Geography exercise books. "That lot could teach the lemmings a thing or two. Aren't you joining them Bethany?"

"After the basketball, Miss."

"Ah yes. Right. Mind you win!"

"Definitely! Goodnight, Miss."

By the time Bethany lent over the railings to catch her first glimpse of the whale, the clouds had gathered. The tide was ebbing and the grey bulk lay deeply wedged in the sand. She took a deep breath. In her mind's eye, she saw the tide turning and the frothy crests surging in to cradle the dark, shapeless form. She saw the water seep into every crease and lap the whale, just like the runt of a litter might be licked and nuzzled again and again, till its pulse was rekindled. She saw the whale respond, invigorated and soothed by the swell. Then, with one thrust of its enormous dorsal fin, it was sea-borne once more, drifting out of the shallows toward the deep. A phoenix now, it rose up and plunged into the pitch and roll of the sea…but then miracles didn't happen on the Abbotsby foreshore, did they?

Bethany knew it would upset her to see the whale but a stronger pull lured her there. Others obviously felt the same way.

Huddled and still with their shoulders hunched against the miserable weather, they reminded her of the Lowry paintings they'd studied in the art class. But the heavens opened and the stick people scurried for shelter. Only one remained, hooded, cagouled; a silent watcher. For those who understood, it had to be that way. Even without an introduction Bethany knew that she would share an empathy with the stranger; the wide drooping shoulders and the still, fixed gaze told her that. Nevertheless, at least for a little while, she stood apart, not wishing to intrude. An image of her mother, a solitary figure in black standing by her father's grave, inveigled its way into her thoughts. She remembered her uncle taking her by the hand and leading her to the big black car. "To leave mummy with her special thoughts," he had said, ever so quietly.

"Does it always rain on funeral days, Uncle Bob?"

"No sweetheart, not always." But there was no well meaning uncle to deflect her grief now. Bethany moved forward, dwarfed beside the grey whale. The almost imperceptible movement of its great hulk told her that its struggle for life wasn't over yet. Bethany wanted to shout out her rage, so much so she could not disguise the audible catch in her breath. It was then that Daniel turned to her.

"Oh…..it's you!"

"Yes," he said more timidly than he would have liked. Normally he'd have squared his shoulders making ready for the verbal onslaught but Bethany's eyes were brimming. Daniel looked out to sea, to the diminishing light on the horizon. He wanted to put his arm around her, to comfort her, but a wall of antagonism stood between them.

"Come on, Danny, make a move, lad!" His father's words clattered around in his ears.

"It…it's awful," he said at last, "such a powerful creature dying like this." Sensing his difficulty Bethany gave him a watery smile. "You don't have to say anything," she said, "it's all right."

"But maybe I want to. Maybe I want you to know that I'm with you on this. I can see why people don't like the idea of them being hunted. They're awesome. Most of us go through our entire lives never making an impression like this." Again Bethany smiled, this time openly wiping away a tear.

"I'd like to say it's the cold or the wind or something," she said, sniffling. "But heck, of all the people, it had to be you seeing me like this."

"Why? Do you think I'll hold it against you? I mean, well…showing me that you can be just as vulnerable as the next person?"

"Maybe, but if I thought you'd understand…!"

"Ouch! I've obviously been giving out the wrong signals?"

"Just a few!" she said, looking at him sideways on. "Anyway, there's nothing to be done, is there and I'd best be going; the cold's getting to me."

"No, there's no point in hanging around. It's time to move on, isn't it?" he said, running his fingers across her shoulders to deflect the rain. Surprised by his own spontaneous gesture, Daniel drew back. Blushing, Bethany looked away.

"I…I suppose," she said.

"As for feeling cold…how about a coffee or a hot chocolate? If we hurry we'll catch the harbour café before it closes. It'll cheer us both up. The bright lights of our great metropolis are calling! My treat…to make up for all those wrong signals I've been giving out!"

"Thanks," she said," but I have to get back. I'm late as it is and mum will be doing her nut. Oh heck!" Bethany pointed to the high point of the road that led down to the sea front. "There's the last bus. I'll have to fly, sorry!" Fiddling to match the Velcro on her anorak she turned to go. "But thanks all the same," she shouted when her pace became a sprint.

"No probs…I'll see you around!" But there was no reply. Bethany was already well ahead of the wind.

Daniel scanned the deserted front, the haunt of day trippers and trigger-happy gamblers looking for hungry slot machines. 'You have to be mad, sad or inspired to be out in this weather,' he thought.

Even dressed like a hoody, Daniel recognized Smithard. He was the school's resident head-banger and weird! Straddling his bike, he seemed to be leering after Bethany. Daniel watched him watching her as she climbed through the railings and hailed the bus. 'OK, so in a deserted street you'd probably watch anything that moved. Yeah, well anyway, she's safely on her way.' he thought. Adjusting his collar and setting his shoulders against the drizzle, he heard the bus gather speed. He turned. Smithard was peddling like fury behind it.

Chapter 7

The hill leading to Penhill Bay was a 'three in one.' Bethany thought how tiresome a trek it must have been for the fisher folk in days gone by. She remembered how her own legs ached when, as a child, she'd ventured out with her mum and been scolded for dragging her feet. Nowadays of course, least ways in the summer, the little 'Up Hill and Down Dale' mini transit bus took the day trippers to and fro. But of course, tonight, she'd missed the last run. Did she care? Well, yes, because…oh God, her mother would be on her case again.

Rounding the bend she cut through the ginnel into Fisher's Row. 'The Snooper' was standing at her cottage gate, her thick arms folded across her ample bosom. As usual she was minding everybody else's business bar her own.

"Hello, luv. A bit late the night aren't yer lass?" Well, if she thought Bethany was going to enlighten her, she thought wrong. Not everyone liked to live in each other's pockets.

"Hello Mrs. Crooks. Well, there you go. There's always something to keep me busy." 'Nosy Parker!' she thought.

Home was the last cottage in the row. Despite the closing in of a grey summer's evening it was without its welcoming outside light.

"Hiya Mum!" Better to be cheerful, better to try and diffuse another set-to. But there was no reply from the kitchen where her mother generally pottered about, always preparing for the day ahead. Bethany sauntered down the narrow hallway and turned into the sitting room. Her mother's dark form stirred in the old, leather armchair. "Hi! Sorry I'm late."

"You need be sorry!" There, the challenge. "You must think I've nothing better to do than worry myself silly all night, wondering where you've got to this time."

"Mum, you know I go to basketball practice on a Tuesday and Thursday night and -"

"That would get you home for six. Teatime. Tea time at six Bethany, remember?"

"Yes Mum but -"

"But what? It's a quarter to eight for goodness sake! You must be half starved and perished by the looks of you."

It was true. Bethany was hungry and beginning to feel the effects.

"I know you worry about me mum, but you shouldn't. I'm fifteen and -"

"Fifteen or not, I want to know where you are!"

"Well it was the whale, mum. A whale beached at Abbotsby. Everybody's been talking about it. I had to go and see it and then I met Daniel and we -"

"Oh so you have been with a lad. I thought as much. Even before Mrs. Crooks told me!"

"Mum! You don't need to listen to her. I'm late because I went to see the whale. And that's it. Never mind what Mrs. Crooks said. She's a busy body, you know that."

"Nevertheless, I like to know where my daughter is before the busy body enlightens me!"

Bethany drew back. Her mother had a point.

"OK...I'm sorry. I just wish you would trust me, that's all."

"Trust doesn't come into it, Bethany. I just need to know where you are."

Bethany couldn't help herself. "Oh, give over, mum. I've said I'm sorry!"

"Yes, and words come cheap sometimes." Bethany glared at her mother. "So now you're telling me I'm being insincere...wonderful!"

"I'm not doing anything of the sort," her mother said. "And you've got no call to be dismissive with your, 'Give over!'"

"Mum! I'm nearly sixteen! What am I supposed to do to convince you? I've got my feet on the ground, right...oh, what's the use!" Anyway, I'm going up to write my diary and think about the English project. I mean, all that fuss over a bit of carved wood the other night. Honestly, mum!"

Sighing, Mrs. Mallinson crossed over to the window to draw the curtains. Her neighbour, still supposedly taking in the night air, shrugged her shoulders and waved. "Well, Bethany's right about you!" she muttered under her breath but waved back all the same.

Dear Diary,

Thank goodness there's always you to come home to. Still, it's a bit one sided, you being there just to listen to me moaning on. Well, if you could write back, I wonder whose side you'd be on. Then again, if I was looking for advice I suppose I'd go to an agony aunt or Ron; she'd tell it as it is! So another day is over and another set-to with mum. Wonderful! Thinking about it though, I might have gone OTT this time. Too much attitude, that's my problem. Well, I suppose it doesn't hurt to put her mind at rest but it's like an intrusion, having to account for every second. Still, I'll try again tomorrow 'cause it would choke me to try tonight. Anyway, I don't think mum's in the mood to make it up either. And who would have thought that the day would end with Daniel and me actually having a normal conversation, well, sort of. Talk about blushing. Heck, 'Be still my beating heart!' What was all that about? I mean, he only wiped the rain off my shoulders. A friendly gesture, that's all. Besides I hate him, I hate him...the schmuck...and...and haven't I just told mum my feet are firmly planted on the ground. God! I really would have liked that hot chocolate as well. Maybe he'll ask me again but maybe not. I might have come across as being a bit defensive, sort of making excuses, but he'd be wrong. He doesn't know my mother, does he? I wonder if he has to answer to his mum as I have to mine. I bet not...

"Ah well, sweet dreams, diary!" she said, sliding into bed but sleep simply wouldn't come. She tried counting sheep, tried remembering the fun she used to have with her mum and dad. Things had been different then. Her mum had been OK, jolly and much more easy going. But now...well, they'd had tiffs galore, but they'd never stopped Bethany from sleeping.

In the end, fed up with tossing and turning, she wrapped the duvet around her, gathered up her not quite a bean bag cushion and staggered over to the window seat. The last of the light had given up its struggle, but she was always happy to listen to the surge of an incoming tide, the crash and slap of the sea seeking its way, the miaow of a cat wanting to be let in and hurried steps that echoed on the cobbled ways. At any moment the street lights would be switched on, the ragged walls of the ruined Cistercian abbey would be illuminated against the darkening sky and the softer, summer magic would indulge her secret, romantic streak. Then, just maybe, Daniel would be in her thoughts!

But just now, wedged in the window seat she felt compelled to search the dark waters of the distant sea. She had heard, yes, there it was again, a forlorn and undulating cry. Perhaps it was a seal's? No, too long, too low, too distant. A whale's then? Yes a whale vainly calling for its mate. Bethany swallowed on the lump in her throat. All the same, her senses probed the night. Then, "Oh God!" Bethany drew back, startled The seagull had landed in a flurry of dust and down. "You're scary," she said, "and I wish you wouldn't do that!" She tried to stare the bird out but it only pecked at the window. It was an insistent tick, like that of a clock in an empty hallway. But the sound became a drum beat in her head, intruding into her personal space and the seagull held her in its gaze with the kind of look that left her wondering.

"OK...OK!" It's sleepy time," she said, snuggling into her duvet but still the bird pecked at the window. She tried to focus her mind, to think about the basket ball final, to imagine herself stacking deck chairs in the summer and to invent ways of getting her own back on The Snooper; anything to distance herself from the feeling that she was being lured towards another place, to be nourished, it seemed, by an emptiness that left her heart aching. Afraid and cold, Bethany yearned for the cosy warmth of her bed but a swathe of mist rose like a sea fret. Behind it, shrouded in a dervish whirl of grey gossamer, a dark form was beckoning. Bethany drew back. A woman...yes, it was a woman with sad, unforgiving eyes, eyes that seemed to be drawing her in...

Chapter 8

Bethany woke to the relentless cries of hungry seagulls.

"Aw, go away…!" but there could be no snuggling up in bed, no lying limp and relaxing. 'I must be mad to have spent the night here,' she thought leaning forward to manipulate a toe that had gone into cramp. Then there was the dream. Bethany shivered; well, it had to have been a dream! Opening the window she gazed over the rooftops. Her bird had gone of course, leaving the sill strewn with matted feathers and droppings. But the fresh air was a tonic. It was a clear day, 'a day for looking forward,' she thought and glanced over to her alarm clock. 6.30. Well, she'd have a bath and hope the cranky old system wouldn't disturb her mum.

But if that didn't, Bethany's clumsiness must have. In the space of five minutes she had knocked over her Complete Works of Shakespeare, allowed the breeze to catch and slam the door and (as if to lend truth to the idea that disasters come in threes) dropped the slippery bath cream into the steaming water. 'Some bath this will be,' she thought as she watched the birth of a mountain range.

"Are you all right up there, Bethany?"

"Yes, mum. Sorry I woke you."

"Right oh."

'Hmm…not quite so cool this time, quite warm in fact!' Bethany thought. 'Maybe she could even tell her mum about the woman in her dream, but then again, maybe not. She would only think I was loopy.'

Lowering herself into the water the snowy peaks embraced her. A hot bath and a quick turn around was what she had in mind. A child's wonderland and the memory of her mother bringing the story of the Pied Piper to life was what she got. Those were the days when her mother's sense of fun had filled the cottage; the days before her dad had died. After that, grief seemed to steal her personality and middle age douse her spirit. After that she always seemed to wear a frown.

Bethany remembered how her mother used to kneel beside the bath to talk, to play and weave her magic. Surrendering to the ghosts of times past she breathed in the fragrance of her mother's perfume. The Hamelin scene was unfolding. Her own sculpturing began to take shape: here the village; there the medieval spires; here the old Town Hall where the Mayor and the Corporation plotted their deception and there, the cobbled ways, down which the rats would scamper and the children skip toward their destiny. Here the Sunday hats from which the rats emerged, and there, the deep sided river Waser with its fast, swirling water. On its furthest side, way, way across the little bridge, the mountain path meandered to Koppelberg Hill. The scene was set.

"Sh... if you listen...," her mother had said ever so mysteriously "you can hear the rats!" With trust and childish wonder Bethany had listened. Now, as then, the faintest rustle and jostle of aerating bubbles moved her imagination so that the rats popped out with their beady eyes and long thin tails to form a squeaky stream of excitement. Now as then, she was beguiled by her mother playing the recorder. The tempo quickened till she could hardly hold the tune. Then the faulty notes became the death knell of the rats plunging into the dark flowing river. Bethany shuddered. Her mother's magic was there still - "Hush, listen!" Now she played a lighter tune, all clefs and trebles. Into Bethany's mind's eye came the children, excited and wondrous at the music they heard. Up, up into the mountain shades they skipped till they faced the cavern.

Bethany scooped out a hollow of diminishing bubbles. This was the cave through which the children would pass, never to be heard of again. Seeking the warmth, Bethany sank further into the water. Again, she thought of the lame boy, alone and friendless and closed her eyes against the reality of her own, sad mother.

Later, urged out of the bath by the tepid water, Bethany wrapped her bath robe around her and scrunched up her hair. Only then did she notice the dainty dried up cheese sandwiches, the cup of cocoa with its thick, wrinkled skin and the left over Christmas serviette.

"Hi Mum! Sorry about the supper," Bethany said, settling the tray with its untried peace offering on the draining board. "I didn't hear you come up."

"No matter. You'll be wanting some breakfast though, I hope." she said, turning the bacon. "And how you slept all scrunched up in the window seat like that, I'll never know."

"Well, for one thing I was upset I don't like going to bed on a row. I'm sorry, mum."

"Me too. And for another?"

"Oh…oh well…" The question had set her heart thumping. Her mouth went dry. Her eyes brimmed over.

"Good gracious, Bethany whatever's the matter?" her mother said, handing her a tissue. And in that moment, weakened by the softer memories of her mother and by the comforting hand on her shoulder, she couldn't help herself…

"I…I had this dream, mum, more of a nightmare really." Bethany paused, unsure of how or whether to go on. "There was this…this woman," she said at last. "She was wrapped in a mist and it sort of held her in. She was writhing about in a torment. She couldn't escape. Her eyes were wild with a kind of longing…and I…she…oh I don't know mum, but it was awful. I knew she was alone on the cliff. I wanted to help her but -"

"But, it was just a dream, Bethany! There's no need to take on so!"

"But was it, mum? I can't put her out of my mind or the seagull. It's always there, on the sill, staring in at me."

"Well, shoo it off, Bethany. I've told you not to encourage it and as for your dream, don't be daft. That whale will have been on your mind I expect. You'll feel better with something inside you." Falling in line with her mother's no nonsense response, Bethany rubbed her eyes and peered over the frying pan. She wrinkled her nose. "Just the egg, Mum."

Frowning, her mother shook her head "I'm not sure all this vegetarian nonsense is doing you any good! You're a -"

"Growing girl. Yes, I know, Mum, but to be honest I'd rather not grow any more," she said, looking downwards. "5 ft 4 in: 36-24-37 "ll do for me."

"Well, if it's the 37 inches you're worrying about, don't," her mother chided. "Ample bosoms have been in the family for generations. It's in the genes. You're not ashamed, are you?"

"Sometimes! You try darting about on the basket ball pitch like a grasshopper in a frenzy and a ton weight up front and you'd know about it!"

"Tst! You should be grateful for what nature has given you. Now come on," she said, squeezing her arm. "Eat up!"

"Thanks Mum. We'll be able to have lots more leisurely breakfasts like this when I break up. Only a bit longer to the hols and then, *freedom*!" Bethany punched the air with a clenched fist. "Yes! And I'll get up earlier. I'll even have time to help with the housework."

"Well, that's nice but not for one minute do I suppose it'll last," her mother muttered as she turned to the stove.

"Have faith mum!"

"Yes Bethany! If all else fails, I'll have to! Now hurry up. Time's getting on." Bethany sighed but at least for the moment, their shared antagonism had been put to bed.

Chapter 9

School couldn't come quickly enough. For one thing Bethany was looking forward to the basket ball final and regaining the cup. Then again, given that her mum was being difficult about the barrel, maybe the others would spark off some other ideas in the English lesson. Daniel would be there of course. So? A flutter of excitement caught her by surprise. Bethany flushed. "Don't be such a nerd," she told herself. "We've been sworn enemies for years so why would he have any interest in me? Or me in him for that matter! Besides, if he was interested he'd have telephoned. Yeah OK, he doesn't have my number? So! How many brain cells does a schmuck need?" Thinking about it though, their meeting had been purely accidental. There hadn't been any gradual build up of interest or messages from interceding friends this time. Worse, no ecstatic realisation that they'd cared for each other all along, like in the films. Well, OK, they weren't kids any more and he did sort of apologise. But could she remember the briefest of smiles? She could not.

'Heck, what am I on about? I hate him, don't I? Yes I do. I do!' Bethany thought as she scanned the school courtyard. No sign of Ron there. 'Oh, hell!' she thought. 'Sooner or later I'll have to own up about Daniel. 'course, she'll say I'm the mother of all hypocrites. Oh well, here goes; she'll probably be by the bench puffing at a ciggy as if there was no tomorrow.'

That was their refuge, their early morning sun trap, the place where they happily endured the faulty notes of the kids having their music practice; the place where they connived and gossiped. It was their fix before the school bell herded them into the classrooms to be talked at by lots of Mr. Chokumchilds. 'Dickens must have understood kids. He'd encouraged them to dream, yes…but there are dreams and there are dreams,' she thought, trying to focus on the long, dark shadows of the poplars stretching out across the green. Instead she was drawn to the dappled light dancing beneath the cherry tree they'd planted in memory of one of the teachers. She closed her eyes to avoid a migraine. But...there...there it was again, that distant voice, despairing, tormented. Someone, somewhere was trying to...to connect with her. Afraid, with her sense of reality clouded, Bethany lent against the wall, her breathing suddenly laboured. Again and again she breathed in deeply, till the ache in her heart eased. While above, a lone seagull hung in the air, a watcher from on high.

"A penny for them!" She spun round.

"My God," she said, turning away to hide the rush of blood to her face, "You startled me!"

"Sorry."

"I was miles away!" she said.

"Where?" Daniel paused, giving her time to indulge his curiosity.

"I...I was just thinking." Bethany pointed to the Lower 6th formers floating in from the locals shop, unconcerned and unflappable, despite the early September mocks and the summer holiday fraught with revision. "That might be me next year if I'm not careful." The lie tripped easily off her tongue.

"Why? Don't you want to do A Levels?"

"Not really. I can't imagine studying for another two years. Mum wants me to. As far as she's concerned the point of the compass is fixed: A Levels... Uni... A profession."

"I know what you mean. I'm OK with it though. Maybe you should think about taking a year out. Go back-packing or something, you'd have a focus then, something to look forward to and -"

"And pigs might fly. Mum would have kittens!" Bethany said, heaving her school bag on to her shoulder in response to the school bell. Daniel held out his hand. "I can take that."

"What! And lose my cred with the emancipated set! Not likely, but thanks all the same."

"Hmm, giving in to peer pressure, hey!" he said with a grin that masked his embarrassment.

The door of the tutor room was open, a concession to 11R for their improved behaviour! '**Their** improved behaviour! I don't think so,' Bethany thought, glaring at the real perpetrator. Graham Smithard sat with his legs sprawled out across the aisle in a shaft of sunlight. He'd been silenced, his cheek curbed and his behaviour modified, not by detentions or warnings from the Form Tutor but by the condemnation of the class; to Coventry he had to go!

"Hey up!"

Bethany glared at him- and his legs. Grinning, he shifted them a fraction but slowly, making her wait. Turning to Daniel, she wrinkled her nose. Smithard had been a nerd forever. She'd learned to ignore him but just lately he always seemed to be around. He was creepy. Since his last fiasco, looking up to the ceiling had become an automatic gesture. Egged on by some of the other lads he'd chewed bits of paper till they were gooey with spit. Thrown up to the ceiling they had stuck becoming distant stars adrift on a fading blue sky. Some of the others moaned but he wouldn't stop. It wasn't even subtle so that when Mr. Harrison had walked into the classroom, detected a 'you don't know it yet, Sir, but look what somebody's done' atmosphere, he just sat back in his chair and waited. That's when the unease and threat of confrontation was really felt.

"What's up, Sir?" Graham Smithard was pushing it.

"Do you mean, 'what's the matter,' Sir?"

"Yes sir, what's up?" he repeated as if it was Mr. Harrison who lacked understanding. Then the giggling began. Mr. Harrison dismissed Smithard with a withering glance. He looked around, suspicion etched on his face

"Right you lot. I know it's coming up to the end of term. You haven't let off a stink bomb, yet! You haven't," he added, glancing across the floor "been throwing paper pellets around and neither have you so very thoughtfully put an upturned drawing pin or whoopy bag on my seat, so what have you done?" Again the giggling.

"Amanda? Luke? Jamie? Oh come on, somebody, do put me out of my misery!"

"Up, Sir. The operative word is UP!" This from Adrian Fletcher, not so much the class boffin as arrogant moron; 11R's resident Clever Dick. Mr. Harrison looked up, sighed with incredulity and continued with the register. Then, with the day's notices read he gave his interdict.

"Right 11R. Since you find it impossible to behave like sensible young adults, the classroom is out of bounds until the end of term." The response was immediate.

"Why, Sir?"

"We didn't do it, Sir!"

"It's not fair, Sir!"

But Sir was adamant and so it was that the early morning sun trap had come into existence.

Chapter 10

It turned out to be a boring sort of day. Double maths and science were not Bethany's idea of heaven. Ron wasn't in any of her sets. Neither was Daniel come to that. Boffins, both! Worse, they had been together all day! Bethany found herself blushing at the unexpected thrill she got when she thought about him. During morning break she'd seen him in the common room playing snooker with Trevor Wilson. He'd seemed happy enough, too happy! What was it with boys? How could he go all day without speaking to her? "Oh well...focus...focus!" she said, gathering up her hair and double flicking it into a rubber band to make a pony tail.

Now she had to get her own back on The Bovine for the foul that lost them the trophy last year; she'd been quietly psyching herself up for it. With her trainers laced up tight she headed across the field strewn with scavenging seagulls. There were rich pickings. Avoiding the chocolate wrappers darting about in the breeze, Bethany tried to put the seagulls out of her mind. Sprinting on to the pitch, a roar of approval made her smile. She looked around. No sign of Ron. Why wasn't she there, gearing up for some serious baying as usual? Instead, when the slouching figure of Graham Smithard caught her eye, she winced. 'What's he hanging about for? As if I didn't know!' But turning around she was surprised to see Daniel standing on the other side. Grinning, he gave her the thumbs up sign. Bethany sort of waved. It was a pathetic wiggling of the fingers kind of wave - not cool!

Ah well, here goes! Standing with her feet apart, her body posture alert, she tried to concentrate. The whistle blew. The ball bounced. Bethany lost it. The Bovine grinned. Her eyes darted this way and that. Bethany confronted her. Jumping up she managed to deflect the ball. It whizzed across the pitch. Side stepping and leaping into the air Bethany tried to intercept the next move.

"Good defence!" someone shouted but from her sprawled position on the ground Bethany could only manage a weak smile. The whistle blew. Play stopped and the PE teacher was at her side.

"It's nothing, miss. Just a twist. It'll loosen up!"

"Best not to risk it Bethany," she said, massaging the offending foot. "Off you go now and try not to put too much weight on it. A paddle in the sea might do it good." Whilst the other girls helped her to her feet the PE teacher's voice rose above the melee. "Right Jenny. You're on!"

"Sorree!" Jenny said as Bethany hobbled off.

"No probs. Just make The Bovine pay, hey?" she whispered. Daniel ambled alongside her.

"Tough luck!" he said.

"You're not kidding. This is how The Bovine was supposed to end up, not me!"

Daniel looked puzzled. "The Bovine?"

"Yeah! Once when she'd scored against us, she dawdled by Ron with the sweet smell of success under her nose. Well, you know Ron; she called her a silly cow. Unfortunately Mrs. Palmer picked up on it."

"And?"

"She got a telling off. Told her to watch her vocab. Furious, Ron stormed off. The funny thing was, later on, Miss sidled up to her. "The word you were looking for was Bovine, Veronica!"

Daniel grinned. "Cool! I'll wait for you if you like," he said when they reached the changing rooms, "give you a coggy and the thrill of a lifetime!" Bethany felt her colour rising.

"Why? Where are we going?"

"To the beach? To give your foot a good soaking, and to see the whale. They've had to get a crane in to shift it."

"I'm not sure..."

"Oh come on," he said, sensing her misgivings. You'll be OK. It's not suffering now."

"Right oh, but you might be sorry! Have you any idea how long it takes a young girl to get ready!"

Bethany hated the emptiness of the changing rooms. Gone, the before and after subdued murmurings and enthusiasms of matches lost and won. Now it was a left over place with discarded tea-shirts, shorts and snapped off laces lurking in dusty corners. Discarded blazers hung on pegs, rejects all. On the bare, green walls health and fitness posters depicted beautiful smiles and even more beautiful, tanned bodies. Bethany hated them. Hurrying, she changed back into her uniform, took one last look around, put her tongue out at the Miss Perfects and closed the door on the smell of stale sweat and the muddy imprints of trainers.

"So this is your bike! Nice one," she said. "You even clean it!"

"Only when dad starts giving me grief. Here, let's have your kit," he said, easing her sports bag over his shoulder. "No one's looking!" Bethany gave him the dead eye.

"So you have one as well?"

"One what?"

"A difficult parent."

"Don't we all! Anyway, hop on!" he said. As if this was her normal form of transport, Bethany eased herself on to the crossbar.

"Just relax," he said when her knuckles began to blanch. "And hang on, 'cause it's all down hill!" But his teasing had no effect. From the moment Daniel lent forward Bethany could feel his warmth, his breath on her cheek and her heart beating.

"Damn!" he said when he finally skidded to a halt. The unit and trailer was already easing its way up the slipway. "We've missed the action."

"Well, thank God for that!" she said, sliding off the bike and giving her bottom a rub.

"Well, how about that paddle and a short walk?"

"OK. I think I can make it to the harbour and back- with a rest in between," she said when a look of disbelief crossed Daniel's face.

"It's a fair distance. Don't you have to get home?"

"Yes, but I'm OK for a bit," she said, watching Daniel padlock his bike to the railing.

"Mm." Half expecting to see Smithard hanging around, Daniel scanned the parade of cheap-jack shops.

"What's the matter?" she said.

"Nothing I suppose."

"Except?"

"Well, Smithard…the last time we were down here, I thought he was watching you."

"Oh, him! Tell me about it," Bethany said. "He's a loser, been like that for years. I take no notice. Come on; let's walk where the sand is firmer. Just a minute though." Bethany knelt to unlace and ease off her trainers. Then, after tying the laces into a double bow and stuffing her socks into the toecaps, she slung the lot over her shoulder.

"That's better. I love the feel of the sand, it's so cool and this is great!" she said, curling her toes round the hardened ripples made by the tide. "There's nothing better than a good foot massage after a tough game of basketball. Agreed?"

"Well, about the massage, yeah, but I'm not sure about the basketball, being a tough game, I mean" and he scanned her face for a reaction to his teasing. But there was no take up, only a half smile and a "hm" that held the promise of dispute in its tone.

Daniel watched her limp toward the water, beguiled it seemed as if by the song of a siren. He watched her standing with the water swirling and eddying around her slim ankles…watched and wondered if like him, she felt the pulse of the moon in the waves that ran so clear, so true. As a little fella he had many a time raced them in, jumping over them as they peaked. He had giggled and screeched with excitement till he saw the froth disperse and the water recede leaving fragmented shells glistening in the sand. Then he had felt lonely and helpless. Till the next resurgence time had stood still, a forever kind of sad time that he didn't understand. Now he watched those same waves swelling the distant sea, waves that would return…again and again. He followed Bethany's gaze.

She was watching the sun struggling against the clouds, clouds that darkened great patches of the sea. Then, in a rare moment, it broke through so that a swathe of brilliance cut through the water and a million gems danced in the shallows. Again he looked seaward, watched the sun combine with the sea, the sea with the sky, a blurred mass of blood red, orange and gold.

Bethany turned towards him. He watched her approach, her hair blowing free, her face pink from the sharpness of the east wind. The school uniform seemed out of place. In his mind's eye he saw her dressed in a flowing shift that clung to her nakedness. She was a Celtic mystic, reborn and due to be sacrificed. A wave of protectiveness overcame him. Oblivious to the piercing cry of a gull overhead, he watched her gravitating towards him, drawn it seemed into his magnetic field.

"Awesome, isn't it?" she said. Daniel thought about the times he'd walked this stretch of sand, a lonely beachcomber teasing out the confusions of his teenage mind?

"It is, and it's a monkey's birthday," he said turning his palms upward to catch the spots of rain. "Come on, but careful now!"

Minutes later they had reached the lifeboat slip way. The curly seaweed and the discarded debris of holiday makers had collected against the wall.

"This is the bit I hate," she said, skimming the sand from her bare feet with her socks.

"Well, let me do it!"

"Not likely!"

"Don't be daft, give it here!" he said, snatching the sock.

"Feet are really horrible aren't they?" she said, as much to hide her embarrassment at feeling like a little girl again as at the personal way he rubbed the coarse sand from between her wrinkled toes.

"Well, they're OK if you're in need of a good laugh!"

"Cheeky! And don't you dare," she warned. "Besides, I'm impervious to tickling."

"Big word!"

"It's what my Dad used to say."

"Used to?"

"He's dead," she said, more matter of factly than she'd expected.

"I'm sorry!"

"It was a while ago... when I was little," she said, her weak smile barely masking the pain of remembering. "And now, if you don't mind, I'll have my foot back!" Bethany glanced at her watch.

"Time to go?" he said.

"'fraid so. I've got some serious grovelling to do. I've been neglecting Ron for one thing and mum's not impressed with the English project. But this time," she said with a determined frown, "I'm going to have my way. Besides, she worries if I'm out late. Pathetic, isn't it?"

"Shall I take you home then?"

"God, no; she'd do her nut in!" Daniel grimaced and looked away. "I know…sorreee," she said.

"OK. Anyway, where's home, Penhill estate?"

"No!" Bethany looked at Daniel as if he had just stepped off another planet. "The bay of course, it's the only place to live!"

"Arguably?"

"Definitely, Daniel." Bethany turned away. It was the first time she had spoken his name and she coloured up. "You can take me to the bus stop though," she said trying to compose herself. "It's too late to walk the cliff path. I rarely do any -."

"What's up?"

"I...I...don't know. It's just that...why ever did I say that?"

"Say what?"

"About rarely taking the cliff path. I never take it."

"A slip of the tongue maybe."

"No, not that. I do love the cliffs though. I've always been drawn to them because they're timeless. Just think, if they could speak, what stories they could tell…"

"You're not kidding. I don't know about timeless though. There's a beginning and an end for everything I suppose, the alpha to omega of life maybe, and as for the cliffs, they're eroding. It won't be too long before the sea claims the castle ramparts."

"Oh, don't...don't say that!" Bethany's eyes glazed over. She turned away, her eyes brimming.

"Hey, come on!" Daniel reached out to touch her shoulder. "What brought this on?"

"I'm sorry. Oh heck, this is stupid."

"Well, stupid or not, something's got to you." Daniel's steady gaze held. He waited, his encouraging half smile giving her confidence.

"It's nothing really... nothing I'd expect you to understand," she said at last."

"Try me."

"It's...it's just that I feel different these days somehow. All mixed up. I mean, I love the cliffs. Up there with the wind blowing off the sea it feels good, as if I'm part of the elements, identifying and bonding with them but..." Bethany's voice cracked. She paused "but these days," she said, fighting back the tears, I sort of have the sense that it's more than that, that I'm being drawn back in time and...and -"

"Come on, let's get you to the bus stop," he said, putting a comforting arm around her. "Your problem is that you take things too much to heart. Seeing the whale probably upset you more than I realised. A jerk is what I am!" Bethany smiled.

"No, you're not. It's more me being paranoid!"

"And as for thinking you might take the cliff path again when you never have, it was probably a déjà vu experience. We've all had those. That's weird enough though, I'll give you that." Bethany shrugged her shoulders.

"It is," she said "and thanks for listening," but her eyes were fixed on the cliff face and the seagull that hovered overhead.

Chapter 11

Bethany dumped her gear in the cupboard under the stairs. Her mobile phone throbbed in her pocket. Heck! Another text from Ron. The third that day!

'Where r u? Call me!!! R.'

Bethany sighed.

"What the matter?" her mother asked as she sauntered by.

"It's Ron. I said I'd meet her after the basket ball the other night and -"

"And you decided to go with that lad instead!"

"Yes, but it hadn't been planned or anything. I'd just met Daniel on the beach. I'd -"

"I know, been to see the whale."

"Mum…don't even go there!" Bethany said, giving her mother a sidelong glance. Mrs. Mallinson shrugged her shoulders. Bethany pouted. "Why do I get the impression you're judging me! Anyway, I haven't seen Ron all day. I even thought she might be off school."

"Hm…so you phoned to see how she was?" The question hit home.

"Come on, mum. Don't make me feel guilty. I feel bad as it is. Things don't always go to plan, that's all."

"Well, what about tonight? She usually watches you play, doesn't she?"

"Yes, but she wasn't there either.. Not early on anyway. When I sprained my ankle, the teacher said a paddle would do it good so Daniel took me and -"

"Aaah, Daniel!"

"Mum! You're doing it again! I'll ring her in a bit, OK?"

"OK but it's not me you need to placate, Bethany!"

"I know. Anyway, I'm going up to rinse my feet."

"Don't you want something to eat? And how is your foot anyway?"

"It's OK. The paddle helped. I'll come down and get a sandwich later on. I might even tackle some ironing."

"Praise be!"

'Well, here goes! Better get this over with,' Bethany thought as she dialled Ron's number.

"Ah, at last! My erstwhile friend!" Bethany ignored the put down.

"Hi, Ron! Where did you get to this morning? I waited for you at the sun trap!" Bethany said, trying to deflect her own guilt. The accusation found its mark.

"Yeah, like I waited for you to call! I told you I had a dental appointment and that I wouldn't be in school or at the match -"

"Whoops!"

"You might say, 'whoops' - or whatever that's supposed to mean, but I hung around all night waiting for that call. We were supposed to meet up, remember?"

Bethany had remembered, too late of course, but she was not going to sour her feelings about Daniel by making him the excuse. At any other time she would have confided in Ron, giggled about what happened or might have happened on a date. This was now. Her time with Daniel was too personal and precious to degrade it with girlish tittle-tattle, suggestive sniggering and the like. Besides, after all she'd said about Daniel, it would be hard to explain and she knew she'd be accused of hypocrisy, but Ron was miffed, miffed as hell.

"We can go for a coke tomorrow night," Bethany volunteered.

"And I suppose that's by way of an apology."

"Sure. I am sorry. It's just that, well, you know, I mean…for a start there's the English project. Have you decided what to do 'cause it's driving me potty. Mum's still being difficult. Maybe we can get together on it. Anyway, look, I'll have to go, Ron. Mum's got the tea ready. Tell you what, I'll ring you later. OK?"

"Yeah, whenever!"

"You'll be pleased to know I've made it up with Ron, well sort of," Bethany said, settling the plate of tuna sarnies on her lap. She'll be OK. Ron always has plenty to say, but she never keeps things on. We might do the English together."

"So what are you going to do tonight?"

"Like I said; I'll do some ironing and maybe sketch the barrel. That's all I can do," she said with a suppressed huff. It was just as well that the phone rang. Her mother picked it up.

"Penhill 830102..." Mrs. Mallinson glanced across at her daughter struggling to set up the ironing board in the confined space. "Yes, she's here," her mother said, passing the phone over. Annoyed by her cool tone, Bethany adopted a more friendly one.

"Hello. Oh...Daniel...hi! I dunno. Is there time? It'll take forever to cycle over. Oh...right. Just a minute." Bethany covered the mouth piece. "OK, mum?"

"I expect so." But resentment hung around her mother's face.

"How long will it take for you to get here? Right. I'll meet you by the war memorial in an hour. Bye."

Picking up the iron Bethany meandered over to the sink and, gauging the tap water flow, began to fill the steam cavity. She glanced across at her mother. Her face was a mile long. "Damn!" The steam cavity had flooded.

"There's no need to lose your temper!" Bethany's sigh was audible. "Or sigh!"

"Is it all right if I breathe?" She had spoken under her breath.

"Pardon?"

"Nothing mum." Bethany turned aside. Her eyes prickled but she wouldn't cry. Gulping on the lump in her throat, she began to sort the laundry; she would begin with her school shirts.

With the iron railings set into the surrounding stone wall of the memorial there was barely enough room for Bethany to sit down.

"Come on, Daniel. Make it snappy!" But the words were barely out of her mouth when she saw him free wheeling down the hill.

"You're mad!" she said as he skidded to a stop, swirling the loose gravel into a heap. "And a vandal!"

Pushing his fingers through a mass of thick black hair, he raised an eyebrow. "Where else can I find my thrills?"

"Yeah, well, there are thrills and there are thrills. Is that the kind you're looking for?"

A wry grin crossed his face. "You show me one better!"

"I will!" she said. "Anyway come on up to the house. You can leave your bike in our front garden."

"OK. Will I meet your mum?"

"No. I think an introduction had better wait."

"Why?"

"This is it," she said, indicating the cottage with a flick of her head.

Daniel persisted. "Why?"

"Why what?"

"You're evading my question, Bethany. I'm not brain dead, you know."

"Well, not quite!" she said, smiling. "Mum's not so good tonight."

"You mean, she doesn't want to meet me. She doesn't approve."

"Of you? No. She doesn't even know you."

"Or want to know me?"

Bethany clicked her tongue. "We've had a bit of a row, that's all. Come on." Bethany led the way to the narrow opening between the cottages. "You'll need stamina for this," she said. Daniel followed her eyes. "The steps go on forever...to heaven and beyond."

"I can't wait!"

It was a long climb, a silent climb, each concentrating on the way ahead.

"And I thought I was fit," she said, rubbing the backs of her knees.

"Here." Daniel held out his hand. "It's all part of the service."

Bethany smiled. She loved the affectionate teasing.

Below them nestled the row of cottages with their red roofs and intriguing garret windows. A few straggling tourists had ventured out making the most of their time and a distant queue of them waited to board the night fishing trawler.

"I used to hang around the lighthouse when I was a kid," Daniel said, "but it never occurred to me to come up here. It's great!"

"Close your eyes then. It's my turn to lead the way," she said. "You only have three more steps to go. Then you'll be in Heaven."

. "Trust me," she said, putting her hand across his eyes and steadying him. "There. Now you can open them!"

"My God, Bethany! You're mad!" She laughed. "I don't mind heights but this is something else!"

"Isn't that the fun part...the excitement? It's the gulls' view. I love to watch them. They're more agitated than usual at the moment. They'll have had a second clutch. Watch Daniel!" Urged on by their parents' cries and reeling acrobatics, the fledglings teetered on the wind swept ledges. "I wonder what it is that tells them it's time to fly."

"Instinct I suppose. Or maybe the parents stop feeding them and it's a case of do or die."

"Well, you wanted a thrill! It's wonderful up here, isn't it? When I want time out, this is where I come."

Daniel scanned the horizon and the fading blue skies. Looking outward across the sea wasn't so bad, but when he took another step forward, his heart missed a beat. Below him the sea foamed and frothed. He watched it recede, watched it swell the ocean, watched the rebirth of the waves and their steady, heaving progress towards the cliff face. When it broke, crashing thunderously on the rocks, he gasped. "It's never still. It's amazing."

"Yes," she said, pitting her body against a sudden gust of wind. "Have you ever wondered what happens to all the noise...the sounds we make here on the planet? They have to go somewhere, don't they? Our experiences as well. I mean, we move on from them and they become history, but...but those same experiences were real enough, so where did they go? Does a trace of them linger on the empty air, unearthly and intangible...and might they come back to haunt us again, like deja vu and all that?"

"Bethany, there you go again! I'm beginning to think you're a bit psychic! I mean, you're always on about that sort of stuff. You'll be telling me you believe in the stars signs next."

"And why wouldn't I? The moon controls the tides so why can't the stars influence us?" she said, turning away and swaying dangerously close to the cliff edge.

"Bethany!" Daniel grabbed her arm. "You nearly fell then."

"Anyway, have you?" she said, dismissing his concern. "thought about deja vu and all that."

"No, no," he said, "there can be no coming back. Once things have passed, that's it."

"Still, you are impressed with all this," she insisted."

"'course. It's awesome! But promise me you'll never come up here on your own again!" he said, taking a step backwards.

"I can't do that. It's my retreat. Everyone has to have one."

"Yes well, you'll have to find a more conventional one!"

Bethany scowled. "Or else what?" she said, throwing down the gauntlet.

"Or else nothing if you put it that way, I suppose. I'd worry about you that's all."

"You've got a funny way of showing it! You sounded controlling and yet..." Bethany looked directly into his eyes... "what are you hiding, Daniel?"

"Hiding?" Daniel looked away, disturbed by her persistent gaze.

"Well, that's not the real you, is it?" she said taking his hand.

"Come on, Bethany. If I need any psycho-analysis I'll -"

"Get your father to book you into a private clinic?" Bethany could have bitten her tongue.

Daniel sighed. "Not you as well!" he said, turning away.

"Now I've upset you. I've opened my big mouth again!"

"To say what was on your mind, yes!" he said, "but I'm not apologising for the fact that my dad has a bob or two!" Anyway, Miss Perfect, it's good to know you're not faultless!"

"I'm sorry, Daniel." Daniel turned back to scan her freckly, open face. "And Daniel..."

"What now, Freckles?" Bethany clicked her tongue.

"Will you do the English project with me? Miss said it's OK to work in pairs so long as we put our own slant on it and it's our own work?"

"What have you got in mind?"

"Well, it's historical. We'd have to do research."

"OK. Maybe. Anyway, what brought that on? A minute ago you were huffing and puffing and on your high horse again, all because I want you to take care of yourself," he said, smiling into his collar.

"Yes, well you deserved it. You're a pompous nut!"

"Easy, tiger!" he said, pulling her towards him. In her shyness she looked away, but at the touch of his hand on her cheek she turned toward him and he kissed her.

It was lighting up time when they arrived back at the cottage. Daniel had insisted on getting her home before dark. "Best not upset your mum," he said, lifting his bicycle over the fence. "Don't want to scupper my chances before we've even begun!" he said with a telling wink. Then he was gone. With a silly grin, Bethany watched him out of sight. Sighing and drawing her shoulders back, she turned to the cottage.

"He's gone then?" The voice from the dark recess had the expected edge.

"Yes. We climbed up to the cliff top and chatted."

"So I assumed. Why didn't you bring him in?"

"I thought…thought that you wanted to be quiet, Mum. That…that you weren't too pleased I went out."

"Well, I'll give him his due. He got you home before dark and long may it continue." Bethany turned her face away, raised her eyes to the ceiling.

"I'm off upstairs to do some homework then. Can I take the barrel?" The pause which followed was irritatingly long. "Mum?"

"If you must." So she had heard! "But be careful with it."

"I will."

Long after the routine sounds of her mother preparing for bed had ceased, Bethany was still sitting at her desk. The spotlight had picked out the relief on the carving so that she'd been able to do a wrap-around sketch of the whole, a bit like an ancient map. Then came the detail, little cameos of each design or lettering. 'Much easier to have an enlarged photo!' she thought blinking away her eye strain. Then, rummaging through her school bag, she located her (no way would I be seen dead in these) spectacles, propped herself up in bed with her diary and slipped into a time zone of her own...

Dear Diary,

Oh my God. I've forgotten to phone Ron again! Well, it's too late now. An insensitive prat is what I am and I'll be in for it tomorrow. She'll go bananas especially when I tell her about Daniel. But Ron, if only you knew how my crazy life is starting to find a momentum of its own. I can see myself having to tell little white lies that turn into whoppers and catch me out with a very red face! Speaking of which, when Daniel made his move on me, thank God the light was already fading! God, Ron, you know well enough that I've broken the 'first man you kiss will be the man you marry' rule yonks ago but this was straight out of Barbara Cartland. Well, you know, the cliff top, the darkening sky and the crashing of the sea on the rocks below! But heck, yeah Ron, the earth did move for me! Still, it was only a kiss! And this is the boy I've loathed...hated for years. Well, you did tell me 'to give it a whirl girl' He's terrific. Different from all the others and so masterful. Well, he'd have to be to interest a bossy boots like me, wouldn't he? I'm going to have to watch my mouth though. I don't know why or how exactly but I obviously touched a raw nerve tonight.

Ah well, lights out time, Diary. Bethany reached over to switch off the bedside lamp. She was tired. 'It'll soon be morning,' she thought, snuggling down and nestling into her cuddling pillow 'and then I'll see him again.' She smiled. It was just like being a child again, willing herself to sleep on Christmas Eve so that the morning with its bulging stocking hanging on the end of her bed would come all the sooner. Excepting **that** Christmas Eve. The memory of her father's last illness came suddenly, uninvited. and she turned over covering her ears. But the sounds that had disturbed her then, came again. He'd been in the next room. Each rasping breath had been long and irregular. Bethany had tried to follow his rhythm with her own but in the in between silences she couldn't hold her breath any longer and her heart had stood still. Then came the death rattle but for all its turmoil it gave her hope. After all, her bronchitis had been like that and she'd got over it. Now she knew better. In the early hours of Boxing Day morning her father had died.

The memory of those haunting sounds kept her awake. She tried to think of Daniel, of life rather than death, of the future rather than the past. For a little while she even played silhouettes against the moonlit wall, celebrating the happy moments she had shared with her dad, but a sudden breeze caught the curtain. The distorted animal magic was lost…lost in the sigh of the rustling fabric and of the woman, for there she was again, veiled behind a smouldering mist. Bethany drew back. Her pulse raced.

"What! What do you want of me!" she cried but there was no answer, just a heavy burden of sadness and longing.

Chapter 12

The next morning armed with her school bag and the scroll, Bethany pushed open the kitchen door with her bottom.

"Hey! Steady yourself, girl!" her mother said, swerving the tea pot away from her. "You'll be scalding one of us!"

"Sorree!"

"Anyway, what's the rush?"

"No rush, but look at this, mum." Bethany laid the enlarged wrap-around sketch of the barrel on the table. Her mother scanned it briefly and returned to the stove. "So, what do you think?"

"Think? I think you must want something to do, sitting up there doodling half the night." Mrs. Mallinson eased the cosy over the tea pot spout pausing long enough to give Bethany a reproachful sidewards glance.

"Doodling!"

"Well, let's face it, you're no Leonardo da Vinci are you now?" she said.

"Yeah OK! But look mum…the engravings. They're amazing. There's a sort of turret and a path running down to the sea," Bethany said, holding the barrel up to the light. "And boats, look…the one that stands out has a name on it. There's a monogram and -"

"Yes well, now get on with your breakfast or you'll be late for school," she said sliding the sketch to the far end of the table.

"Mum!"

"Yes dear!" her words were laboured, weighted with frustration.

"You might show more interest."

"Maybe. But first things first. I'm out tonight. It's the church committee meeting. We're planning the summer fete."

Irritated by her mother's crazy logic Bethany shook her head and frowned. "So?"

"So I won't be able to get your tea, and knowing you Bethany Mallinson it'll be rabbit food or nothing, if indeed you do finally decide to eat."

"God, mum!" she said, running her fingers through her hair. "That's outrageous!"

"What?"

"Well I mean, here am I goggle-eyed from peering all night at your precious barrel and here you are -"

"Exactly my point. You're obsessed with it, and you've got shadows under your eyes!"

"So I didn't sleep very well."

"Not again! So what was it about this time?"

"Dad. I couldn't get him out of my mind. Then there was the -"

"The what?" her mother asked. Bethany stopped short. No way could she tell her mother about the shifting images that had teased her mind into believing she hadn't been alone…Gathering her thoughts she reached over for a piece of toast. "It's just that when I dream about dad it's as if he's still alive."

"So do I," she said, her voice softening, "but it's better not to think about things past and gone if you ask me, especially when you're trying to get to sleep. Anyway, what plans have you got for tonight?"

"Daniel's coming over after school. We're going to plan our project."

"Oh, so it's *our* project now? I see. And what about Veronica?" Bethany shot her mother a ' thanks for reminding me' look!

"I forgot to phone her again last night. She'll be manic."

"I don't wonder. I like that girl." Her mother spoke with conviction.

"I know."

"She's open. Honest too and she speaks her mind."

"Then you'll like Daniel!" Bethany's smile was meant to be encouraging.

"Will I now?" her mother said, with a doubt that hung in the air. "Well, if he's coming here tonight just remember I don't want him upstairs."

"Mum! He might have to go to the loo." Bethany's impatience threatened to spill over.

"And that's all. I don't want any hanky panky under my roof, or anyone else's for that matter," she added with a dire tone and warning glance. Bethany's sigh barely hid her anger. "Besides, you can be sure 'you know who' will be poking her nose in. She'll be all agog! And you might sigh! You wouldn't be the first young girl to get into trouble and you wouldn't be the last! But not my lass!"

"Mum!"

"I know. You think I'm jumping the gun. Nevertheless," she said with an air of foreboding, "there's nothing like a bit of straight talking about these things, besides, forewarned is forearmed!"

"Straight talking? These things!" Bethany couldn't help herself.

"Come on mum, tell it as it is... you're talking about sex sex sex!"

"That'll be enough! And you can put that barrel back now you've done with it. I don't want it broken," she said with an air of finality. Resigned, Bethany tossed her mother a look of forced disbelief.

"Yersss, mum and OK...I won't break the barrel!" she said. ' But why, oh why, she thought, 'was her mum so closed in, so unapproachable?'

It was close to the end of break when Bethany finally caught up with Ron but the sudden onslaught of hyperactive first years stampeding toward the door interrupted their conversation. "My God, what are they like! Don't tell me that once was me!" she said and, at the sight of Miss pint sized 'O'Donahue (newly appointed Biology teacher) straining and twisting her elongated neck like a demented ostrich, she grinned. "Anyway, like I said, I'm sorry, Ron!"

"Course you are!"

"All right, I deserved that," Bethany said, picking up on her sarcasm. "But -"

"No buts, don't even try to make excuses. You're out of order and you damn well know it!"

"I'm always out of order it seems."

"Yes and my heart is bleeding! Excuse me whilst I get my violin! *And* I don't care if you had another barny with your mother. I don't care if you were feeling sad and woe-be-gone and wanted some space. I don't even care if you had a heavy date and a bloody pimple sprouting on the end of your nose!" Bethany turned away, her eyes rolling in annoyance. She hated being accountable, especially to her mate. "And like I said before, I thought we were friends, but apparently not." Bethany drew in a long breath. The escaping sigh could have filled a wind sock.

"Yeah, OK...but there wasn't a pimple! Right?" Bethany waited for the pause to take effect, waited for Ron to pick up on the innuendo.

"Ah ha! But you did have a heavy date! So that's it. Well, go on. Which magnificent, acned specimen turned you on this time!"

"He's not acned." Bethany paused, unsure of how to go on. Veronica's impatience brimmed over.

"Well...spit it out!"

"He...he's not even the arrogant twit...I...I thought he was," she said, screwing up her face with embarrassment.

"Who is -? Oh my God it's Daniel? Daniel, the Moron! Daniel, the Schmuck!"

"Go on, scoff, why don't you? That's exactly why I couldn't, well, didn't want to tell you. I knew you wouldn't understand and I felt such a hypocrite."

"So you bloody well should! You've bleated on about him since Junior School. It's been a running -"

"Joke. Yes, I know but -"

"It's not anymore!" Ron said, rolling her eyes.

"No. Things are different. He's -"

"Cute!" Veronica said, widening her eyes and smiling mischievously.

"Come on Ron. Give me a break!" Bethany shifted from one leg to another. "He's an OK kind of person. Really! I...we were wrong, that's all. It's OK to be wrong now and then, isn't it? And people change!"

"So that's it. Fine. See you at the wedding, if you can remember to invite me!"

"Don't be daft! And don't give me a hard time; you're just like mum."

"Oh yes, mum. She'll be over the moon!"

"Exactly...so get off my case, Ron! Anyway what about this English topic?" she said, changing the subject.

"What about it?"

"Well I thought you, me and Daniel could -"

"No way! You can count me out of that one. Two's company and three's a crowd, remember? Never let it be said that I came between star-crossed lovers."

"Star-crossed? God, what a misery you are, Ron!"

"Hm...maybe. Still, I'll be there to pick up the pieces. What are friends for after all? No, don't worry about me, about the project, I mean. I've found a pair of my great, great grandmother's mother-of-pearl binoculars. She was in service; a scullery maid. The master thought the chauffeur was seducing the upstairs maid so he asked her to spy on them." Bethany's interest peaked, Ron's eyes lit up, the drama queen instinct dying to take over.

"Well, get on with it, was he?"

"No, he was sleeping with the mistress!"

"So what happened?" Ron lent over, "Murder most foul!" she whispered. "The master did her in and stuffed her up the kitchen chimney. The broth was never the same after that...and the maggots, well -"

"Yeah all right, Ron!"

"Good story though, don't you think?" she said between giggles. "Anyway, I'm going. Let's get together sometime. We need to talk some more...intimately, you know. Give me all the gory details!!" she said with a 'wink wink say no more' glint in her eye.

"Hm! Somehow I don't think so! Not this time my old mate!"

Chapter 13

"This is an unexpected pleasure. I thought you didn't like to be seen with me!" her mother said when, that evening, they strolled down to the church together.

"Don't be daft, mum!" 'course, it was a lie. If any of her friends (Veronica apart) had bumped into them, she'd have died a thousand deaths. Her mother wasn't particularly old and even if she had been, that wouldn't have mattered. It was more the look of her. The fashion. Ever since Bethany could remember, she'd made most of her own clothes from obsolete Style patterns.

"Why don't we go to town in the holidays, mum? We could buy you a new outfit!"

"Why? What's the matter with this one?" she said, readjusting her collar. "A nice bit of cloth, this. Made to last!"

"You can say that again!"

"So what would you have me wearing?"

"Oh I dunno. I can see you in a good country style suit. That would be more like you mum. A zip up bomber jacket and let me think -," she said, turning her mother round and looking her up and down.

"Get away, Bethany. You half dream life away!" Mrs. Mallinson shrugged her daughter off.

"I know. A make-over and a new hairdo. When I get a summer job later on, I'll treat you."

"You'll do no such thing. My hair is fine just the way it is. Besides what's the use of spending all that money just to flatten it with a hat?"

"Exactly! Go mad, mum. Get rid!" When all was said and done, it was the hat that took the biscuit. That and the terse remarks her mother dropped. "No. I don't think so Bethany. Anyhow, in case you've forgotten, this is the ladies' church meeting, not a jaunt!"

"Sorree. Only trying to help. So what time will you be finished?"

"Why?" she asked with an air of suspicion.

"We'll come and meet you, that's all!"

"What? You and that lad?" Mrs. Mallinson sniffed.

"Why not? We can't have you walking home in the dark...all alone! You never know what might happen," she said with a cheeky grin.

"Tst! Half past ten then. Really, you're incorrigible, Bethany!"

"And mum!" Bethany called her mother back with a curled, conspiratorial finger.

"What now?"

"Don't forget. No hanky panky with the church warden whilst I'm away!"

"You may well joke but mark my words. 'There's many a slip ' twixt the cup and the lip!"

Bethany watched her bossy, spirited mother close the church doors behind her. She glanced at her watch. 7.00 o'clock. Just enough time to get back to the cottage and change.

'So what should I wear?' Bethany thought as she rummaged through her wardrobe shelves. Casuals of course. What else? No point in wowing him with girly, romantic gear: a tiny narrow strap skirt with a stick on tattoo strategically placed on her thigh and knee high boots of course; maybe even a pierced navel! He's got a hope!' she thought, grinning at the unlikely image she'd conjured up for herself.

Fingering through the little choice she had or ever wanted, she picked out her comfortable, plain white, turtle necked top and denim jacket.

"Boring!" said her alter ego as she looked in the mirror sideways on.

"No, I'll dress to suit myself," she said, dropping a mini skirt onto the bed in disgust.

"Coward!"

"Huh. You're not wrong," she said and bent to tie the laces on her trainers.

"Bap....bap...bap!" That couldn't be Daniel! It was. She rushed downstairs and opened the door a fraction. "Sh!" Bethany pressed her index finger to his lips. "What's up? Is your mum asleep? I thought you said she'd be out. I'm only announcing my arrival."

"And how! Do I really want The Snooper spreading it around that my boyfriend's a yob! Anyhow that contraption does nothing for your image. What is it?" she said, opening the door wider to let him pass.

"It's my hooter!"

"Well, why can't you have a bell that tinkles like all the other little boys?"

"Hey, steady on girl! This 'ere hooter is a mark of my individuality. Besides, I have to make an impression somehow!"

"That's true!" Bethany's head nodded like a gimmicky boxer dog in the back of a moving car.

"Hey. Like I said, steady on B! I'll have none of your cheek. I'd rather start where we left off!"

"And where would that be?" Bethany said with a capricious toss of her hair.

"Come here," he said, reaching over and encircling her in his arms. "Oh, that!" Bethany pushed him aside. "No, not tonight!" she said.

"Why, have you gone off me already, Freckles?"

"'course not. No, it's just that I promised mum -"

"What? That you wouldn't kiss me?"

"Something like that!"

"Well then, **I'll** kiss **you**. You don't have to kiss me back!" he said, reaching for her again.

"But -"

"No buts! Friends kiss each other hello, don't they and in France, it's three times. Comme ci," he said, planting a successive kiss on each cheek. Bethany flushed.

"Ah...but you are blushing, ma petite!" he said in a broken French accent...."and I ' av to control myself. Come, let us get on wiz zis business of ze Englis project." Then after a pause - "but what is ze time zat your muzzer will come 'ome?"

"You're mad," she said, scuffing his ear. "I know not. She may stay a long time wiz ze church warden!"

"Ah! So when ze cat is away ze mice can play. It is ze same all over ze world n'est ce pas?"

"Idiot, come on!" she said and led him to the cabinet.

"There's the engraved barrel I was telling you about; on the top shelf," she said, pointing through the other bits and bobs.

"Oh never mind that! Let's have a gander at the miner's lamp and that George Stevenson paper weight! It's great. Can't we work on that?"

"No, Daniel, the barrel!" Bethany reached up, fingering beneath the lace cloth on top of the cabinet. "That's odd." She patted the surface. "I don't believe it!"

"What?"

"My mother. She's hidden the key so I can't get in. Well that's great. Thanks mum!" Bethany sat down on the arm of the chair. Her despondence and anger spilled over into the little room.

"She wouldn't have done it on purpose."

"You don't know my mother and you never will do the way she carries on!" she said with an unflattering pout.

"Well, it's no use getting hot under the collar. People always do things for a reason. Think, Bethany. Why would she hide it?"

"I suppose because it's an heirloom!"

"So she doesn't want it tampered with. Our place is full of them, but they're left lying around. People are different, aren't they."

"Maybe. This is her 'everything special' cabinet," she said but the edge of resentment was still there.

"There you go then. Anyway, I thought you did a wrap around sketch?"

"I did." Bethany reached into the sideboard. "There," she said, carefully un-scrolling and re-scrolling it the opposite way. "It's not good, but it'll give you an idea." Daniel scanned the illustrations, finger pointing the detail.

"And remember, we have to write a biography." Bethany said.

"So who could have carved it?" he said, standing back to take in a wider view.

"I don't know and if mother does, she's not telling!"

"Oh well, we'll just have to look for clues." Daniel's logical mind had been tapped. His self assurance surfaced. "When was it carved?"

"I don't know that either but look, there's a ship with a name on it. We could start by going down to the harbour and asking around. There's old Walt, the salt! He's always down there smoking his pipe and mending nets. He's lived round here since the year blob and what he doesn't know isn't worth knowing. He's a bit of an eccentric though, talks to himself and all that. He's our own resident Methuselah and an old friend. He may know."

"OK, it's a start. What's the ship's name?"

"I can only decipher a bit of it. The engravings override it. See, it's here. It begins with a 'J'; there's an 'i' and what looks like an 'r' at the end," she said, trying to trace the lettering with her finger.

"So we need to find out what it was called, its history, who it belonged to, what it carried and when. We can get started on that at the library."

"Yes but that wouldn't give us a biography, would it?"

"Right. So what's this?" Daniel said, pointing to the interwoven lines.

"It's my attempt at drawing what I think is a monogram but without a closer look I couldn't make it out! I think that's an R but what with all these curly bits I can't be sure about the rest."

"OK, this'll be fun!" Daniel's enthusiasm caught Bethany by surprise.

"I'm glad somebody can get excited about it!"

"Hm. Tell you what, I'll bring my Digital camera over."

"Yeah…but give it a couple of days - Mum, you know," she said with an apologetic half smile.

"No, I don't really, but it's your Mum, your call."

"Don't be upset, Daniel. I just have to take it slowly, that's all. You'll know what I mean when you meet her."

"And when will that be?"

"Tonight. I said we'd meet her at half past ten and walk her home from church."

"So what's the matter with the church warden doing that!" Daniel said managing a weak smile.

"Some chance! I sort of teased her about it. She nearly had a fit."

"OK. Well, how about spending the day together on Saturday. You have a bike so we could picnic somewhere, spend the afternoon at the library and then you could come over to our house for supper. We'll see you home."

"That'll be great."

"OK, so where's the loo?" Daniel said. The sudden change of subject took her off guard.

"The loo?" Bethany's large eyes grew larger and she blushed.

"Now what's the matter? It is all right if I have a pee?"

"C…'course! Up…upstairs on the right," she stuttered. Daniel put his finger under her chin tilting her face toward him.

"Look me in the eye B. What is it?"

"Have I to be honest?"

"Always and absolutely," he said, a confused look beginning to form.

"Mum said she didn't want you upstairs!" Daniel sighed.

"Well I can always pee in the garden."

"No! No... it's not that, it's -"

"Oh. I get it! She doesn't want *us upstairs together, snogging!* No problem, Freckles. Grab your jacket and we'll be on our way. I can nuzzle into your softer recesses out of doors just as well as in!"

Chapter 14

"It's a bit chilly on the butt!" Daniel said, easing himself off the dry stone wall and taking her hand. "Still, it'll cool my ardour!"

"Just as well then. We're in the spotlight under the street lamp and you can be sure The Snooper's peeking through her nets, so never mind your ardour; think about my reputation!"

"Does that mean I don't get a good night kiss?"

"Just a peck. I don't want to be known as the tart of Fisher Row!"

"A tart, you! Hardly," he added with a convincing smile.

"Well you know how people gossip, especially her. It's how she gets her kicks! Anyway, what do you think of mum?"

"She's OK. A bit on the cool side. Then there were those predictable questions. I mean, why do adults always ask what you're planning to do when you leave school? It's like being asked about the birth of the universe! How many of us have the slightest idea what we're going to do? They just don't get it, do they? Life's for living isn't it? Why do we have to be bound in by plans, plans and more bloody plans!"

"So why didn't you tell her that!" Bethany snapped

"Oh yeah, and scupper my chances with you! Besides, she's protective of you, and you of her, by the sounds of it. I wouldn't want to upset her. She'll mellow; it's probably the one parent syndrome," he said.

"Excuse me!" Bethany's voice crisped like the sound of a footfall in the snow. "She's always coped so there's no need to patronise."

"Brr! Do I detect a draught or are we heading for a gale force wind? I was just going to say that she's bound to be doubly concerned being on her own. I mean, my parents go on endlessly about how to cope with me and my erring ways. Anyway, I can feel the way the wind's blowing, there 'll be no fond farewell to warm me as I cross the moors on my lonesome tonight, so I think I'll be on my way."

"OK!" Bethany proffered a petulant cheek.

"So be it!" he said, giving her the briefest of pecks. "See you on Saturday!"

"Fine!"

Daniel shot off, rattling down the cobbled way until he became a diminishing black spot. Bethany was miffed, but angry with herself mostly for jumping to conclusions. How could she have been such a nerd?

Sighing, she turned toward the house. But the still, soft night held her. Breathing in the salty air she scanned the heavens. 'Somewhere up there is my star...I wonder what influences are at work for me?' she thought...'what inescapable circumstances will shape my life...my ideas and Daniel's?'

Then there was the cliff, a dark, larger than life promontory clothed in midnight blue but -

"Oh...no! God...no!" A sudden rush of adrenalin held her fast in a saga that had no beginning. "No...no...don't let it end that way!" she moaned when the woman of her dreams teetered on the edge of the cliff, her red hair flowing out behind her. Bethany closed her eyes against the dishevelled image silhouetted in the moon glow, and her ears against the tortuous cry that cut deep into her consciousness. "Please, please...don't," she cried. Stunned by an indescribable sorrow Bethany opened her eyes. The woman had gone and the cliff had become a dark, dangerous and forbidding place. Bethany turned back to her tiny front garden...to the scent of roses and the welcoming light of home. Home...inside, in the warmth, 'Yes, that's where I need to be,' she thought.

"Goodness me you look pale, Bethany. That's what comes of sitting on the wall. Apart from that, you'll get cystitis, and then you'll know about it, my lass! I'll get you a cup of Horlicks, hot and sweet. You look as if you could do with it."

"Thanks mum. I'm OK. Just a bit shivery" but her heart was pounding. She would never understand why, when the woman came to her, she felt an immense urge to accept her as a reality she could not fathom. Then, all she wanted was to close into herself, to block out the weight of responsibility and an unease she could not define. 'Oh, mum,' she thought, curling up in the armchair; 'if only you knew how much I need to talk to you... if only dad was still here!'

"About this boyfriend of yours," her mother said as she tinkered in the kitchen.

"It's Daniel, mum! What about him? Don't you like him?"

"He seems a decent sort of lad, I suppose. No, it's just better if you say your good night indoors."

"But I didn't think..."

"Yes, well you thought wrong young lady. This is where you entertain your friends, not in the street for the entire world to see!" Bethany sighed. There she was again, thinking about what the neighbours would say. Why couldn't she just welcome Daniel for himself?

"Well, he's coming over on Saturday. We've decided to do some project research in the library. Aunty Barbara will help. She always comes up for me," Bethany said, then wished she hadn't; the fact that her mother had taken the key to the cabinet still rankled but the comparison was churlish.

"Now don't you go bothering Barbara when she's at work!"

"Come on, mum! How can we be bothering her? It's her job for goodness sake! It's what she does. After that we're going for a ride across the moors. I'm organizing a picnic so will you make an egg and bacon pie for us?"

"I expect so."

"Then Daniel's asked me to supper," Bethany said, trying to sound up beat.

"Is that a fact? It's all planned then!"

"More or less. Maybe next time, we could do something together?" Mrs. Mallinson lowered the tray onto Bethany's lap.

"We'll see," she said.

"Great. Thanks, mum," she said, nibbling on a digestive biscuit. "You do look after me!"

"Yes, well, drink up!" Mrs. Mallinson said with just a hint of a smile. "You looked as if you'd seen a ghost when you came in."

"Do you believe in the spirit world, mum?"

"Good heavens, girl. What a subject to raise just when you're about to go to bed. You'll be giving yourself nightmares again...but yes, I'm sure there's an after life. As for ghosts though, spirits crossing over, restless spirits...no, I don't. It's a lot of nonsense if you ask me! Why?"

"Oh nothing. Just wondered. Anyway, I'll be off to bed," she said, giving her mother a peck on the cheek, but as she climbed the stairs, the lump in her throat grew and her face creased up. 'If only someone would be on the same wavelength as me,' she thought 'but who...Daniel? Maybe he will be the one.

Approaching his home, Daniel slowed down. The crunch of his tyres on the gravel was the only man made sound he heard. Without a breeze to disperse it, the night-scented phlox was intoxicating. Daniel lifted the latch on the side door, pushed it open, wheeled his bike through to the back garden and propped it against the wall. He turned to scan the shadows playing on long stretch of moonlit lawn. Beyond was the orchard gate. Odd. He strained his eyes to see what was barring its way. Dad must have left his coat hanging on the archway.

"Hey up! 'bout time!" Taken off guard, Daniel felt the rush of adrenalin.

"Hell Trev, what d'ye think you're doing propping the gate up like some bloody gargoyle." His tone was critical.

"Cool it, mate! Gargoyles aren't as good looking as me!" Trevor's joke went down like a lead balloon. "Put it another way, I wouldn't have to if you answered my text messages or opened your e-mail once in a while."

Daniel nodded. "OK. Point made. Still, why didn't you wait inside?"

"Your mum asked me to but it was late. They'd just settled with their gin and tonics."

"Come on in anyway. Want a beer?"

"Sounds good."

The pool table dominated the room, its green felt illuminated by the focus light. It was a man's room, all angles and dark, polished mahogany with none of the softer touches you might expect; no curtains, only Venetian blinds, no vases filled with flowers, only ashtrays. Along one side, the glass fronted cabinet displayed a variety of sporting trophies shining in the reflected light; on the other was the gun cabinet, locked and all the more intriguing for it.

"Some sportsman, your dad," Trevor said, admiring the array of team photographs.

"I suppose," but Daniel could not disguise the grudging tone. "Here mate," he said, handing over a beer and wiping his damp hand on the front of his jeans. Trevor sat back in one of the leather chairs. They were expansive, cold. Straddling a sit-up-and-beg chair, Daniel turned towards him. "So what's up?"

"Nay mate, what's bugging you, you mean! Where the hell have you been? I haven't seen you since you took off that night. The lads wanted me to organise a match, but you're like the bloody scarlet pimpernel these days! Are you up for a game or what?"

"'course I am!"

"Anyway, why did you take off at the bowling like that? If it's something I've -"

"Don't be daft! You're on the wrong tack. It's not you mate. It's me." There was a long pause. It would be difficult admitting he was seeing Bethany. "I suppose you could say I'm smitten!" he said, a sheepish grin forming.

"Smitten? You've got a woman!" The possibility caught Trev unawares, but in that instant everything made sense. "Of course...!"

"Well don't sound so surprised!"

"Come on then. Who is it?"

"Bethany."

"What, Bethany 'the bleating soap opera wannabe?'" Daniel flinched, angry at the insult, embarrassed by its origin and the Micky-taking he knew would come.

"That's the one. And I don't need any grief from you, mate."

"Grief? Me give you grief? Would I? Remember me? I'm your personal shrink; I told you you'd got the hots for her!" Daniel grinned.

"It just happened. We were on the beach looking at the whale."

"Yeah. I saw them take it away. It was awesome. They used a heavy crane, put it on a flat bed trailer and by God, did it stink! Remember that poem we did last year. Something about the 'lugubrious death of a whale?' It all came back to me. Never heard what they did with it though. So what then?"

"What then?" For a moment Daniel was nonplussed. "Oh yeah, well then we decided to do the English project together. You were right, Trev. There's another side to her. Yeah, she's got her feet on the ground, she won't be pushed around. She can be bossy -"

"And to your cost, mate. Remember that!"

"Yeah but she's sensible, quick off the mark...and sensitive deep down... just doesn't wear her heart on her sleeve, that's all! Good sense of humour and - "

"Yeah, all right, mate. I get the gist. I can see that you find her sexually appealing!"

"Her sexual appeal has nothing to do with you, mate! You had the chance, remember. Too late, my old buddy. I'm in. You're out!"

"It's that serious?"

"Might be." Daniel shrugged his shoulders. "At least it was, up until about an hour ago!"

"Had a tiff eh? Been putting your foot in it!"

"Something like that!" Daniel conceded. "She's touchy, hard work sometimes. There's some sort of struggle going on there."

"Trouble at home, thoughts of exams maybe."

"No, it goes deeper. She's weird. Sort of mysterious, but whatever it is I have the strangest feeling that maybe I'm a part of it."

"Sounds a bit odd, but then 'all the world's queer, except thee and me and even thee's a little queer!' Isn't that what they say? Anyway, I'll be on my way," Trev said, knocking back the dregs of his beer. "Besides, far be it from me to keep you up. Now you've got a woman you'll be tired out!" Trevor's lascivious grin erupted into an enormous chuckle. "So what shall I tell the lads? Do you want a match or what?" he said between spurts of laughter.

"I suppose."

"I tell yer what! This is bad news! If you can't manage a bit of cricket and a woman, give up the woman I say! She's wearing you out, taking over your life!" Dodging a back-hander, Trev ducked. "You know what to do when you catch a weasel asleep, mate!"

"Yeah, piss in its lug oile. Now ger out of 'ere!"

"I'm going! Give me a ring when you want some more therapy or a session in the nets! And thanks for the beer, mate."

"No hassle. See you, Trev."

"Is that you, Daniel?" His mother's voice drifted into the hallway.

"Yes, mum." He opened the door to the lounge and surveyed the scene. His mother was propped up at one end of the settee with a book. Her gin and tonic sat on the coffee table, barely touched. She would savour the thought of it and sip it slowly. His father's drink, possibly his second or even third, was clutched to his chest. He lay sprawled in his armchair with his head tilted back, his earphones on, his eyes closed. Daniel meandered over to the CD player and picked up the disc cover. Elgar, as he suspected. Approaching his mother, he turned her book over.

"Les Miserables?"

"Hm. It's hard going though. The print's so tiny and this subdued lighting doesn't do much for me."

"Look, mum. All right if I bring that other strange bee home for supper on Saturday night?" Smiling, Mrs. Foster gave him a knowing look.

"Of course. I'll look forward to it," she said. "What time?"

"About six, but tell dad not to -" he whispered but not quietly enough.

"What j' ye say, Janny Boy? T'shell dad shwat?"

"Nothing, it's nothing! Go back to sleep, dad!" he said, gently tapping his bald patch, and the light intermittent snoring continued like a well fed pig snuffling amongst the swill.

"So you'll tell him, mum?"

"I know. No smart remarks!"

"We're doing our school project together. Tell you about it tomorrow. I'm whacked. A quick shower and I'm off to bed. Say goodnight to baldy for me!"

"I will. Good night Daniel."

Chapter 15

For the remainder of that week it rained. Getting to and fro from school was a dreary affair; school even more so. Bethany had been told off loads of times for not paying attention or gazing out of the windows. By Friday, she had had enough. Ron had been wrapped up in Home Economics preparing lunch and afternoon tea for visiting dignitaries. 'Serves her right for being such a swat,' Bethany thought. As for Daniel, he might just as well have been the Invisible Man. Apart from in English she only saw him now and then in the corridors, head and shoulders above most of the kids. Then, every time she blinked, he'd disappeared, probably scooped up by some visiting alien, curious to study earth male schmucks and their apparent lack of interest in females. 'Who cares?' she thought when she finally arrived home. Taking off her coat, she glanced up at the notice board in the kitchen. "Gone to the shop. Won't be long. Put the kettle on, Mum.

Bethany hated it when the house was empty and cold from the damp. It seemed to permeate the cottage walls so that the curtains hung limp and the panes ran with droplets of rain that turned into trembling tributaries. 'I know,' she thought, curling up in the arm chair. 'I'll ring Ron. She'll cheer me up!'

"Hi Ron. It's me!"

"Ah...Beth, my erstwhile friend again!."

"I know. Anyway, I'm here now! So how's life, groovy, exciting or what?"

"Busy. I was doing my practical all day. It goes toward the exam."

"I saw you. Up to your eyes in pastry. How did it go?"

"Not bad, I think, I hope! As for life being groovy or exciting, I don't think so! I am going to Northern France for a long weekend though."

"Sounds OK to me," Bethany said, fiddling with some loose cotton on her school shirt. "Paris?"

"Probably not. In any case it wouldn't be much fun without you."

"Hey! Don't be so daft. It's a family holiday and come to think of it, probably the last you'll ever take with your mum and dad."

"Yeah, Mum said I ought to ask you along. I thought we could parade up and down the Champs Elysee strutting our stuff!" Imagining Ron's lascivious grin, Bethany smiled.

"I'm sorry, Ron."

"I know. I told mum you were in lurve! It would have been great though. Next year maybe? Unless of course you're still going out with Daniel. How are things anyway?"

"OK. He's been round helping me with the English project. We want to get it over and done with so's we can take on a bit of casual work through the summer."

"Work!"

"Yeah, why not?" Bethany said, curling her legs up into the chair. "It beats hanging around. I'll start saving up for next year. If we're going to Paris I'll need some stuff to strut! Can't rely on my fashion sense to pull anyone!"

"Oh I don't know. You've managed to pull Daniel."

"Yeah, but he doesn't count. I've no taste - only joking! He's great. We'll have to fix you up with his mate!"

"Oh yeah!"

"Don't you fancy him then?" Bethany made a face, fully expecting an ear full.

"He's OK. Never thought about it really. Till last night."

"Veronica! Tell all!"

"Nothing to tell really. He nearly knocked me over with his bike. I'd been down to the off license for dad just before closing time. He came careering round the bend and nearly sent me flying. Of course he was full of apologies and sort of walked me back to the house as a kind of sop I suppose. He'd been to see Daniel."

"Did you make a date, you being a fast mover and all that!"

"No Beth! He just wanted to make amends really...talked about Daniel mostly and your budding romance!"

"I'll bet!"

"He did! Anyway he's in Scotland for the hols, Youth Hostelling. We won't even be in each other's orbit!"

"Do you want me to put in a good word?" Bethany said, picking up on just a hint of regret.

"Absolutely not. I told you it was just a friendly chat. Besides, we're not thirteen any more. I don't need an intermediary."

"Suppose not." Bethany glanced at her watch. "Well I'd better get off this phone else Mum' ll be on my back. So no hard feelings then?" Bethany said as much to assuage her own guilt as to make up for neglecting her friend.

"About what?"

"Me neglecting my best mate."

"Ah! You do admit it then! But no, none at all. A best friend is one thing; a boy friend, another, and I know when to butt out! You never did get round to telling me what's bugging you though."

"No... well...another time."

"Yeah, OK, but if you have a fall out and get bored, go build a rook's nest up your bum! That will keep you busy! Tarra!"

"So what's that sigh in aid of?" her mother said as she came through the door to see Bethany gazing out of the window.

"Oh I dunno. I suppose I still feel guilty about Veronica. I've just rung her. She wanted me to go to France with her parents."

"Well, that would have been better than sitting around here poring over some silly barrel!"

"No, you're wrong, mum. It's interesting, and fun. I mean, think about it!"

"Oh no. Don't start on that again! I've got better things to do with my time and it's a pity you don't think the same way! Anyway, let's be having a cuppa,"she said changing the subject. "It's that windy out there. It'll be all right for your picnic though or so the weatherman says," she said as she busied herself unpacking the shopping.

"Yes, but why won't you talk about the project, mum? Why are you being so difficult?"

"Difficult?" she said, rounding in her daughter. "No, Bethany, you've got the wrong word. Annoyed is what I am. Annoyed that you should choose to mess with the past, and worse, make it a public affair! You know how I've always kept family matters close to my chest. It's in my nature I suppose, or maybe the way I was brought up."

"That's daft, mum. If it was something recent, I'd understand but come on! It's not as if we've got anything to hide and even if we had, it would be a long forgotten skeleton in the cupboard!"

"And if that were the case, it's exactly where it should stay!" her mother snapped. "Well, you'll go ahead with it all the same, but as I said, don't bring me into it!" Bethany stared into the cup of tea her mother had put into her hands.

"And now I suppose you'll be storming off to your bedroom!"

"No!"

"Well, it's what you usually do when we have a set-to."

"I get frustrated, that's all," Bethany conceded.

"And I don't, I suppose?" her mother said, matter of factly. "Anyway, let's get on with the tea. I'm as hungry as a hunter and you must be ready for something."

"I am. And thanks for doing the picnic shop for us, mum."

"That's all right," Mrs. Mallinson said with just a ghost of a smile and she turned to chip the potatoes.

Later, after struggling with a couple of Sudoku games, Bethany left her mother dozing by the fireside and made her way upstairs. It was late. She was tired and flopped, fully clothed onto the bed. But the minutes turned into hours; she couldn't sleep. She'd forgotten to pull the curtains as well. A mistake. The moonshine was bright. She tossed and turned, reluctant at first to look out over the roof tops to the promontory. Bethany closed her eyes against the memory of the woman standing on the edge of the cliff, her shift clinging to her body, her arms flailing against the wind, her hair aflame. Still she sidled over to the window. Taking an intake of breath she tapped on the window. The seagull stirred. Drawing its head out from under its wing, it fixed its eyes on her...soulful eyes that burned laser-like into her own. That was when she thought of it! Risky, yes but the house was quiet. Why not? And her mother would be so busy with the baking tomorrow, she wouldn't even notice that the barrel was missing.

Chapter 16

"Lovely day tha knows, Lisa." The snooper's voice drifted up to the bedroom.

"It is, Mrs. Crooks." Bethany wriggled down under the duvet. For once her mother's crisp, no nonsense tone made her smile. It must be late though. Rubbing her eyes, she peered at the alarm clock. "Nooo! Ten past nine!" Bethany swung out of bed. In mega time she had showered, dressed and dried her hair. For a moment she wondered why her mother hadn't called her as usual. Then she remembered. Maybe she'd already noticed the barrel was missing. "Oh God! Please…please not," she muttered when, with each step on the staircase, a pang of guilt surged through her. Each step brought her nearer to the moment when their eyes would lock. She'd know in an instant if she'd been found out.

"Ah! At long last!" her mother said, "Another bad night?" Bethany breathed a quiet sigh of relief. So far so good. As expected her mother was well ahead with the sandwiches.

"Hi, mum. Sort of, but let me do that," she said, taking the butter knife off her mother. "Have I to boil a couple of eggs as well?"

"What for? Won't the ham do?"

"It's all about choice, mum. Mixed with mayonnaise, pepper and salt they're yummy!"

"Baby food it you ask me. Go on then but I'll tell you one thing, it'll be a long time before I listen to your bright ideas again, my lass!" Bethany glanced up from taking the eggs out of the refrigerator. 'What now?' she thought.

"You should have seen young Molly's face when I asked her for a French stick and some pate de whatever…!"

"You all right, Mrs.Mallison?" says she, peering over the counter.

"Why shouldn't I be Molly?" says I.

"Well, you'll 'ave to go to the Promenade des Anglais for that there foisse de grasse," says she sniffing. "This isn't the French Riverera, tha knows!"

"And everybody...everybody I say, sets off laughing. The cheeky faggot! But never again. So it'll be potted meat, same as it always was. It's those French teachers again. Instead of teaching you to read and write, they're having food tasting sessions, food you'll only eat once in a blue moon. What is it anyway, this pate de foisse grass?" she said, enunciating the esses with great flair.

"Pate de foie gras! Mum! You don't hear the ess and by the way 'faggot' isn't a word you should use these days!"

"Oh!" Mrs Mallison tutted. "I can't imagine why not, it's just a Yorkshire expression."

"Anyway, it's goose liver."

"You mean to tell me they breed hundreds of geese just for a bit of glorified potted meat?"

"'fraid so."

"Well I never. It shouldn't be allowed. Patey der foyer gra in Penhill Bay if you please! And you of all people, you, foregoing your principles for that lad!" Bethany blushed. "I should have known; you're just out to impress! Any road, that lass made me out to be as daft as a brush so don't you ever send me out on a wild goose chase like that again! And it's no laughing matter...especially when it's at other folks' expense!"

"No Mum," Bethany said, stifling a fit of giggles "I'm not laughing at you. It's the pun."

"The what?"

"The pun; goose's liver...wild goose chase. And the image of you going hell for leather after a wild goose honking its head off and your skirt tangled around your legs, both of you in a flurry and a scurry and all this in Penhill's own riviera!"

"Well I'm glad someone can see the funny side of it," she said, stifling a smile. "And now...oh...here's your friend. You'd best make it snappy, hypocrite that you are!"

Bethany opened the door before Daniel had had a chance to knock. She was still red in the face from laughing.

"Hi," he said, standing back and warming his hands on her face. "You were red in the face and miffed when we parted the other night. Now you're blushing at the very sight of me. You've got it bad, Freckles."

"It's Mum making me laugh."

"Never."

"Sh! And stop calling me Freckles. Coping with a carrot mop is bad enough! Come in," she said, "and behave!"

"Hello, Mrs. Mallinson."

"Now then!"

"We've chosen a good day for a picnic, haven't we? And thanks for making the sarnies."

"Yes," she replied, glaring at her daughter. "And mind you take care on the roads. These mad-cap tourists 'll be the death of us all."

"Don't worry, Mrs. Mallinson."

"But I do worry!" Well put in his place Daniel gulped. "And mind you get home before dark young lady."

"Mum!" Bethany said in a cringing tone. "You'll be asking me if I've got my hanky next! Besides, Daniel's dad will be driving me home."

"Is that so?" she said, handing over a bottle of pop. "Well, be off with you else the fizz' ll have gone out of this before you get to wherever it is you're going!"

Chapter 17

"That wasn't too painful, was it? Mum, I mean," Bethany said as they peddled hard up the hill. She was already starting to puff and pant. "Let's stop at the promontory. Give my legs a break."

"What a wimp! But no, she was fine...like you, a bit outspoken!" Bethany gave him the dead eye.

"Lovely, isn't it?" she said, laying her bike down on the verge and crossing over to the viewing area. Despite a fresh breeze, the concrete seat had already warmed in the sun. Instinctively they gravitated toward one another. Daniel wrapped both arms around her and she snuggled closer, molding herself to him.

"You can say that again." The double entendre was not lost on Bethany and she gave a sideways grin.

"It's perfect, the way the bay curves. It's a natural harbour. I love being here watching the gulls circling and the fishing boats sallying to and fro. Look, there's a guy sketching on the cliff." In the silence that followed Daniel knew she was absorbing the whole scene, her senses inter-playing.

"It's in your blood isn't it?" he said.

"I suppose, but -" Daniel waited. He knew that her qualification would be important.

"But what...?" Still Bethany remained silent.

"The cliffs," she said at last. "Just lately I've the urge to get up there. Couldn't we walk along the ridge?" Shading his eyes from the direct sunlight, Daniel scanned the coast line."

"It's dangerous; there isn't a path and like I said, the coast is still eroding."

"Still?"

"Yeah! I remember dad telling me about Little Penhill. But I shouldn't be telling *you!* You must know about the cluster of cottages way past the headland?" he said, pointing into the distance. "It was a tiny hamlet. When the cliff fell most of the cottages went with it, except one. There's nothing there now, just a few dry stone walls."

"Are there any roads leading to it?" Bethany's interest was palpable.

"There used to be cart tracks across the moors but nature's taken over. Anyway, let's be off!" he said, standing up and stretching.

"And you, a southerner!" she said.

"What's that supposed to mean?"

"You know more about it than I do and I've lived here all my life!"

"I only know because one of dad's business friends took us for a jaunt in a light aircraft. He was a local history fanatic. Anyway, we followed the coast line and he pointed out the landmarks."

"But you make it sound as if I'll never see it, never go there and I've got to, Daniel. Somehow I've got to."

"Well it won't be me who takes you. Like I said, it's dangerous and I don't want your mum breathing a tornado down my neck! Now, about our picnic." he said.

"Yeah. Let's find somewhere special that we can make our own."

"Hey steady on girl that sounds a bit heavy to me!"

"Don't be so daft. I didn't mean -"

"I know you didn't. Come on, I've found just the place. I did a recce the other day. You'll like it! So let's get a spurt on!"

An hour later and well into the countryside, Daniel rode ahead to the brow of a hill. He looked back. Bethany was struggling.

"Come on, keep up!" he shouted. "Isn't it you who always yaks on about the equality of the sexes?"

"Don't set me off," she said in between puffs. "You just can't get through the day without annoying me, can you!"

Daniel laughed. "Well, let's see if this pleases you!" he said when she caught up with him.

The view was breathtaking. There were no peaks to sharpen the softness of the hills brooding against an azure sky. Bethany marked the subtle change from the white limestone fells to the undulating emerald landscape with dry stone wall divides and rock-strewn surfaces. But she was impelled to look back, to scan the ocean of heather that reached almost to the cliff edge. Sighing, she turned again, this time searching the distant hills. An isolated homestead nestled between the ridges and a man was tending the dry stone wall, but in the forefront a more secret place caught her eye.

"That's it isn't it?" she said, marvelling at the gnarled, persistent growth of a few trees amongst the limestone rocks. "All is forgiven. Come on, race you!" Taken off guard Daniel struggled with his pedals. "Wait on!" he shouted but Bethany was gone, freewheeling out of sight down the snaking road. He found her sitting on the wall.

"And who was it rabbiting on about women being inferior to men?" she asked with forced innocence and a cheeky grin.

"Oh, *some* poor, misguided chauvinist, I expect!" Daniel said, smiling at her gentle ribbing. "Anyway, where's your bike?" he said, ignoring the subtle signs of a pout.

"I heaved it over the wall. If this is to be our Shangri-La, there can be no clues as to our whereabouts."

"Right," he said. "Mind out!" and with an easy swing lifted his own bike over. Scissor jumping, Daniel followed.

"I'm impressed!"

"You should be, and now it's your turn to impress me. What's for lunch?"

Bethany delved into her rucksack, pulling out a crisply starched white and blue tablecloth. "Grab some rocks and anchor the four corners," she said spreading it on a smooth patch of grass. "Then go and brood. Have a wander around our estate and leave me to it!"

"OK boss!" With one leap Daniel was back over the wall. Out of earshot and anonymous in the landscape, he sat and watched this girl who had suddenly come to mean so much to him. Trev had been right when he'd told him to "get confident." There had been other girls, girls as keen as he was to practise snogging. It was an unwritten agreement. You had to get your experience somehow. Then, meaningful conversation wasn't necessary. Along with the trivial chatter, he'd learnt how not to fumble. Not that he'd ever gone all the way, but the desire was there all the same and he felt guilty about the wet dreams, the laundry and his mother noticing. However much he told himself it was only natural, the stains were proof of something that should be private, proof that it was time to get a place of his own. Daniel watched the easy way Bethany moved. 'It's not as if her figure's something to drool over, come to think about it, she always dresses in jeans, T shirts and sloppy jumpers; nothing to accentuate. No, it was something else. Trev's sarcastic jibe sprang to mind: 'I can see why you find her sexy!'

'So she's athletic, but her supple body language is something else,' Daniel thought. Her movements flowed and, for all the basketball, she was not muscle bound. He remembered the softness of her arms and felt the gentle slope of her shoulders when his arms had encircled her at the viewing stage. There the contours of her body had molded into his, naturally, without embarrassment as if it was meant to be. Then there was the kiss the other night. 'Yes! A goal scored, a challenge won. It was inspirational. 'So what now...?' he thought. Daniel looked across the jagged limestone rocks to see her waving. It was time for lunch. He stood up and scrambled down the slope. Then when her broad smile welcomed him, he felt his heart turn over.

With the ease of a hurdler, Daniel vaulted over the wall. "This is great. Fit for a king!" he said, helping himself to a sausage roll with one hand and a bite sized Scotch egg in the other. "Home made too."

"Mum. Mum did it all."

"Well I take back everything I ever said about her. She wouldn't have done all this unless she approved of me!"

"Oh yes she would. Mum likes everything to be right. I'm sure she believes that somewhere in her far and distant past, her ancestors lived the life of Riley. It's the little things. She still uses lace-edged handkerchiefs and spends hours embroidering them. I keep telling her to change the habit of a lifetime and enroll on a computer course, French-anything! But no, she's in a rut, my mum."

"All the same, she can bake for me any day. These are terrific. Here, want some quiche?"

"You mean egg and bacon pie! In our house, despite mum's airs and graces, it's egg and bacon pie. But no, I'm vegetarian, remember." Kneeling down in front of him, Bethany looked directly into his hazel eyes. "We're like chalk and cheese really aren't we?" she said with an edge of regret.

"I suppose but it's not a prob. You'll soon get used to my ways!"

"You've got a hope! I am me. I'll never be or do anything that isn't me. It's instinctive. It's as simple as that," she said, reaching out for a handful of crisps and an egg sandwich.

"Oh yeah! Sounds a bit arrogant if you ask me."

"I'm not arrogant! Anyway, talk about the kettle calling the pan, 'grimy bum!' I just think it's important to be yourself that's all."

"So, does being yourself mean that you can't or shouldn't have a mind open to other people's ideas? You want to be careful, Freckles. You might find yourself stuck in a century all to yourself!" Feigning annoyance, Bethany scrambled to her feet. "Now what's wrong? Hey, come on; don't even think about getting in a huff! We're having a picnic remember? Besides, I've brought something special along. I stole it, just for you! Here, a bottle of dad's best plonk." Bethany's pout faded away. Her face blanched.

"Me too!" she said.

"What?"

"Stole something; well, borrowed it- for you. I had to. I had to let you see it in the daylight so's you can take some photos. Mum will spit blood if she finds out. Look!" Bethany reached into her pannier. She had protected the barrel in a cocoon of bubble wrap "There," she said.

"So this is the famous barrel!" Holding it carefully, he turned it round and around. "Yeah, you're right, it is interesting. And look at the work that's gone into it. All this fine detail, even down to the spirals on the mast ropes. Talk about craftsmanship; it's great. Does it open?"

"No, I don't think so. Besides mum went ballistic when I tried. So don't; it's bad enough me sneaking it out of the house. I just hope to God I can get it back before she realizes." Daniel rooted in his rucksack for his camera.

"You're worried."

"I am. If she finds out, I'm dead," Bethany said, slicing her finger across her throat. She's paranoid about it. Come on. Best pour me a glass of wine; it'll help me to forget. I suppose you could say we're partners in crime now and I thought you were supposed to be the toff in this relationship!"

"True!" he said, grinning and turning the barrel around in Bethany's cupped hands to get the best shot, "so out with the wine glasses!"

"Plastic cups you mean."

"Well standards must be dropping, that's all I can say! Here, have a swig of this. 'Chateau Neuf du Pape.' Anything else is vinegar or so dad says. But that's something else...a different kind of arrogance, I suppose."

Bethany glanced across. For a fleeting moment he looked serious-even sad. Perhaps, after all, his life wasn't so perfect. And why all the bluster? Perhaps...well, what did she really know about him, his thoughts, his feelings, his plans for the future. There were so many things she wanted to ask. But in that moment, for some unknown reason, her heart went out to him.

"Well," she said, leaning towards him, "a kiss is what I need!" Surprised, Daniel turned, steadying the open bottle of wine in a natural recess. "I think I can handle that," he said, gathering her into his arms.

Chapter 18

Their bikes secured, Daniel pushed open the heavy library doors and stood aside for Bethany to pass through. The entrance was dingy, even more so coming out of the bright sunshine.

"It's time this place was done up, modernised," Daniel said, peering through the gloom at the utility green paint work. "Electrically sensitive doors wouldn't come amiss when you've got your arms full of books and your head full of God knows what."

"You're not wanting much. New doors? Forget it!" Bethany said with the air of a boardroom rep. "They can barely keep up with the book budget."

"How about a new librarian then?" he said, indicating the middle-aged woman hanging over the desk. Her several double chins resembled a concertina. She was concentrating and the intensity showed in her pout.

"A younger version perhaps!" Bethany snapped. "Would a blonde bimbo be more to your liking!" Daniel cringed. 'Talk about shooting yourself in the foot,' he thought but pushed his point all the same.

"Well, cheaper to employ!"

"Maybe!" Bethany snapped, "but this one knows everything there is to know or knows where to find the answers. Haven't you ever noticed?"

"Don't come up here very often, no need, especially now we're on line."

"Ah well! Spoilt brat!" she said, giving him a withering look and, with a broad smile, turned to the lady behind the counter. "Hi there, Mrs. Slater!"

"Her face matches her name," Daniel thought, but thought again when her preoccupied expression gave way to a wide grin.

"Good gracious! Mrs. Slater indeed! Aunty Babs to you, luvvie! Your mam' ll be across next week. It's her turn! But who's this young man?" she said, raising a quizzical eyebrow.

"Oh sorry, this is Daniel...my sometime boyfriend!" Bethany muttered under her breath. Aunty Barbara looked searchingly into his eyes. She took his outstretched hand.

"My word, that's a strong handshake," she said. "I always say you can tell a lot about a man from his handshake!" Bethany shot a false smile in Daniel's direction. He winced. "Hello, Mrs. Slater," he said, with as much charm as he could muster.

"So, what can I do for the two of you?" Bethany glanced at Daniel, her hesitation giving him the chance to take the lead.

"Um...er...well, we're doing a school project on local history and we need some information on ships," Daniel said.

"Hm...Ships in general or one in particular?" she said, linking her finger tips.

"Well, we wondered if you had anything on the types and names of ships running around the late eighteenth century."

"Now there's a strange choice of a word," she replied. "Running what? They were into smuggling in those days of course but that's not what you meant, was it?"

"No, not especially. Operating. I suppose that's what I meant, but we can gen up on smuggling whilst we're at it, can't we Bethany?"

"Well, your mam would be able to tell you about that. There's very little she doesn't know about the sea, local affairs especially, when you get her going."

Bethany flushed. "*If* I can get her going," she said, flinching at her own disloyalty.

"Ah well, your mam's never been one for talking since...yes well, never mind. Have you anything to go by?"

"A sketch. We've got a rough sketch." Daniel nudged Bethany. "Come on, cough up, Leonardo," he said with an encouraging smile.

Grinning, Bethany delved into her bag.

"I hope you're ready for this!"

"It's nay se bad gel!" her Aunt Barbara said, reaching over and squeezing Bethany's arm. "Now I'd say that's a lugger. Fast little boats those, two masted usually with square sails. For speed they added another mast. See, there it is. You've captured that! They manoeuvred well, and needed to, mind you. The Excise men were up to snuff as they say. All the same, revenue was lost, but..." Her aunt paused. Her frown deepened. "You know I'm sure I've seen this somewhere before. By the life of me though I can't think where. It'll come to me, probably just as I'm about to drop off; it always does." Bethany's heart raced.

"So a ship like that would be into smuggling?" she said, seizing the chance of distracting her aunt.

"I'll say, and the devils would smuggle anything! We think about it differently nowadays. The romantic image lingers on I suppose, but it's no difference from today's scroungers. When all's said and done, it's still thieving," she said, disdain written all over her face. "Well, don't get me going. Our Bethany understands though, don't you, pet? We're alike as two peas in that respect, putting the world to rights I mean. A regular couple of suffragettes!" she said, chuckling to herself. "Now, as for the names of ships -." Mrs. Slater waddled across to another section of the library. They followed. "If you write to Lloyds, the insurers; here's the address," she said, picking up and flicking through the early pages of a directory "and ask them to send you a list of all the luggers operating along this coastline from about seventeen fifty, you might be lucky."

"Well, we think this one begins with a 'J' and we've sort of identified a few other letters."

"Oh well, you'll need a lot of patience," she said, clearly impressed by the thought of all the hard work ahead. "Still you're keen by the sounds of it."

"Oh and have you anything on local monograms?" Daniel asked.

"Yes and no to those two questions, luvvy. Again, there are plenty of them but if you have any loose change you can photocopy the ones you find interesting." Again Mrs. Slater waddled away. Clearly fascinated by her beam end, Daniel smirked. Bethany caught his expression. She stared at him, her fixed, false smile acknowledging his insensitivity.

Daniel blushed.

"Don't worry," she whispered, "we tease her at home. We tell her that her hips sway like a battleship in distress!"

Daniel dissolved into a fit of laughter.

"Sshh! Control yourself!" she said, digging him in the ribs. Floundering, Bethany's aunt reappeared.

"Now I'm off to work behind t' stacks," she said, handing over a book "and you've obviously got a lot to do as well. Don't forget though, the library closes in an hour and I for one won't be sorry, so cheerio the pair of you."

"Bye Auntie, and thanks."

"Goodbye, Mrs. Slater."

Later Auntie Barbara peeked through into the reading room. Bethany and Daniel were still note-taking. 'Hmm. He'll do for our Beth or I'm a monkey's uncle. It's only to be hoped that our Lisa thinks the same way,' she thought.

Chapter 19

"Sorry about the faux pas!" Daniel said as they pedalled away. "Your aunt's great, really."

"OK. I believe you. I believe you!" Bethany said, a huge grin forming.

"All the same, what a dope!" she joked, "but don't worry I won't tell anybody! Anyway, if it's any consolation I'm going to have plenty of time to make an idiot of myself tonight. I'm not sure I can cope with all this," she said, looking around at all the up-market houses. 'No wonder Mum was worried!' she thought.

"It's the welcome that counts and Mum's looking forward to this." Daniel turned into his driveway. Bethany followed. She bit her lip in mock terror. "I think I want to go home!"

"Don't be daft!"

On either side the borders were a mass of colour. Red antirrhinums dominated the cluster of white allysum and blue cornflowers. "It's lovely," she said looking around.

"Hm. You could be forgiven for implying we're over the top patriotic!"

"Well, are you?" she said, braking and hopping off her bike.

"Dad is."

"Even down to the flower arrangements?"

"Yeah. It's his fad. Correction, one of his fads!"

Expecting to share in the funny side of his father's eccentricity, Bethany turned to him, a wide, disbelieving grin still on her face, but Daniel wasn't even smiling. She wondered at that. In fact, looking back, he hadn't been himself since they'd left the library. He was quiet, less chirpy.

"Are you OK about this?" she said, following on through the wrought iron gate at the side of the house.

"Sure," but Bethany wasn't convinced. His reply was too matter of fact, lacking the nonchalant tone she had come to expect.

"So this is the back garden!" Her eyes swept across the well-tended lawns and flower beds. "However do you manage it all?"

"We have a gardener."

"Aaaaah, I should have known!" she quipped, but Daniel didn't take up the challenge. "Come on, I'll introduce you to Mum."

They found her in the kitchen putting the final touches to a home-made gateau. "Hello, there! I hope you like fresh cream, Bethany?" Her welcome came with a broad smile; it was warm, natural. There was no need for an introduction. The smile and her easy way were sufficient. "I'm afraid so, Mrs. Foster."

"Me too. So I can rely on you to help me see this off then!"

"Yes but, if I ate what I like and I like most sweet things, I'd be like a barrel!" Bethany's heart jumped into her mouth; in all the excitement she had forgotten about the barrel. Suddenly she was in a court of her own making, her mother both judge and jury. Her pulse raced. 'Guilty as charged' she thought.

"Well I hope you'll tuck in and enjoy yourself tonight."

"I will. I'm looking forward to it."

"Oh good. Now Daniel, why don't you show Bethany around? Dinner will be about sevenish and I'm sure you'll want a wash and brush up before then," she said with a raised eyebrow.

"Oh yes please!" Bethany coloured up at her own spontaneous show of enthusiasm. "It's been a great day but I'm whacked. All that fresh air!"

"Well, have a shower and make yourself at home. You'll find everything you need in the bathroom. Help yourself, and don't be shy! Take a bath if you prefer and wallow."

Bethany did have a bath, luxuriating in the corner shaped tub that was also a Jacuzzi. Surrounded by bubbles and exotic fragrances she had never felt so pampered. Aromatherapy was a phrase the girls bandied about at school. Bath oils, body lotions and sprays were always on top of the Christmas lists. Now and then she had even treated herself. But this, this was pure magic, a magnolia wonderland with the evening sunlight pouring through the frosted glass, making diamante patterns on the wall. For all its peachiness, the décor wasn't really twee. Against the green and apricot hand towels, alternately rolled and arranged on the open shelves, were deeper, plum and aubergine colored candles, pomegranate shaped jars and lime bottles. In pride of place in the corner was a maiden hair, its fragile ferns cascading and reflecting in the mirror. 'I could get used to this,' she thought.

An hour later, Bethany surfaced, refreshed and excited. Adjusting the front of her mauve cardy across the skimpy matching vest, she made her way downstairs. It had been an age since she had had reason to dress up, especially after wearing jeans for so long. Self-consciously, Bethany pulled her short skirt down.

"Hey Beth, how much longer are you going to-?"

"I'm coming. I'm coming!" Rounding the stairwell Bethany smiled. She was impressed. Daniel had spruced himself up. He looked great, colour- coordinated in his brown army trousers and open necked khaki sweat shirt. He was blushing too.

"Been too near the sunlamp?" she said, indicating his glowing face.

"No...I...I. Yes...!"

"Well make up your mind. What's up?"

"You well know what's up. Don't play cat and mouse with me!"

"So say it. Spit it out. Since when have you been lost for words?"

"Since now...you look terrific. I never thought...I didn't know...!"

"There you go again. Be careful, Daniel. You might slip up and say you really thought you'd fallen for a tomboy! Well, I'm not a tomboy and I'm glad you approve."

"So you'll want a drink to go with the celeb image. Some wine, a gin and tonic...a Pims No 1 with all the trimmings?"

"A bitter lemon with ice will be fine, thank you kindly."

"No probs." Daniel crossed over to the drinks cabinet where the crystal glass shone in the subdued lighting and the port, deep ruby red in the decanter, made its own enticing statement. "There you are, but it's a bit of a come down!"

"Cheers! It could be champagne," she said, the sparkle tingling her nose.

"Champagne? Did I hear someone say champagne? Ah, so this is the little lady you've been keeping to yourself since Junior School! How are you my dear?" Mr. Foster said, taking and squeezing her hand. Bethany smiled. Daniel bristled. "This is Bethany, dad."

"Well, I didn't think it was Father Christmas!" Danny cringed. When his father clasped his arm he pulled away.

"So what have you given Bethany to drink? Good God, lad, couldn't you find anything more interesting! Let me make you a snowball, one of my specials."

"Thank you, but no. I'm fine, really."

"Decisive too. Well, let's see if I can tempt your mother instead," he said with a twinkle in his eye and disappeared into the kitchen.

"He doesn't mean any harm!" she whispered in the awkward silence that followed. "Come on, show me round the garden."

"Bethany. I'm not a child to be distracted -"

"I'm sorry. I didn't mean to patronise. I can see you're upset, that's all."

"Maybe. But what the hell. It's no big deal. I'll take you round the garden later. Besides, dinner 'll be ready soon. And don't worry, I won't make a scene. But one thing's for certain, if I know my dad, you'll come away knowing more than you did." This time though, his words were tinged with pride.

"You do admire him then?"

"Admire *him?* After a fashion. He's so embarrassing, that's all!"

"Daniel was telling me that you want to walk up the coast by way of the cliff, Bethany?" Mr. Foster said when they sat down to eat.

Taken unawares she found herself floundering. "Yes...yes I do! I expect it's really beautiful, wild and rugged and I enjoy that."

"I'm sure it is. I know it is...but it's also very dangerous, my dear. On certain stretches, the cliffs have been eroding for years. Daniel told you about Little Penhill?"

"Sort of…"

"It was a terrible disaster. The locals responded as best they could, but of course there were no lifeboats as we define them today and as Fate would have it, the one they did have was being stripped and repainted. So the poor devils were drowned...every man jack, or buried alive, the kiddies too." Mr. Foster paused. "Well that's how the story goes." For a moment they were all subdued. "Well, I'd better kill this one," he said emptying the last of the wine into his glass. Daniel cringed! "Should you go along the cliffs, though I sincerely hope you won't," he continued, "you'd see a plaque...if it's still there of course. It's not much, but it's a kind of recognition that people died there...that they counted for something. Better than the last time if the truth be told."

"Why? Was there another cliff fall?"

"Many, but one was supposed to have sparked local interest. No one ever really knew what happened. Rumour begot rumour, but try delving. What! They clam up. You'd have the devil's own job getting any information out of the locals - so my colleague told me. Unusual really; in the normal way they like to spin a yarn. They'd talk a hind leg off a donkey. Well, you'll know that, Bethany, living amongst the fisher folk. Anyway, it's a long time ago. I don't suppose we'll ever know now. It was a different world then of course. High and low, most folks around this coastline were involved in a smuggling racket: gin, brandy, coffee, tea. They even reckoned Lord Rossitor at the Castle was involved. I can see why the poor would do it of course, but the gentry, no. Sheer greed if you ask me. I suppose it might have been an exciting diversion. Still, forget the romantic image...moonlit stretches of sand, secret tunnels leading to the dark ginnels and the landlords sympathetic to the cause. Read Daphne Du Maurier if you want that. No, it was a bloody trade; often violent. A cat and mouse game between the smugglers and the Revenue. Especially when they'd been tipped off, as was the case occasionally. They'd lie in wait, but for all the smugglers' guile and their network of contacts, they were sometimes caught red-handed. The crackle of musket fire would echo along the beach and in the coves then all right. They rarely found the ring leader of course! The locals would be tight-lipped and God help any informer if he was ever caught! But you need to get to the Customs and Excise Records if you're interested in that. And what's changed I ask myself? Nothing as far as I can see. The fat cats are still there reaping their ill-gotten gains."

"You can't make sweeping statements like that, Dad!" Clearly irritated, his father drew on his Havana cigar. He sat back expansively. "I mean, **you** could be viewed as a fat cat!"

"Daniel!" His mother's reproof fell like a boulder down a well; the rising water, the unease that followed.

"No, Helen; let him go on." Bethany shuffled uneasily in her seat. "Make your point, son!"

"I said you could be viewed as a fat cat, Dad. I didn't say you were one. You're a business man; you're in a controlling position. You're wealthy. You make all the rules and live the good life."

"Dead right, Danny boy. Everything you say is true. The difference might be that I work hard for my living. Besides, there's no comparison. I'm not talking peanuts; I'm talking big money, big big money, gained on the backs of the fisher folk."

"Yes but it's all relative. You can hardly describe your salary as peanuts."

"So?"

"So..." Daniel's reply hung in the air. "So...I...I suppose I get your point."

"Well, that's a relief, Danny boy. For one awful moment I thought you were about to criticize me in front of our guest. Now how about you two doing your own thing for a bit whilst your mother clears up and I make a few phone calls."

Bethany was quick to reply, "Oh, I'll help with the pots, Mrs. Foster."

"No need Bethany, really. The dishwasher takes the strain. Besides, this is your treat. Now off you go. Perhaps we can have a nightcap together before we take you home."

"I'd like that...and thanks for the meal, it was great!"

"Hmmm." All the same, her warm smile didn't quite dispel the air of sadness that hung about her.

"We'll be on the computer in my room then, mum."

"Fine. Shout if you need anything."

"That was a bit fraught!" Bethany said, pulling a chair up to the computer.

"No sweat."

"But you always gave me the impression you were a happy family."

"So we are, mostly," he said, logging on. "It's no big deal." Dismissed and clearly annoyed, she turned to look out of the window.

"Oh come on Bethany," he coaxed. "Don't let him spoil things. He's always like that but it's not a problem. I can hack it, and you don't have to."

"That's the point. I suppose it's none of my business but I don't like to see you arguing with your dad."

"It's not unusual, you know. Most teenagers do. You do," he said, pointedly.

"Yes, but it's different. We banter. It's not serious stuff."

"Well, you could have fooled me! You're as hung up about your mum as I am about my dad. Anyway, come on, let's not get heavy. Look, I've designed the jigsaw," he said, bringing up the drawing facility. If we can fill in the blanks we'll get a much better picture of what we're about -."

"Fine," she said, cupping her chin in her hand.

"It is fine. Now come on, Freckles, don't go all miserable on me!" There it was again, the nickname, the calm encouragement, the warm link with the Daniel she knew and loved. And the thought was out, free and spontaneous. Grinning, she moved closer to the screen. Her open smile had suddenly become a secret one. "What? What's up?"

"Oh, nothing really," she said, linking her arm through his. Feigning interest, she tried to distract him from the sudden rush of heat to her face. She knew her cheeks were glowing.

"So how are you with the graphics?" she said, already tired of considering her navel.

"So so." he said.

Good. Daniel hadn't noticed her discomfort. "Well, I'd like a castle, with turrets and a path running down the cliff to the sea."

"No probs," he said, sketching and colouring in the grassy headland, the keep and the ramparts. "And let's head it up with the monogram. We're sure of the R aren't we? Now, the ship. The ship without a name. A lugger with an extra sail. There. We'll give it a capital J and we know there's a p and maybe an I, but that's all we've got. Still the shipping manifests might throw up some ideas. I'll write to Lloyds' if you like?"

"OK. And I'll pop down to the bay and have a chat with my old friend, Walt."

"Shall we get together again tomorrow?"

"Best not..."

"Here we go again!"

"Come on, Daniel. I've been out a lot lately. Mum gets lonely. Next weekend though. If mum goes to Appleby to see Aunty Barbara, I'll come across on the bus with her and we can spend the afternoon at the castle, have tea and -"

"OK but how about taking in a movie, mid week?"

"Going to the flicks, you mean!" Bethany laughed. "I don't think we'll ever make a team. Like I said, we're like chalk and cheese. What star sign are you anyway?"

"Leo... Lord of the Jungle," he said with a growl.

"Hell's bells! Leo's should never get together with Librans."

"Why, what's the matter with Librans?"

"Cheeky! Leos like their own way and you have the dominant sign. We're a disaster waiting to happen!" she said.

"So when's your birthday, Daniel?"

"September 29th. Yours?"

"August 26th. There we are then, closer to one another than you thought. Your problem, Freckles, is that you're all doom and gloom!"

"Mm. Sometimes, I suppose. But only when my equilibrium's all at sea!"

"Big word!"

"An important word. It's all about balance. When my heart is heavy it's because I'm at variance with nature," she said, answering his sarcasm with an arrogant turn of her head.

"Gobble de gook!" Daniel waited for another reaction, but Bethany didn't bite. "Don't tell me you actually believe all that rubbish?"

"I just read the signs," she said, getting up and looking out of the window. For a while she stood there, lost to the skyline. Beyond the gardens were the roof tops and the castle illuminated against the darkness. Beyond that, the cliff, cruelly jagged and clothed in a shifting mist. "Yes, I suppose I just read the signs..." Daniel turned, surprised by the soft eeriness of her tone, but Bethany was beguiled yet again by the insubstantial vapour hovering there. Against the midnight blue sky she watched it taking shape...a tormented soul fading in and out of the real world and always, always reaching out to become part of Bethany's own longing.

"Penny for them?" Daniel said, encircling her in his arms. He felt rather than heard her beating heart and her deep, lonely sigh. "Bethany?" Turning her around he searched for a response in her eyes, in her face, but she only smiled, a mysterious half-smile that left him unsatisfied and excluded.

Chapter 20

Bethany watched the black Mercedes roll down the cobbled way. Separated from his parents by sound proof glass, it had been a private drive home. She had been glad of that. It was late, too late to make small talk, and she was tired so, for the second time that night, she had found herself luxuriating. After the hectic day, what more could she have asked for? It was a new experience, intoxicating in its way. She had accepted the suggestion of his Enigma Variations and snuggled up close to Daniel. Holding his hand throughout the drive along the coast road she sleepily wondered at the moon, so full, so awesome in the night sky.

Turning back to the cottage, Bethany peeked through the window. The Chinese lanterns nestling among the gourds glowed deep amber in the subdued lighting

"Hi, mum! I was just thinking how cosy you make everything look."

"I do my best," she said, but her words had a defensive ring. Bethany sighed. The last thing she wanted right now was a row. "So how was it?"

"I had a great time and your baking went down a treat."

"All the same, I don't want you getting ideas above your station; there's no way you can keep up with that family," she said, flicking her head toward the window.

"That family? You haven't met 'that family' mum, so how would you know I have to keep up?"

"Come off it, Bethany. Let's not play games. Folks don't have flash cars like that unless they're top drawer."

"But there are lots of ways of being 'top drawer.' Money isn't everything. That's what you've always taught me, that I've to hold my head high and be proud of my background."

"Exactly my point. You'd be better setting your sights a bit more down market if you ask me. You want an ordinary lad, like yourself."

"Daniel is an ordinary lad. He wants to make his own way, do his own thing."

"Really? Well that's not the impression I got. The last time I asked him what he was going to do, he said he didn't know."

"I don't either. It's not even an issue yet, mum. We've got lots of time -"

"For idleness, yes, and in my experience mischief isn't far behind." Bethany flushed. Her heart contracted. Was that her mother's way of letting her know that she had taken the barrel. Turning away, she paused and waited for the onslaught. It didn't come.

"Well I'm going to bed, mum, I'm whacked. We found a super place in the middle of nowhere for the picnic though; you'd have loved it. We saw Aunty Babs in the library as well. She said not to forget it's your turn to go across next week. I thought we could go on the bus together. Maybe we can do a bit of shopping and have a coffee. I've arranged to see Daniel in the afternoon; we're going up to the castle. But afterwards we can have a rickety ride home together on the rattle trap. It beats a Merc any day!" she added with the ghost of a smile. "Anyway, what was your day like?"

"Magical! We'll talk about it when you can spare me two minutes of your heavy schedule."

"Hey, that's hip, mum!" she said, determined to keep the conversation upbeat despite the sarcasm. You saying "magical" I mean. You know, teen speak. You're not letting that church warden lead you astray, are you?" she said, giving her mother a hug. "Anyway how old is he? You haven't got a toy boy lined up have you, mum?"

"Tst! Certainly not! A pick me up is what I need."

"Whisky. Call a spade a spade! It's whisky. Face up to it; you're becoming a cool dude with an addiction. A lethal combination!" But before her mother had a chance to remonstrate,

Bethany was gone, secretly glad to get away from her mother's prickliness.

Dear diary,

Phew! What a day. I mean, 'how does a body cope?' as mum would say. Well yes, let's start with the body, shall we? His? OK then, if you insist! It's so athletic! When he puts his arms around me, I feel so safe, so warm and protected. It must be all that sport. So I must remember not to dampen his spirits and moan at him when he wants to spend time with Trev. And my body? Limp! At least when he's close to me there's no other word. It's a pathetic cliché, I know, but limp is definitely the word for it! I know, it's terrible. I'm losing my grip. Help! After the picnic, I lay down on the travel rug watching the clouds scudding by. He must have seen it as an invitation. Well, I suppose it was. Naughty Naughty! He lay on his side, resting on one elbow at first, just looking at me really, and tickling my face with spear grass. We kissed a lot till my lips were puffy...oooh! Did I say my body was limp? Definitely an understatement. Then he sort of half rolled over and I felt the warmth of his thigh on mine and well, the upshot is, I've decided to put a stop to all this canoodling. It's going to get me into deep trouble. Besides I shudder to think what mum would say. She'd probably call me a trollop for starters. I couldn't bear that.

Shoving her diary under the mattress, Bethany scrambled into bed and lay there, desperately trying to stay awake.

"Come on, mum, sup up and come to bed!" she whispered into her pillow, but it was a while before she heard her mother's step on the stairs. Even then, she had to wait until the sound of her gentle snoring told her the coast was clear. Easing herself out of bed she tip-toed over to her bag and took the barrel out of its bubble wrapping. She had left her squeaky door ajar and, avoiding the creaking steps, shifted her weight; childhood escapades and midnight feasts when Veronica had stopped over had left her with an intimate knowledge of those. But this was no childhood escapade. Bethany cringed. As if in a minefield, she shifted her weight this way and that; as if in a minefield, her heart thudded against her ribs. Clutching the barrel against her chest with one hand she manoeuvered her way downstairs.

'The key...the key...oh, thank God!' she thought. Moment by conscience-stricken moment she slowly opened the cabinet, and fingered her way among the artifacts.

"There. Done, all done!" she said. The burden of guilt lifted she made her way into the kitchen. 'It won't matter if mum hears me now. I can say I'm just getting a drink,' she thought, reaching into the fridge, but in the semi-darkness an adrenalin rush stopped her short. Someone was there watching her. Blushing, she stood up. She turned. "I'm sorry, mum," she said, but there was no reply...there was no one there...only a cauliflower on the kitchen table, the green frill of a house-maid's bonnet setting off its round, white, smiling face and cheek bones you would die for. "I don't know what you've got to smile at!" she said, but somehow she knew...knew that her "sorry, mum" had more to do with being found out than feeling genuine remorse.

"You're a first rate hypocrite," the cauliflower said with a disdainful, disapproving smile.

"I know...I know, don't remind me," Bethany muttered as she made her way back upstairs.

Chapter 21

Daniel woke to the buzz of the hedge cutter. 'Dad...oh God, I forgot!' Turning over he glanced at the clock; it was ten past nine. He tried to feel indifferent; it was Sunday after all, but the persistent revving was the reminder; he'd promised to help in the garden.

Normally, he would have been up at the crack of dawn heading down to the foreshore and giving Trev a knock up. They'd always take the narrow path that ran to the sea front and run the length of the beach if the tide was down. Their serious running phase had begun as a challenge to their personal fitness. They had joined the ranks of the early birds-the church goers, the beachcombers, the newspaper vendors and the night trawler men landing their catch. It had become routine, 'a religion of sorts,' he thought as, in a kind of silent communion, they had breathed in the fresh, salty air and watched the daylight grappling with the invariably grey sky. It had been preferable to lying in the pit virtually brain dead from the night before. They'd tried that. No thanks. So what now? He *could* stay in bed and think about Bethany, even fantasize about ' doing it 'with her. Well, it would have to be that way. Fantasizing and experimenting was one thing. Making it with a girl like Bethany was another.

"It will happen, take it slowly; feel your way!" The sex education teacher's Freudian slip had had them rolling in the aisles. Remembering, Daniel grinned. 'OK...OK...but when...where?' Daniel wondered. It was all right blowing up condoms when you were thirteen. So long as the girls kept their giggling under control, it was sort of OK easing a condom on the plastic penis and it was definitely OK practising at home, but how are you supposed to do that when it's your first time and you're faffing about with zips and tight fitting jeans and whispering sweet God knows what in a girl's ear!

"Daniel!" His father's impatient tone jarred his nerves.

"Coming dad!"

"I thought we had a deal, son? The garden. Remember?"

"Like I said, coming dad! Just give me five."

"It'll be a bunch of five if you don't get a spurt on."

"Yeah, you and whose army!" Daniel muttered under his breath. Then, "I'm on my way!" he shouted, but tried to recapture just one more highly charged, image-making minute of Bethany seductively unbuttoning his shirt and easing it off his shoulders. But no. Too late. "Thanks, dad!"

Instead, he conjured up his father...a globe fish, a puff ball of a fish. A swollen to nearly bursting fish with an evil pug face, diamond shaped beak and barbed skin. A puffed out hollow on the inside, prickly on the outside, fish. An expansive fish, a fish that's so full of wind it can beat the sound barrier. 'A blown up condom's got nothing on you, dad!' he decided as he jumped out of bed into the shower, selected the jet stream and waited for the shock of the cold, needle- sharp spray to ease the blighted feelings he held for his father if not the hot ones he felt for Bethany.

Sundays. Bethany loved Sundays, the 'no rush' days when she could lie in a while, doze and will herself to hang on to some pleasurable dream. This time it had been tortuous. Out there, somewhere in time and space someone had called her name...called, and with a curling finger beckoned her to leave the comfort of her bed....to follow...to search. But for what? For whom... and where? In a maze of crumbling castle walls, Bethany had been lost and confused by the sameness of everything. She could only move forward, beguiled by the shifting shadow of the woman, by the sound of the sea crashing against the rocks and the swirling backwash of surf. Then there had been the cry, that so sad cry that might have been the gull's swooping and diving in front of the cliff face, but was not. In that moment the maze had ended and she was thrust forward to teeter on the edge of the cliff with a yearning so strong that her own cry came like an invocation,

"Where are you…"she'd cried. "Robert, my love…where are you?" The buffeting wind held her then, tight in its grip…held her for one last, agonising moment. When, suddenly it stilled, she fell into the churning waves, her mournful cry dying on the salty air.

"Come along now, Bethany!" Her mother's soothing voice drifted in and out of her consciousness. She stirred. She was, after all, lying in her bed. The hungry sea had not claimed her and when she felt the cool flannel on her forehead, opened her eyes and saw the concern etched on her mother's face, she knew she was safe.

"Calm yourself, Bethany, throwing yourself about and crying out like that. And look at the pillow slips all damp with sweat. Do you wonder why I worry about you, my lass! You've been that restless lately. I seemed to be awake all night listening to your ramblings."

"Why? What did I say?" she asked, wishing she hadn't. What if she had talked about Daniel…about their relationship…those little intimacies…her taking the barrel? Her mother would go spare! Flushing, she half sat up, lodged a pillow behind her, yawned and ran her fingers through her unruly hair. Distractions, all.

"Say? Now you're asking me. I don't know, Bethany. It sounded like gobbledegook, that I do know. Now look. I'm off to church. I'll be visiting Mary Jessop as well. She's going downhill fast, poor old thing. Still at ninety eight it's a blessing. She's still got all her wits about her though. The Grim Reaper'll have all on making an impression on that one! Anyway, you have a lie in and pull yourself together. You'll be making yourself poorly." Then in a blinding flash, as if the angel Gabriel had suddenly appeared, her eyes narrowed…"but you haven't got anything special you want to tell me, have you now?" Her mother's fixed stare gave Bethany the heebie jeebies.

"No mum," she said, the memory of her sneaking off with the barrel surfacing again.

"Because if you have…well, what I mean is -"

"I know what you mean, mum, and no, there isn't anything worrying me," she said pleased and surprised at her own composure.

"Right. I'll be off then. Dinner will be at two. Late, I know, but it's all in a good cause. Get yourself something to bridge the gap."

"The way I'm feeling I couldn't eat a thing. Sorry mum. I think I'll wander down to the harbour and get some fresh air instead, it'll do me good."

"More like knock you out. Anyway, I'm tired of trying to make you see sense!" And with a sniff she was gone, her Sunday best shoes clearly giving her some gyp as she clomped down the stairs.

'So much for the 'no rush' Sunday morning,' Bethany thought when she could relax around the house, enjoying her own space, listening to her own music, thinking her own, uninterrupted thoughts whilst her mother flirted with the church warden.

'As if!' Sighing Bethany knelt up to look out of the window. It was a 'can't make up its mind' sort of day. The bland grey sky had given way to a few uncertain brighter patches, but Bethany was not convinced. She had seen those so-called promising signs before. 'Well,' she thought, pulling her thick Aran sweater out of her drawer, 'this will see off a north easterly!'

Chapter 22

It being Sunday, Bethany knew that as night followed day Walt would be down at the bay mending nets; everybody's nets as it happened. It was all he could do with his failing eye sight and arthritis; both had taken a hold on his once strong physique. But his hands had been spared. His fingers could shoot and loop the shuttle as nimbly as ever; it was robotic. And yes, there he was, perched on an upturned lobster pot puffing at his pipe, watching the smoke carry on the wind. He was staring out to sea, absorbed, thoughtful.

"Hello, Walter...Hello," she said again, "penny for them!" This time he turned, surprised and pleased to see her.

"Now then luv. I'd know that voice anywhere. The gig lamps may be running low, but there's nowt wrong with me lugs!" It was wishful thinking, but Bethany didn't argue! "Any road, where 'ave yer bin hiding yerself? By t' life o' me, I don't think I've set eyes on thee since t' storm brok up me little boat. A rare un, that storm; nature were agen us that day, by Jove. Ah well, ere, 'ave a bit o' crab," he said, thrusting a tiny pink claw towards her.

"No thanks Walter. Isn't it a lovely day?" she said, breathing in the salty air as if it was her last.

"It is an all. And we were born to live by t' sea. You're like me, lass. It fair breks me 'eart when I think ont' fishing trips I've missed. There's nowt I'd like better than a trip round t' headland in me own boat. But there y'are. Lads say they'll tek me any time but I knows they reckon I'm a silly old bugger - excuse me french luv- and a liability like."

"Now, Walter, don't tell me you don't enjoy sitting here keeping an eye on them all?"

"Aye. I reckon I do for t' most part, but I'll turn inter a land lubber, niver mind a couch tatty if I'm not careful, lass. Any road, will yer bide a while and chow the fat wi' an awd salt. You'd as soon be with a young un though; I'd bet me life on 't!" Bethany gave him her best 'don't be silly' smile.

"I will Walter. I wanted to ask you something anyway. I'm doing a project for school."

"Oh aye!"

"And if anybody can help me, you can."

"Crikey. Tha's got a lot of faith lass. Things 'ave changed since I were at school. Come to think on it and if truth be telled, I did me best not to go! Came down 'ere all t' time. Kid catcher went arse over 'ead trying ter get me back in." Walter paused. "Sorry luv," he said with a Pop-eye sort of grin..."it's being short o' female company that does it! I'll give 'im 'is due though. He tried all right but even when me dad landed me a clout round me ear'ole and marched me back up ter school agin, they couldn't learn me owt. Book learning...naw! I was 'appiest down 'ere watching t' boats going out with an open sea in front o' me and squawking, 'ungry gulls arguing over t' tit bits. Like bairns they are, fratching and fighting over t' scrapings in t' rice pudding dish! Well now, luvvy. Give you an 'and? I'll do me best. Never let it be said I didn't try to 'elp a Mallinson out."

Walter tapped his pipe on the heel of his upturned boot. The ritual had begun. She would have to wait, wait very patiently for him to settle himself to another smoke. Bethany watched him suck on the old pipe, testing it and tapping it again. She listened for the crackly sound of air and saliva in the cleared stem. Easing first one buttock, then the other, he delved into his pockets.

"'ere, od on ter that," he said, handing her an old penny. It was covered in the gritty bits of burnt tobacco.

"Don't you ever turn your pockets out, Walter?"

"Nope. Why would I want to do that? The muckier the penny, the older it looks. Besides, I don't 'av ter look at 'er miserable face then," he said, nodding at the scowling face of Queen Victoria. "I ask you? Who'd want ter wake up aside 'er ivery day that dawned! She were a right tarter an all by all accounts."

"Well, I think you need a good woman to look after you!"

117

"Niver. I'm not 'aving any woman telling me where ter ger off! There'd be ructions t' live long day and night. Nay lass...with awd Nick wandering this 'ere earth, there's more than enough trouble unless *you're offering* o'course!" he said with a chuckle.

"Walter!"

"Well, yer mam then!" he said, giving her a wink.

"All right I'll ask her!"

"Ye'd better not be doing that, lass. She's a cracker of a woman, your mam. I awlus 'ad a soft spot for 'er, like. But no, it's to be our secret! Besides I'd 'av ter get toffed up and empty me pockets out else she'd be chowing t' fat! No thanks! Besides," he said pointing to the worn image of a seaman on his tin of Capstan tobacco, "this 'ere could be a picture o' me! Fading clean away we are, the pair of us!" Struggling to ease the lid off with the blackened coin, he frowned. "He's as stubborn as me an all. D'ye think he might be trying to tell me summut?" he added with a chuckle that quickly turned into a cough. Ah well, I'm not long for this world, so I'll carry on and die 'appy." Bethany reached out for his gnarled hand, heavily veined and bruised. She watched his weathered face wrinkle when he smiled and heard the rattle in his chest when he breathed. She turned away. From the earliest, even when she played on the sand as a toddler, Walter had been there. Ever in the background, but there.

Taking out a good finger and thumb's worth of tobacco, he rubbed it into the heel of his hand, filled his pipe and firmed the crinkly tobacco down. Then, turning into the wind, he struck a match. Bethany could hear the intermittent plopping sound and knew that the glow would soon be there. Turning back towards her, he tipped his captain's peak and sucked on his pipe with an air of contentment and authority. She waited until the moment had been savoured.

"Well lass?" he said at last, "What's to do?"

"I just wondered if you know what this is?" Bethany slid the rubber band off the scroll and rolled it the other way. "It's a monogram," she said, "but I can't separate the letters." The old man got his glasses out and studied it less carefully than she would have hoped.

"Aye- it's an 'ard 'un, that!" he said. Bethany sighed. She had had such hopes. "I seen 'em before though," he added. "Common as muck, but you 'after know where ter look."

"You mean there are lots, lots of the same design?"

"Somebody 'ad a fetish you might say. Somebody who were good at carving and 'ad too much time on 'is hands. But I'm no scholar, lass, so why bring it ter a dumb cluck like me!" Bethany was caught unawares. She didn't want to tell even Walter about the barrel. In a way it would have been a betrayal of her mum too.

"I found it...It was embroidered...it was -"

"Aye. Well when yer ready ter tell me t' truth, you'll know where ter find me, lass." Bethany felt herself blushing. "Truly, Walter. I just came across it and thought it would be interesting to do for my project. I suppose I was intrigued. Thought it might have belonged to someone local. That's why I was a bit unsure of what to say. I didn't want to seem to be prying that's all. But where are the other ones? Will you show me?" Bethany tried to hide the excitement she felt. Any time now Walter would be wanting to settle to his mending again. Nothing would interfere with that.

"Well, it's got to be local, I can tell yer that, so yes, you'd best not blunder in like a bull in a china shop. I suppose you've a young man as can take yer in t' pub?"

"I can go in myself, Walter."

"Nay lass. It ain't fitting. Too much o' that sort o' thing going on I say. Much better if you go, escorted like. Come to no 'arm then."

"Oh Walter, you sound just like my mother!"

"Aye. She's a good 'un, your mam. Knows what's what. Your dad an all. 'e wouldn't 'a wanted yer in't pub on yer tod!"

"All right Walter. Just to please you. I'll go with my young man!"

"Well now. Yer need ter be in t' Cod with a Fish in its Gills, up on t' cliff top. Set theesen up wi a glass o' cider and sit in t' snug,

119

right in t' corner. It's where all t' courting couples used to get." The old man stopped short. Half smiling he buried his chin in his jumper. "Why Walter, you're blushing!"

"Not me, lass! Nay, nay..." he said with the discomfort of being found out. "Now it be time I got on with me nets and more to t' point, it be time you went 'ome for your Sunday dinner."

"So I...we have to go into the snug."

"Aye, most as do look into each other's eyes. They see nowt else! Sit with t' setting sun be'ind yer. It's better that way."

"So who do you think carved them?"

"Like I said, I dunno. Whoever...'e were smitten all right. Obsessed as yer might say. Now then, lass. Don't let the cows come 'ome afore yer come ter see me agin and bring that young man so's I can 'ave a gander at 'im."

"I will and I'll treat you to a flagon!"

"There yer go agin. I's think not, lass. A right little Jezebel yer tonning out to be. If there's any buying ter be done, it'll be me that does it, or that young man," he said with a twinkle in his eye. "We'll salt 'im, shall us? I'm not known as 'Walt the Salt' for nowt! Away yer go now, lass and leave me to me mending!"

Chapter 23

'Oh well, teacher training day or not, I suppose I'll have to get up!' Bethany flinched. The early morning sun was shining through the knife edge gap in the curtains. It's laser warmth was fine, but when the breeze conspired with the shaft of light, it played on her face and she turned her head into the pillow, enjoying the smell of sleep and warm bed clothes. She was so relaxed, as if her body had shut down leaving her mind to wander at will. Dream-like, she was floating it seemed in a sea of white mist. But the strong sunlight and her mother's insistent call won her over again.

"For goodness sake, Bethany. I hope you're not going to moon about all day!" she said when Bethany finally appeared down stairs.

"Is that a question or a criticism, mum?" she said, collapsing into the fireside chair. Feigning tiredness so as her mother wouldn't see the resentment, her finger tips played carelessly around her eyes. A response was certain to come.

"Both as it happens, and less of the lip young lady!" Bethany shifted uneasily. She knew she was out of line. All the same her mum was annoying her, making her feel guilty and putting her on edge. Bethany watched the fine needle deftly working away. She was sure her mother was the only person in the entire universe who mended tights. In the past hour she would have made breakfast, cleared, washed and dried the dishes, mopped the kitchen floor, watered the house plants and made out the shopping list.

"Don't you ever stop!"

Looking at her daughter over her spectacles, her mother paused.

"Would that be a question or a criticism, Bethany?"

"All right, mum. You win!"

"Really? I didn't realize we were competing. All I ask is that you stop moping about and do something useful!"

"Useful? Why does it always have to be useful?"

"There you go again. Why not useful? Creative then! Physical! Why not go for a walk and take your sketch pad. It's a long time since you did that and it's a lovely day."

"Because I don't feel like it I suppose."

"That's the trouble. You don't appear to feel like doing anything these days. Frankly, you're getting on my nerves and I suspect the feeling's mutual. Besides, having a long face isn't going to make whatever's bothering you go away. Where's that lad got to this week anyway?"

"I told you. We're not seeing each other till next Saturday, except at school maybe." Bethany's long face became a pout.

"So that's it," her mother said, "well, why not?"

"I thought...I...we..."

"Come on spit it out, girl!"

"Ooh...it doesn't matter," Bethany moaned with an impatience that matched her mother's.

"Fine!" she said, glaring at Bethany. "There'll be no reasoning with you today! Well, come what may, it's time I went to the shop!" Mrs. Mallinson snapped off the thread with her teeth and rewound the loose strand on its reel. "How this gets into such a mess I'll never know." Bethany watched her mother scramble out of the chair. Briefly glancing in the mirror, she tidied the loose strands of her hair then took her coat from behind the door.

"Do you want a hand?" Bethany said when she saw her mother struggling to find the armhole of her coat.

"I can manage, but dare I suggest you make yourself useful tidying this!" she said, indicating the tangle of cottons and wool in the needlework basket. "I won't be long." Then, snatching up her shopping basket and without so much as a glance at Bethany, she closed the door with an undisguised huffiness.

"Hello?" Bethany had been impelled to answer the phone. Besides it might be Daniel. Bethany sighed, waiting for the crackle of a poor line to ease.

"Ron...Ron... is that you?" she shouted above the static.

"Yeah. God this line's bad!"

"Well, what do you expect from the froggies?" Animated, Bethany tucked the phone into her neck and resettled in the chair.

"So how are things?" Veronica sounded up-beat.

"Not bad, I suppose."

"Oh my God!" Veronica sighed one of her 'Here we go again,' sighs. She had the measure of her friend all right. "And is that it?" she snapped, clearly disgruntled. "Bethany, you're pathetic! *What-about-Daniel*?" Her idiot speak did the trick.

"Oh...I'm not seeing him till Saturday."

"Zat was not ze question!"

"We're fine!"

"So...az ze love bug bitten? 'ave you -?"

"No, we have not! And you're one hell of a nosy parker! Also you've got a one track mind and I wish you'd shut up with that stupid accent!" she said remembering Daniel's attempt at the same thing.

"Sorree!"

"Yeah, I bet you are! What have you been doing anyway?" Bethany's put down had had its effect.

"Museums and battlefields."

"Too many by the sound of it!"

"You can say that again. Interesting though. It's just that I can't take anymore. It's harrowing. All those cemeteries!" Veronica's disbelief hung in the air.

"I know."

"You don't. You can't. You have to be here...it's different."

"Yeah. I suppose. So what else do you do? Any night life?"

"Walk, talk, drink and eat, the usual stuff. Wish you were here though. There's this waiter...a dark, Mediterranean type...mysterious...broad shouldered. Cute bum too -"

"Yeah, OK. I get the picture!" Bethany chuckled. "You're incorrigible, Ron! Anyway, what about Trev?"

"Trev? Who's Trev? Oh yeah, Trev...I've got a date. We're going bowling when I get back!"

"You are! Tell me more!" Bethany said with an air of conspiracy.

"Now who's minding other people's business!" Veronica jibed. Glad to have got a dig in, she continued, "Anyway, don't sound so surprised. I'm no oil painting, I know, but -"

"Don't be daft!"

"Well, think about it. He's lost his best mate to you and he's got to do something with his spare time!"

"Yeah. My heart is bleeding for him...and you. Come on, Ron, stop putting yourself down!"

"Being realistic, that's all. Anyway, look, let's go out when I get back. The four of us."

"Cool! Catch up on each other's news," Bethany suggested.

"And how's mum?"

"Cool! If you'll forgive the pun! Well, what's new? She's OK I suppose. It's me. I'm a little -"

"Prat?" interrupted Veronica. "Yeah. I can go along with that! Well, look. We'll be home in a couple of days. I'll give you a ring."

"Great. See you then but don't do anything I wouldn't."

"You've got to be joking. I want some fun!"

"See you then, Ron! And keep your hands off that bloke's bum!" Bethany grinned.

"I'll try! Oh and give my best to your mum. Byeee!"

Sighing, Bethany put the receiver down. She always enjoyed a good banter with Ron but suddenly the house seemed empty and she, lost in it. Stretching out in the chair, she yawned. Well, it had been her own choice not to see Daniel. She had wanted to be with her mum, to reach out to her...to talk about him and…and about the barrel and the uneasy feelings that seemed to be sapping her energy but - 'Oh, God, some chance,' she thought.

Another thing. Since Daniel had come on the scene, each day brought new, stronger feelings, each day she felt change was in the air and welcomed it. So why did she also feel disturbed? Yes, that was it, disturbed, even tormented. Sometimes she saw herself shedding her skin like a snake. It would be a symbolic act of renewal... a hopeful act, full of promise and excitement. So why did she so often feel she was drifting back in time, to somewhere, but where...where? It was weird; weird enough to want to share her feelings with her mother, but no way. Not an option. She'd only brush them aside or suggest she was sickening for something and send her to bed!

The untidy sewing basket nudged her conscience. She began to wind the stray cotton on to the reels, picked up the pins and collected the buttons. She remembered her mother had used them to teach her the colours, the difference between thick and thin, large and small, textures, so many things. She remembered learning to count and to set.

"Well, that was the past too." Bethany stopped short. Why had she said that? As if there was something else, something she should remember but couldn't. She shivered. Someone had walked over her grave. "My God I'm talking to myself now. I must be going bonkers. Do something, girl! Get a life! Mum was right!" Sauntering into the kitchen, she scrawled a note and left it on top of the neatly arranged work basket.

Mum,

Sorry about earlier. Really! Have gone for a bike ride. It'll blow the cobwebs away as dad used to say. Have made some sandwiches. Don't worry, Love Bethany, xxx

Chapter 24

Cycling up the hill against the wind brought tears to Bethany's eyes so she stopped at the viewing seat to catch her breath. Sometimes it was good to be alone, to enjoy the sense of freedom, to capture the thrash and the crash of the sea against the rocks or sit on the old sea wall as far away from the day trippers and holiday makers as possible. Then she would try to catch the colours of a fading sky on the sea.

But this afternoon the upland acres beckoned. There, she would engage with the contours that softened the horizon. Still, there was only a glimpse of sunshine. It was around, sulking, skulking behind a dark menacing cloud like a shy child peeping out from behind a mother's black, voluminous skirt. "Oh gerraway yer daft cat! Off you go and play!" and so it did till the cloud began to grumble and wonder at the child's whereabouts. Then the shifting shadows on the hillsides scudded by. 'Well, what was a bit of rain anyway?' Bethany thought.

Three quarters of an hour later she felt the first intermittent spots. She didn't care. She would soon reach the sheltered hollow Daniel had picked out for their picnic. If she could not be with him, she would imagine him, sense him, feel his presence and the tingling excitement of knowing she would see him soon.

And there it was. Bethany came to a standstill halfway down the hill. As before, the pasture land, the interconnected dry stone walls and the haphazard beauty of shape and colour that lay between, took her breath away. Free wheeling once more, she located their very own spot. Heaving her bicycle over the wall into the secluded dell, Bethany scanned the area again. Yes, she was quite alone. Delving into her back-pack she unrolled her old cagoule and spread it out. The doubled-over tartan blanket gave her the extra comfort she needed. And so to her book. The sandwiches and coke could wait, Wuthering Heights could not.

Later, numb from lying in the same position, Bethany rolled over onto her back. Joseph's dialect had tested her concentration, but she had persisted and been rewarded. She had loved the descriptions of the wild places, the sense of isolation and the madness that drove Heathcliff on in his pursuit of Catherine. Now Bethany lay with her arms outstretched, her palms turned upward. It was her tried and tested way of relaxing. Above were the darkening skies; beneath, the hard, colder earth and all around a sense of the beyondness of things. 'This could so easily be Wuthering Heights.' Bethany closed her eyes to dispel all other thoughts and feelings. The trick was to suspend your senses, but even here in this timeless place she could smell the damp grass and the fragrance of the heather carried in the wind. Somewhere in the distance a curlew called, a foraging bee droned relentlessly and a lone sheep bleated. At first, as if in a kind of defiance, her eye-lids flickered but she soon felt the familiar twitches of her tired body relaxing. Bethany paced her breathing and felt the tension ebbing way. But how to still the mind? Outside of herself, outside of the here and now, what was there? Time before, time after? And what happens to all those lost, unspoken words, all those unrealised hopes and dreams? Are they cast upon shifting waters? Are they doomed to ride the crests like a rudderless boat...simply drifting...or are they buried, deep in endless time where a man can only scratch and claw his way to a truth that might never be told? But the truth has to be told! Bethany's need to wander along the cliffs, to explore and to feel the fresh breeze, grew. She ached to hear the restless squawking of the gulls *on the eternal rocks beneath*...because...because she didn't just love Robert. She was Robert...Robert...

A strong gust caught the branches of the tree. They creaked. She woke with a start. Bethany wrapped her arms around herself. The damp was rising. The dark clouds seemed suddenly darker, the wind suddenly stronger. She squinted at her watch. 'My God, it's twenty to seven! Mum'll be having kittens!' Even so, confused and light headed, she lay back. Knowing only that her dream was important and that there had to be a reason for her deep sense of loss.

Breathless and tired, as if she had been on a long, long journey, she roused herself. A storm was brewing. The light was fading. Wandering over to the edge of the dell, she peered through the fast waning light. The wide open spaces that had beguiled her would soon be in deep shadow. Then it would become a forbidding place for wild imaginings, dark and exposed. Picking up her belongings with a greater sense of urgency, she looked to the sky. The dark clouds edged with the silver lining were behind her; ahead, the black, ominous ones were gathering.

Bethany had just topped the first hill when the drizzle turned to rain. She stopped to pull and tie the draw-string of her cagoule hood. It was preferable to turning up at home looking like a drowned rat though she knew the wet knot, under her chin would chafe her. She wished she had a tail wind but the squalls came in sudden gusts and the rain lashed out, blinding her with its sharpness. She would have to shelter under the tiny bridge that spanned the stream if it hadn't flooded. Only another quarter of a mile, but her soaked jeans were clinging to her legs.

At last, the bridge. Stopping abruptly, she left her bike with its wheels whirring and spinning and jumped aside to avoid the spray, her trainers squelching in the soft earth. She could hardly keep to her feet on the slope and fingered her way down. A sudden scramble of shapes in the dim light caught her off balance. The adrenalin rushed to her head but she was on the move and could do nothing. Slithering on her bottom, she found herself up to her ankles in cold, muddy water staring into the eyes of a sheep.

Well, sheep or no sheep, she was going to sit out the worst of the storm. If they wanted to leave they could but they stood, stock still, their black, empty little eyes peering into her own. Bethany glared back. She had slithered on a soft carpet of what she thought was damp grass. Her nose told her otherwise. Slimy, green sheep dung! Too late of course, her hands were covered with it too.

"Disgusting!" she said, bending down to the stream and winced as the cold water washed over her hands.

'Mere...Mere!'

"And merde to you too," she said. "If you're a throw back from the invasion, p'raps even you'll get the gist of that one!"

It was already growing dark when the heavy rain eased. Four miles of hard slog lay ahead before she would be home, home to her understanding mum! 'I wish!' The thought came with a sigh, like a lamentation for a lost cause. She knew she would be in for a mega telling off, but home really was where she wanted to be.

True to form her mother was peering through the window. When the light brought her face into focus, Bethany sighed. Relief and anger were clearly vying for supremacy. Anger won. Her mother was not pleased. Understatement. Her mother was mad, really mad. Bethany wished herself far enough. This was no time to be waving a damp white handkerchief.

"My God, girl- get in here!" she said, opening the door to let Bethany through. "Where the dickens have you been, worrying me to death! Well, I'll tell you something for nothing, my lass, it'll be the last time. I'm sick of this carry on!"

"Sorry mum!"

"Sorry are we? For goodness sake turn the record over will you? Bring a bit of variety into your life, why don't you! It's just the word of the week as far as you're concerned. If you did things properly in the first place you wouldn't have to say it so much! Any road, I repeat, where have you been, traipsing out God only knows where!"

"My note, didn't you get my note?" Bethany pleaded, surprised at her mother's anger.

"What note?"

"In the sewing basket. I left it on top."

"No. No note!"

Bethany scanned the little room. The tip of a piece of paper jutted out from beneath her father's chair. "I left in a hurry. The draft must have caught it when I shut the door!" It was a lame attempt to put matters right. Bethany handed the note across.

"Yet another 'sorry! Oh I do beg your pardon - a 'really sorry.' We've moved on. Don't make me laugh, Bethany! And where did you go gallivanting to this time. Where? Where!" The emphasis and her raised voice took Bethany by surprise. She was used to her mother whittling on, but sustained anger was something else -

"The back ways, toward -"

"Oh yes, I see. On your own, half way across the county and without the brains you were born with. You foolish girl! Just look at it out there! Now get yourself up those stairs and into a hot bath before I really lose my temper. We'll pick this little matter up in the morning- the back ways indeed. The back o' beyond more like. And I thought you had your head screwed on! And another thing. The next time you want something of mine, you might ask for it!" Bethany blanched. Her heart raced. "Of all the things…of all the things. Bethany…you disappoint me," she said, her eyes brimming over. "I…I'm just lost for words."

"I'm sorry, mum, I shouldn't have…" Bethany said reaching out to her mother but she drew back turning her face to the window.

"I'm just…just very sorry," Bethany said, closing the door quietly behind her.

Chapter 25

The next morning Bethany had expected another telling off. It didn't happen. Instead, they sat opposite one another, each keeping their own council. It was awkward and Bethany began to fret.

She watched her mother ambling around in her carpet slippers. On any other day she'd have already been up to her elbows in flour. Bethany thought of the times she had come home from school to the smell of warm bread and pastries ranged on the cooling trays. Today her mother wasn't even in first gear and the more remote she seemed, the more guilty Bethany felt, knowing that she really shouldn't have gone out on her bike all day without so much as checking the forecast. She knew the weather could turn without warning. Going out like that had been an act of madness.

It was the chime of the clock, more strident than usual in the quiet of the morning that finally broke the silence. "It's cup of tea time," her mother said, more out of habit than interest and stood up to draw the curtain against the morning sun.

"I'll get it mum." Except by way of a nod there was no reply. Minutes later, Bethany was back.

"It's been a long time since these surfaced," her mother said, tracing the gold rim of a cup with her index finger. "Your dad picked the set out in a charity shop and oh, you've managed to find a bit of cake," she said, with a telling catch in her throat…"I thought we were out of it!"

"We are now but we can make a batch tomorrow night after school. I'll help."

"Oh, I don't know. You'll want to make plans of your own, I expect."

"Not all day…nothing that can't wait and I am sorry about yesterday and…and for taking the barrel."

"Well, let's just put the matter to bed, shall we?" she said sinking back into her chair though the echo of her sadness was still there. Bethany cringed. "And about coming in late. I've been thinking...you don't need me breathing down your neck at every turn. You'll be wanting your independence, I know that. It's nature's way." Bethany was taken aback. She had thought this was all about her mother being hurt and disappointed in her. "It's just that...well, what with -"

"No mum, it's OK. I know I shouldn't have gone on my own. I was fed up and nothing seems to be easy anymore, straightforward, you know. As for Daniel, I really like him, mum. He's an OK sort of person, good fun and, well I..."

"Bethany!" Responding to the old, authoritative tone of her mother's voice, she stopped short, secretly glad of the interruption. She had been floundering to get the words out. "I spent most of last night reminding myself that you're almost sixteen...and oh, how the time flies," she continued with a sigh. "It's been hard to let go I suppose. If your father had been here, it -"

"Yes, but you don't have to let go, mum. I don't want you to. I just need you to understand." There, it was out. She hoped her mother would not see it as a criticism. "That's all."

"Oh, I understand. I understand only too well. But when I met your father I was twenty six. By then I was sure I knew about life. I didn't. Not at all. And here you are, almost sixteen and wanting to be independent. Sometimes your confidence frightens me. Well, I expect I've got to accept that times have changed, but I hope you'll look after yourself...in every way," she said with a raised eyebrow that came like a warning.

"I will. Of course I will. Anyway I've had the odd boyfriend before mum, and you haven't worried about them."

"I know."

"So why do you worry about this one?"

"Well, I'm sure you could tell me that, but I won't ask you to." Bethany blushed. It was true. Daniel was the first boy she had ever really been close to. Once she had lived a busy, sporty, uninvolved and uninterrupted life. Boys were definitely on the periphery but she had been in control. Now? Now she was soaring with the eagles one minute and digging herself, mole-like, into a hide-away the next. Then there was her pulse racing like mad every time she saw him.

"Mum, when you..." She paused, the old uncertainties holding her back. Unsure of what her daughter might say Mrs. Mallinson waited. She had embarked on this new openness. She would have to see it through. "Yes, Bethany?"

"With dad, did you ever feel that...that every part of your body held a secret just waiting to come out?" The question was unexpected and for a few moments her mother seemed to wrestle with the answer.

"If you mean did I ever feel excitement..." Again she paused, "a kind of fear, wanting and resisting at the same time? Oh yes! It might even surprise you to know that I still do. Sometimes, in my quiet moments, I lie in bed and think about your father. I remember how much I loved him and how close we were. I could scream out for the loss I feel and, if I close my eyes and will him back again, I can bury my head in his pillow and smell his smell. Oh -" she said, suddenly getting up and reaching deep into the pocket of her apron for a hanky, "this won't do, this won't do at all! And now you know why I tell you not to look back into the past too much. It's a veritable Pandora's Box. I mean, look at me now," she said between sniffles, "and that's just thinking about your father."

"I know, mum..." Bethany reached for her mother's hand, "but if it helps to clear the air. If it helps us to understand why we are the way we are, it's got to come good in the end, hasn't it?"

"Aye maybe, but that's your youthful spirit talking. You might see it differently as time goes by. Any road, just you take care of yourself. Perhaps I don't say it as often as I should, but you're all the world to me, my lass!"

"That's more like the mum I remember!" Bethany said, reaching over to give her mother a cuddle.

"Hm. Well now, the mum you know needs to see you getting ready for school." Bethany pouted.

"Do I have to? This project's doing my head in. I can't seem to concentrate on anything else…I -"

"That's true, which is exactly why you shouldn't be mooching around the house. Being at school will distract you. Besides, you'll see Veronica and Daniel. They'll take your mind off it and if you ask me, that would be a blessing."

"No, mum…I just need time to think. Time to…oh come on, mum. Besides, we've only got a couple of weeks before we break up; everybody's winding down now; it'll be manic. It's a short week anyway, what with another training day on Friday and it's yonks since I had any time off." Mrs. Mallinson frowned. She shook her head. She sighed. She looked at the dark shadows under Bethany's eyes.

Well, all right then, but only on the understanding that you don't go out. If Mrs. Crooks sees you, she'll talk. Another thing, the moment you start moping about and giving me attitude, you're back to school, my girl. Right sharp!"

"You're on! Thanks, mum!"

The following days seemed almost unreal. Bethany had lost her taste for the great outdoors preferring to stay home and indulge the sudden urge to give her bedroom a deep clean. Off came the faded posters with their ragged edges. "Sorree!" she'd said, casting aside the heart throbs of her early teens. Out came the plastic bags full of yester-year's trophies from her Brownie days, evidence of the little successes that had indulged her growing sense of pride. Each stirred a special memory. Selecting a couple as keepsakes, she put them aside. Then, wading through the wardrobe and chest of drawers she side-lined everything she had out grown. The pile of has-beens grew too. And could she help it if the fashion world was fickle! She'd never discard anything because the colour was out of season; style was different though. It seemed important to keep up with that. What she wore and how she wore it reflected her individuality and the way she felt at the time.

"Good gracious Bethany, you can't get rid of those!" her mother said when her curiosity finally got the better of her and she popped in armed with a mug of coffee, a heap of protestations and unhelpful suggestions.

"Oh, mum. They have to go," she said. "I can't believe I ever wore them. How embarrassing. Anyway, you've always whittled on about me being a hoarder, well, this is your lucky day. I'm ditching all the clutter. I've decided. I'm making a new start. If Veronica can, so can I!"

"Don't tell me you've made a pact!"

"'course not!" Bethany said. "Veronica's decided to stop fooling around. Oh I know you never thought she did, but trust me, she did! Now she's going to work harder. She wants to go to Uni and study Psychiatry," Bethany said, holding up a size ten top and sighing with the memory. "Well, that, or she wants to be a social worker!"

"And all this when it isn't even the season for new resolutions. Well I never did! But there's hardly any comparison is there? I mean, Veronica carving out a career and you doing a spot of long overdue spring cleaning! Just as long as you give a bit of thought to *your own* future!" she said, turning on her heels.

Bethany fingered the curtains. Thin and faded! An understatement. They may as well have not been there. Still, if they could stand a wash they would have to do.

"Here, mum," she said, dumping them into her lap, "let's make hay whilst the sun shines!" Sighing, Mrs. Mallinson bundled the curtains into the washer. Only when Bethany re-emerged dragging the bedroom rug behind her did she give in to the inevitable.

"And I suppose you'll want to give that a good hiding! I've got just the thing," she said as they struggled to hang the rug over the washing line. "Your old tennis racket. It's in the cupboard under the stairs."

"Good thinking, mum!" Bethany disappeared. Her mother sat down on the bench her husband had pulled together all those years before. She rubbed her hand along the seat. It was badly in need of some varnish. The mental note made, she listened, waiting for the clatter she knew would come. It did - "*Another fine mess you've got me into*," Bethany said when she emerged, the old tennis racket lodged under one arm and the black dusty bowler perched stupidly on her head. She patted it down more firmly. Remembering her father's impersonations at Christmas time, Bethany's eyes brimmed. She turned to wipe the tears away and began walloping the rug.

"Give it to me, girl!" Mrs. Mallinson said, taking the tennis racket off her, "You'll need a bit more umph than - hey come on now," she said, putting an arm around Bethany's waist.

"I'm sorry, mum," she said, wiping her eyes on the back of her sleeve. "I just hate it when I think that the older I get, the less I remember dad...all the little things. Then suddenly I'm reminded like just now and it's awful."

"I know. But that's as it should be. You have your own life to live. New things to occupy you. You can't live in the past. It's time to think of the future- that's what your dad would have wanted. He had such big ideas for you!"

"But I do both. That's the point. Somehow they're both mixed up...the past and the present. I mean, I wanted to get stuck into the cleaning, I really did but only to get the other stuff out of my mind -"

"You mean Daniel"

"Daniel? Sort of, but..." The pause was significant. "The barrel...what about that, mum?" Mrs. Mallinson straightened her back. She breathed in long and hard.

"What about it? And what's that got to do with all this? I thought you were upset about your father," she said, but a light frost had settled on her words.

"I was...I am...but this is different. I can't get the barrel out of my mind and I'll never get any peace until I know the truth."

"The truth is that the sooner you put all this nonsense out of your head the better. You have too much time on your hands, that's the problem. A part time job's what you need, young lady, then you wouldn't be in this pickle. Why can't you just accept that it's a family heirloom, handed down for our safe keeping, that's all?"

"Because it doesn't make sense, mum. In the first place why should we have a barrel with somebody's monogram on it? Who did it belong to? Why did someone bother to engrave it? What's the connection with the castle? Why is the same monogram up in The Cod and…and why can't I let it go? It's as if I'm compelled to find out -!"

"You've let it become an obsession, that's why and you always did have a rich imagination!"

"No. No it's not that and Mum…were we ever connected to someone called Robert?" Mrs. Mallinson's shoulders sagged. She sighed, staring out across the roof tops to the sea beyond, to some world far out of reach of that too and Bethany had pushed her there.

"I can't take much more of this," she said between sighs. "History is just that, Bethany, a few facts, related or otherwise, but history just the same. And better left that way, my lass, judging from your state of mind. I've said as much time and again. Life, your life, mine too, will bring enough problems without delving into the past to look for more. And where on earth did you conjure up the name of Robert anyway?"

Bethany shrank back. The straightforward question had thrown her. How could she tell her mother that she'd heard his name spoken on the wind in a way that made her heart heave into her mouth with the same loneliness and longing she felt for her father?

"Remember all the poetry you used to teach me, mum?"

"I do indeed…every line," her mother said, "but what's that got to do with anything?"

"Well, there was one "There are…there are more things in this world than are ever dreamed of…""

"Well, fancy you remembering that," her mother said, but then her smile faded clean away. "Then I'll just have to be prepared for anything, won't I?" It was as if she had been stung. Patting Bethany's knee she disappeared into the kitchen. The conversation was over. Suddenly, her mother had some summer cleaning of her own to do.

Chapter 26

"This is great…a first; us going out together, I mean!" Bethany said when the ramshackle bus turned into the bay, with clouds of diesel fumes in its wake.

"Yes, I've been looking forward to it. There should be a law against this though," she said, holding a hanky to her nose. "Still, I suppose it's better than shanks's pony. Now, what was the arrangement? A spot of window shopping and a cup of coffee?" her mother said.

"Absolutely! Daniel will just have to wait his turn!"

"Well, I never! Good morning, Joe!"

"By eck! Going on a shopping spree are we?" Cheerful as ever, Joe handed over their tickets. "Tis a bonny day you've chosen an' all. Tell yer what tho, it's a crying shame ye don't do it more often, once t' winter's out o 't way, like. Aye, it's not often we see thee gadding off tergether."

"It is, it is- and you're right," Mrs. Mallinson said, moving along the aisle and settling into the window seat. "Just look at the sea, how it sparkles, it's too beautiful for words!" she said as they crested the hill. "And this can take as long as it likes for me!" The old rattle trap took her at her word, never hurrying and ever struggling up the inclines. Bethany smiled, pleased to see her mother so animated.

"I know. I wouldn't want to live anywhere else."

"Oh get away! You'll be on your travels in no time. This is no place for an aspiring young woman. Besides, I expect there are other beautiful spots out there. The world is your oyster, Bethany."

"You wouldn't be wanting rid of me already?" Her mother reached over, took Bethany's hand in hers and squeezed it tightly. "Oh no! But I've come to my senses. You must be free as the gulls," she said, watching them circling at will above the cliff edge.

"Now that's where I like to be! I always want to be up there, just lately I mean. I don't know why...it's as if -"

"Aye, sometimes it seems the world and his wife is out there sketching, writing poetry, walking..." Mrs. Mallinson's voice trailed off, like a sprinter running out of breath.

"Mum, d'you know anything about the cliff falls?" Her mother seemed not to have heard. She leaned over onto one buttock and rummaged around in her pocket.

"Do you want one?" she said, rattling a bag of mints under Bethany's nose.

"No thanks." Bethany waited. She would have an answer!

"Well, do you?" she insisted.

"Do I what?"

"Know anything about the cliff fall...at Little Penhill?"

"Yes, Bethany." In her mother's resigned tone Bethany detected a faint sigh. "It seems part of the cliff fell into the sea. Most of the cottages were lost. It was tragic. It was a long time ago. Mostly forgotten, best forgotten...," she said, a wistful look crossing her face.

"And what about the next time? Wasn't there another fall?"

"Oh I don't know about that," she said, turning her face to the window. "So, whilst I'm with your Aunty Barbara, what will the two of you be doing?" Bethany frowned. Her mother had changed the subject again.

"We're walking up to the castle. We'll quiz the curator at the castle museum, he might know something, about the monogram, I mean." Bethany paused, long enough for her mother to react, to show some interest, but it didn't happen. "It'll be fun," she continued. "I can remember you and dad taking me up there when I was little. Dad used to lift me up on the edge of the well and walk me around it. Remember?"

"I do! Encouraging you in your hair raising schemes! Goodness, girl, you used to scare me silly. You were fearless, running ahead like a pointer, nosing into everything. One minute you were there, and the next gone! Till you got hurt, then it was a different matter. You wailed something terrible till your dad picked you up and cuddled you. Quick as a flash you dried up then! Crocodile tears, all!"

"Didn't you comfort me, mum?"

"Comfort you? Not a bit of it. Couldn't get a look in anyway! Your daft- bat father was always the one. A proper daddy's girl you were, from start to finish. I used to warn him you'd come a cropper, but he wouldn't listen. I'd have fettled you with a slap, my lass, frightening me to death like that!"

"Ouch!"

"It was ouch as well! So mind you be careful on the ramparts this afternoon. I don't want to have to slap your leg again!"

"You'd have to catch me first, mum!"

"Hm!" she said with an affectionate nudge.

"We thought we'd see if there's a path running down from the north turret." Bethany tried to ignore the goose flesh tingling she suddenly felt on her arms. "There's one on the barrel, isn't there? We wondered if it was real and where it led to."

"Delving again, hey?" her mother said, almost in an acceptance of defeat.

"I have to do my project, mum. We're well into it now. Besides, it's fascinating. Daniel wrote to Lloyds the other day to try and find the name of the ship and we're going to ask about the monogram this afternoon."

"Well. Don't say I didn't warn you, Bethany. It's like peeping through a keyhole. You never know what you'll find on the other side and you might not like it if you do!"

"Oh, mum! You're always on about that. It's only an old heirloom. According to you, nobody even knows where it came from!"

"That's as maybe," she said, straining her head above those of the other passengers. "Any road, we're almost there."

141

Their outing wasn't so much of a shopping spree as a jaunt. 'It couldn't have been any more fun even if they'd had some spare cash,' Bethany thought as they wove their way through the crowds. They were out together, mother and daughter. That was all.

"Come on, Mum!" she said, heading off past Queen Mab's way-out shop that definitely had Bethany's head turning. Then, towards the rich aroma of proper coffee, round, glass-topped tables, cups with pretty coloured doilies in their saucers and a selection of home made cakes and cream gateaux.

"That was just lovely." Bethany watched her mother, ever the lady, dab her perfectly clean mouth with the serviette. "These are too nice to throw away," she said admiring the cosmopolitan motifs. "I've never seen the like, a different one for every blend of coffee. Look, there's one from Brazil, Columbia, and Kenya and oh look, even one from Turkey. Do you think I could sneak one out as a souvenir? I could even impress Mrs. Crooks with that!"

"Honestly, mum! You need to get out more! I'm sure the management can spare the odd serviette!"

"Oh right oh!" she said, rooting in her copious handbag for her purse.

"A-a! My treat, mum!"

"Bethany your bit of an allowance won't stretch to this kind of frivolity!"

"You know me mum! I always have a bit put by. Besides, what's a bit of frivolity between friends!"

"All right- but my turn next time."

"Done!" Bethany said, offering her open hand to be smacked. "Slap it to clinch the deal, mum!"

They had arranged to meet outside the castle entrance. The bench had been taken up by a couple of pensioners watching the steady stream of visitors. Not a word passed between them but they seemed content gazing down the hillside that lead to the harbour below. Now and then, they turned to look at Bethany sitting on the wall in the full glare of the sun. She smiled. They nodded and went back to their sandwiches, neatly unwrapped and set out between them. For a while Bethany was absorbed, watching the sparrows flitting to and fro. They were there to share in the picnic but must wait their turn.

Daniel appeared at last, pushing his bike round the bend. Her sullen look at being kept waiting disappeared. Jumping off the wall she ran to meet him.

"Sorry I'm late!" he said, indicating the flat tyre. "Stopped over at Trev's last night."

"And?"

"His relations were there so we camped out. Used the pump to blow up the air bed and left it there, didn't I?"

"That'll teach you to play boy scouts in the back garden!"

"Hey, watch it m' lady! We did a twenty miler in the afternoon and crashed out."

"Under canvas? How romantic!"

"Yeah, but Trev wasn't up to lying out under the stars! Besides he was all muscle so I gave him a wide berth! We had a few beers and turned in, knackered," he said, drawing abreast with the old couple. The birds scattered. Bethany smiled by way of apology. They nodded. Daniel smiled.

"Friends of yours?" he asked when they were out of ear-shot.

"Could have been if you had taken longer! So what did you and Trev talk about?"

"Footy, bowling and you know, man to man talk!" he said with mock confidentiality.

"Oh yeah?" Bethany's interest peaked.

"And we talked about your mate, Veronica!"

"They're going on a date."

"I know! Look, let's walk around the perimeter walls till we get to the headland," he said, coming back from locking up his bike. "There's a little place I know!" Daniel indicated the rolled up blanket tucked under his arm and his eyes twinkled with mischief.

"Really! Well tough! It's not your lucky day for tampering with a young girl's innocence!" she said. "You might lead me astray, then where would I be?"

"Where would *we* be!" Daniel corrected. If Bethany's sideways glance bore a trace of disbelief, Daniel didn't notice.

"Well, that's nice to know!" she said as coquettishly as she could but somehow the teasing seemed suddenly inappropriate and for a while they walked on in silence.

"Come on," he said, holding out a supporting hand. Bethany took it, allowing herself to be led through the tiny gap in the castle wall. Breathing in deeply, she scanned the horizon. The sea seemed endless. Except for a trawler or two nothing interrupted the air-force blue expanse. A pleasure boat seemed to be hugging the shore line but closer still the waves crested and broke in rhythms as endless as time.

"It's so, so..."

"I know," he said, slipping his arm around her waist. It was one of those special moments. Bethany would never forget the beauty of it, nor her overwhelming sense of well-being. She wanted to hold on to it at least for a little while, but the old restlessness came like a yearning to be somewhere else. Bethany wrapped her arms around him and buried her head in his chest.

"Hey, what brought this on?" he said, squeezing her gently, but he had to wait, wait quietly for her crying to stop.

"I'm OK now," she said at last, "really!" but Daniel still detected a catch in her throat. Stepping back from her, he took Bethany's hands in his and looked directly into her eyes.

"Really?" His question was emphasized, its tone held an edge of disbelief. "Have you and the mater been rowing again? I didn't ask how you got on."

"Oh no, mum was brilliant," she said, snuffling into a tissue she'd rooted out of her denim jacket. "We had a great time."

"So what's the matter?"

"I don't know." Bethany sat down on the blanket Daniel had spread out in a natural recess; it had been formed by a rock fall and was flanked by a couple of trees, survivors, just, of the bitter east winds. Bethany drew her knees up to her chin, thrust her face into the still cool breeze and shivered.

"You're cold! Here." Daniel said, taking off his anorak and draping it over her shoulders.

"It's the ghost." But her words must have drifted on the air. Daniel hadn't heard. 'Perhaps it's for the best,' she thought.

"Too damn right- the ghost of a North Easterly." So he had heard.

"No! A ghost, a proper ghost...an entity that you know is there but can't see..." Daniel turned to Bethany expecting a wry smile but she was still gazing far out to the distant horizon.

"You're serious...and you're blushing!"

"I am? Then you should be more tactful and not mention it. I've been crying, remember? And it's a keen wind -"

"That's not it though, is it? You're embarrassed. You mean it - about the ghost. I -"

"Yes. So now it's your turn to feel awkward. It's not every day a girl tells her boyfriend she not only believes in ghosts, but that she's seen one, well sort of. It's hardly normal is it? Kid's stuff you'll say? Well no, not this time. This time it's for real!" Daniel lay down, his hands covering his face. "This is not happening to me," he said. Running his fingers through his hair, he sighed. "Look. Come on Bethany. There's no need to get so hung up about it. Lots of people believe in ghosts and yes, even claim to have seen them. It's no big deal. And you do. OK. Cool!"

"Wrong again!" she said, picking up and resenting his patronising tone. "This isn't about your regular chat about ghosts. It isn't about your regular girl friend's over-charged imagination after a night with the Ouija board. It's about me. Oh, I know you think I'm demented. I can see it in your face and I know you feel uneasy. Well, sorry Daniel, but you did ask me what was the matter. Well now you know and the day's ruined." Bethany stood up, handed him his coat, wrapped her arms around herself and climbed slowly back up to the gap in the castle wall.

Chapter 27

"Women!" Daniel muttered when he thought about the beer he could have been enjoying with Trev, the two of them spending the afternoon watching the cricket. As it was, Bethany was struggling. Climbing the slope to the gap in the wall she lost her balance but squared her shoulders all the same. Not for a moment did she look round. "Jeez!" Now she would go off in a sulk. But no, he had to admit sulking wasn't her style. She'd huff and puff all right. It was in her genes, judging by the things she'd told him about her great grandmother, to say nothing of her mum. Still, thinking about it, how did she expect him to react! Yeah…OK…but not like a wally; a patronizing one at that. I mean! Had he asked her who she was supposed to have seen or where? No! Had he bothered to ask her how she felt about it? No, he hadn't. So what now? "I'll have to grovel!" he muttered, glancing at his watch; five past three. Well, he couldn't let her wander around the streets till she was due to meet her mother. Scrambling up, he pulled the blanket after him, shook it free of grass and tucked it under his arm.

"Wait on, Bethany!" he shouted as much to break the ice as to get her attention, but she didn't react.

He found her sitting on a bench, deep in concentration. The west side of the keep towered above her and the semi-circle of jagged crumbling walls, golden in the sunlight, were shored up with modern masonry. The stage was set, a mix of the old and the new, but for all the grandeur, Bethany's tiny figure dominated. Daniel flinched at the thought of the drama waiting to unfold. He meandered over, unsure of the reception he would get. The shadow he cast put her in the shade. She looked up, like a forlorn has-been missing the spot light. When he sat down beside her, she turned and buried her head into his chest.

"Ghosts!" he said, taking her hand and examining the thumb nail she had been nibbling. "Let's talk ghosts. Your ghost!"

"Why? You've made your point; apparently it's just a load of rubbish."

"You said that."

"But you thought it!" she said. Daniel ignored her petulance.

"It just takes a bit of getting used to, that's all. I've never met anyone who really believed in ghosts. You're right. Usually, it's kid's stuff. Still, if it's you that's saying and believing it, I'm listening..."

For a long while Bethany toyed with her nail. Occasionally he heard a quiet intake of breath, as if at last she might have found the right words, but they died on the air.

"When you're ready. Just when you're ready; I can wait," he said drawing her closer. And wait he did, till the early evening shadows threatened to envelope them.

"There's a voice calling me to the cliffs," she whispered. "It's weird I know and it only began to happen when we met...then and when my seagull died."

"So you hear a voice;" he prompted.

"Sometimes, yes. At first there was a shape, just a shape behind a swirling mist. It writhed about as if it was tormented. Yes...that's it, like a lost, tormented soul and it was calling, calling out to me. Every time I saw it, it took on a more definite shape. Someone was there, Daniel. Behind...behind the mist -"

"OK, who? Who was it?" Bethany began to wring her hands in desperation.

"I don't know...except...it's a woman, definitely a woman....beckoning to me." Daniel raised his eyebrows and scratched his head. "Yes, yes that's it," she persisted. "Sometimes I see a mist drifting on the cliff edge. At first it seems weightless, like white gas swirling, but I know she's there and that she wants me on the cliffs...so I have to go Daniel...can't you see? I have to!" Daniel wrapped his arms around her.

"Hmm. Anyway, where do I and your seagull come into it?"

"I don't know. It's just that, well, a pair of seagulls started to roost on my window sill. Then one of them flew into the window. It died -"

"And knowing you, you'd be upset."

"I was. It left an imprint. With the rain it has faded, but...I can still see it. It's ghostly, a powdery impression and yet...so real. And its mate still settles on the sill. It looks at me with its empty eyes and well...it's strange...that's all."

"Come on now, Bethany, you're trembling," Daniel said, pulling her close to him again. "Relax. Enough is enough."

"But do you believe me?" she said, turning towards him. Daniel paused before he answered. It was a difficult one. He didn't want to lose her.

"I believe *you believe* what you see and we'll work it out," he said.

"And will you take me on to the cliffs? Will you, Daniel?"

Daniel looked at his girlfriend, so animated, so hopeful and expectant. She was like a child, unable to cope with disappointment.

"We'll see," he said, but immediately regretted his patronizing tone.

"You won't! I know you won't! You're just humouring me."

"Bethany! Look at me. Read my lips. If I can help you, I will. Let me think about it. I need to think about it. Leave it with me. OK?"

"Right," she said but her smile was weak, her face pallid as cheese.

"Come on, let's go and have a hot drink. Then, if you're up to it, we can see what the Curator has to say about the monogram."

The castle tea room, manned for the most part by volunteers from the local history group, was as busy as ever. Daniel opened the door and guided her through. This was a Bethany he had never seen before. The wild look in her eyes when she spoke of her ghost had fazed him. This was not the cool, logical thinking girl with a practical view of things. This was a bewildered, passionate girl, even insecure and Daniel was worried; still, the lively chatter and the background music were welcome distractions.

"Feeling better now?" he asked, when they finally settled to a Cappuccino but her toasted tea cake sat there, untouched.

"I'll be OK. I've never told anyone before. I just can't let go. I want to... but I can't. And I need you to understand." There it was again, the desperate tone. Daniel lent toward her. "I'm trying," he whispered. Then, after a long pause, "Remember when we first got together...?"

"When the whale beached?"

"Yes. Later, you took your shoes off and meandered down to the sea to paddle. You were in your school uniform, remember?" Bethany smiled. "I watched you gazing out across the water and..."

"And what?"

"Well, I..." Daniel paused. "It was strange really. In my mind's eye I saw you...a different person. You were dressed in white. You were of another time and ethereal almost...lovely with the shift clinging to your nakedness. This is daft. Since when did I use words like - oh heck, how did I get started on this! Well, I thought you were a bit of all right! OK? That's what I thought! My imagination working overtime I suppose. But whoever said sex was overrated didn't know what the hell they were talking about!"

"But was it sex?"

"What! You'd better believe it!" Daniel grinned. "But...but... tenderness too."

"You're embarrassed now," she said with a half smile.

"Dead right. At the same time I knew that image of you was unattainable. *That* Bethany was already committed to something or someone out of her reach, out of this world even. *That* Bethany was yearning for something lost. It was weird. It was sad...it...was overwhelming."

"Then you've seen her!"

"No. No! Just a beautiful image of you. Like I said, my imagination going haywire."

"And the sadness?"

"Well, you were feeling sad, remember?" Bethany did remember. She reached over and took his hand. "Thanks," she said.

"No prob! Let's make a move," he said, taking her hand.

"OK." Smiling, Bethany looked into his deep set eyes.

"What? What's up now, Freckles?"

"Nothing. Nothing at all." Trying to hide her embarrassment Bethany looked away. How could Daniel know that his warm, reassuring gesture had been a defining moment; in that instant, she knew he would be her only true love. "Come on, the museum should be open soon."

"I know I shouldn't pigeon-hole people, but my guess is the curator will be a stuffed shirt in a moth-balled suit breathing fusty air and killing off everything but his sense of order, even an inclination to share my excitement!" Bethany said.

"Maybe, so don't you go getting him all worked up!"

"Who ME? As if...!"

"Yes, you. If you'd spent your life with the permanent whiff of camphor under your nose, you'd know what it was to be one of the living dead! I mean, think about it. I know camphor is supposed to repel, but it would take a barrel of it to keep you away. So Freckles, give the poor geezer a break!" Daniel fully expected a clout, but Bethany's withering look was just as effective.

"What a party pooper you turned out to be!" she said, sliding her hand around his waist and tucking her thumb into his back pocket.

But the man leaning against the Castle Museum wall enjoying the sunshine was anything but stuffy. He wore light cords and an open-necked chequered shirt. His sleeves were rolled up neatly, a concession to his public role, Bethany supposed. Reaching into his pocket, he took out a handful of keys.

"He's hot!" she whispered.

"Mebbe, but he could be your granddad!"

"Oh I don't know," Bethany said with a mischievous grin that showed her dimples. Daniel raised a quizzical eyebrow.

"Daniel Foster! Don't tell me you're a yengsa belly! Yorkshire speak for jealous!" she added with a touch of pride.

"I know! But no, I'm not!" he said with a look that cut her down to size.

"Ah! At last...customers! I'd just closed up to get myself a cuppa."

"Are we too late?"

"Not at all. If you're curious about history, great. If you're keen, it's a bonus! Come in."

"We're after a bit of local info," Daniel said, taking the initiative and spreading out the photos he'd taken. "It's this monogram."

"Oh that's an easy one!" Wide-eyed and hopeful Bethany glanced at Daniel, smiled and squeezed his arm

"Here we are!" he said, taking down a leather bound volume. Scanning the chapter headings, he located the point of interest. "It's the Rossitor's monogram," he said, turning it around: Richard Rossitor and the Lady Elizabeth. *R&E*" His tone was one of personal satisfaction. "I know it's intricate but -." He reached across into his desk drawer, pulled out a piece of tracing paper and secured it to the page with paper clips. "Look." The curator switched on the magnifying lamp and fingering his desk tidy searched for a pencil. "If you follow through the inter-twining decoration at the bottom here, you can just see where the bottom of the letter R begins. Follow it round, very carefully and...Bingo!" Away from the strong light, the barely perceptible pencil lines were thrown into relief. "The ' E ' is more difficult, but the same monogram is on the tombs, carved this time. If you do a rubbing you'll see the E clear as day because the letters are more pronounced than the leafy bits."

"That's it! That's it!"

Enjoying a moment of amusement at Bethany's expense, he grinned. "Why the interest?"

"Well, all these engravings are on a barrel!" Bethany said.

"OK. Well, maybe it's commemorative. Until he died Rossitor made something of Elizabeth's death every year as far as I can tell. There were plaques and portraits, silver cups, all sorts, so why not a barrel? Probably a local engraver doing his own thing. One of your own family probably, if it's an heirloom or maybe one of your descendants was a servant in the castle. Who knows? Interesting though and it's different so it might have some local value. Bring it along, let me have a look."

"I can't. Mum…well…no, I can't."

"Ah, OK," he said.

"But we have photos that we can print off," Daniel said to help cover Bethany's embarrassment.

"OK. Meanwhile, you should take a look at the chapel, well, what's left of it. They're both buried in the chapel grounds, side by side. Simple graves really, considering his colourful character." Distracted by the door opening, the curator looked up. "Ah, my second customer of the afternoon!"

"Oh...right. Yes well, thanks a lot."

"No probs, and feel free to call again. You've got me intrigued too. Let me know the outcome."

"We will."

Chapter 28

The chapel was open to the heavens if not the four winds though the outer walls were crumbling away too. Bethany looked up at the Gothic arches. She tried to imagine the stained glass and the biblical story that would have formed the back cloth to the altar and the play of colour that had so often intrigued her when she had knelt in church with her mother. These arches framed a clear blue sky.

"Do you ever go to church?" she asked, glancing around.

"Gave it up. Used to, with Scouts and all that," he said and immediately regretted it. Bethany grinned. "I'd like to have seen you in your woggle or toggle or whatever you call it!"

"Hey, less of your cheek," he said. Snaking his arm across her back he followed the line of her bra.

"Gerroff!" she warned.

"But Freckles! You know you'll never get to heaven on a Platex bra 'cause a Playtex bra won't stretch that far!"

"So that's what the scout masters taught you when you were sitting around the camp fire!"

"Yep! Preparation for the real world," he said, putting his arms around her.

"Daniel! We're in God's house remember, and there are people wandering around," she said, resisting a kiss that set her heart racing.

"It doesn't count. The place is derelict - and who cares, they're human, they'll understand."

"No. No they won't...Daniel Foster will you stop that!"

"This then," he said, pulling her collar aside and nuzzling her neck...

"No Daniel!" she said, leading him out of the secluded niche he had backed her into. Daniel sighed, his frustration clear to see.

"Come on!" she said, "Time and place and all that!"

"So can I make an appointment?" Bethany turned towards him, a challenge emblazoned on her face.

"Sorry...Sorry," he said, raising his hands in submission.

"Well, that's all right then! Now come on. I need to cool it...that's all."

"You do fancy me then!"

Her "Um" hung in the air…"a bit," she said, grinning. "But if you believe that you'll believe anything!" she said, dragging him toward the iron railings round the grave site.

"Well, I suppose there can't be any doubt they belonged together," Daniel said, pointing to the interlinking distinctive monograms on the sides of the tombs.

"Hmm. Who knows? Maybe his colourful character included a dalliance or two!"

"I doubt it. I mean, why would the same monogram turn up in a local pub? It doesn't make sense. Lord and Lady Rossitor would hardly have been likely to pop down to the local for a flagon of beer!"

"What do you mean? You've lost me," Daniel said, scratching his head.

"Oh I haven't told you...the other day I went down to the harbour. I had a chat with Walt. He'd seen the monogram as well. He said we'd find plenty of engravings in The Cod, if we took the trouble to look."

"But that's miles out of the way. It's up the coast."

"When shall we go?" Daniel and Bethany laughed. They had spoken simultaneously. "It'll have to be the weekend for me," he said, "I promised mum I'd help her tidy the garden. Besides, if I'm to keep you in the style to which you're accustomed, Freckles, I need my allowance! And I don't need dad breathing down my neck."

"You don't like him do you?" The question was unexpected. Daniel flinched.

"I'm sorry... I -" Bethany waited for him to answer but the silence seemed to pulsate in and out of an empty space till the cry of the gulls took over. "We haven't a lot in common," he said at last. "I suppose he's OK when there isn't an audience."

"And when there is?" Bethany said, linking her arm in his.

"Then he's prickly, with me at any rate, arrogant and bombastic. You know, you've seen it," he said matter of factly.

"He's a business man. Maybe it's the pressure."

"Maybe. But I'm not a competitor."

"Does he think you are?" Daniel looked down at his feet. He scuffed the turf, like a scolded child, awkwardly.

"Where mum's concerned maybe. Anyway," he said, glancing at his watch and suddenly cutting off the conversation. "It's twenty past five, we'd best be on our way. Can't displease your mum now, can we? Besides we need to eat. I'm starved. All this fresh air. How about you? Would m' lady like a pizza or shall we be like the day trippers and 'ave us a fish and chip tea?"

"Yer, that will be great. I know just the place and this time I'm paying!"

"No, Dutch, let's go Dutch!"

"I'm paying!" she repeated. "Besides, you need to save your pennies to keep me in the style to which I'm accustomed, remember!"

"Joke. It-was-only-a-joke!"

"Hm. Did nobody ever tell you that sarcasm was the lowest form of wit?"

"Yes, and that it exalts the fool."

"In his own low esteem!" They had spoken simultaneously again. "My mother told me that," Bethany said. "I was forever repeating it at school just to sound clever!"

"You should be ashamed of yourself, Freckles."

"Yeah, it was a bit pretentious;" she said, pulling her sweatshirt over her burning cheeks.

"You need bury your head! It was definitely not cool! Now listen up...are you ready for this?"

"What?"

156

"Well, you wanted to follow the turret path didn't you?" he said, grinning.

"You've already done it!" she said. "Good man!"

"Yep, I came up after school like all dedicated scouts should," he said, wagging his head with childish pride.

"You are amazing. Just when I think you're rioting the nights away with Trev, you're on a mission!"

"Just indulging my adventurous spirit," he said with a second wagging. "Now it's pretty steep. God knows what your mum would say if she knew where I was leading you right now. So hold my hand and don't let go!"

"My pleasure entirely. Lead on Macduff! Lead me where no woman has gone before!" Daniel stopped in his tracks, turned round and gave her the dead-eye. "OK. OK. I get it. No more larking about till we get to the bottom!" she said.

"If we get to the bottom!"

Bethany had to admit the descent was dangerous. Apart from being steep, the way was strewn with slack and small boulders so that even in trainers she felt as if she was on shifting sand.

"It's hard to believe this is the path," Daniel said as he turned to steady Bethany for the umpteenth time "but I let the contours decide. There could be no other way."

"It can't have been used in years."

"Don't even think about it!" Daniel said, responding to her backward glance. "We've come too far to turn back."

"So who in their right mind would make a habit of doing this?"

"I dunno, someone desperate I suppose...someone with a known access to the castle and someone who was fit. It would have been easier and safer to take the normal road up to the castle even in the days when it would only have been a dirt track!"

"So, why would anyone choose to take the most dangerous way?"

"For a personal challenge, I'd do it. Trev would as well."

"Just for the hell of it?"

"Yeah, and because it's there. And I'd do it for you," he added.

"Really! You'd climb up here just for me?" she asked coquettishly... "and regularly?"

"Regularly? Hey, steady on girl. Well, if I had to! Anyway, come on; let's rest up for a bit. It levels off through here." Daniel pushed his way between the overgrown gorse. "You'll have to be careful. Breathe well in and keep your hands above your head!" he said, holding the bush back with the weight of his body.

"Oh my God! Ouch." Bethany pulled away, but her T shirt was held by the thorns.

"OK, keep still. You're all right. Believe me it's worth a bit of pain - and pleasure!" he said with a grin and half-baked apology. Bethany raised her eyes to heaven.

"Watch it!" she said as he slid his hand under her T shirt.

"Oh shut up Freckles. This is no time for false modesty. In any case, you're in no position to argue! At last I have you in my pow-ow-ow-er! You are about to be ravished and don't laugh, otherwise I'll have to start all over again." But the more she tried to stifle her giggling, the more she spluttered, the more her shoulders shook and her breasts wobbled!

"God, this is so embarrassing! Daniel will you hurry up! My arms..."

"Oh, it's your arms you're worried about. Well, why didn't you say so? Just put them round my neck," he said, finally releasing her from the thorns. "You'll see, my embrace isn't nearly so horny...thorny...er... thorny..."

"You-did-say-thorny!" she said, accompanying each word with a backhander. Daniel grinned stupidly. "A Freudian slip...really Freckles. I didn't mean...I -"

"Well, I'm glad to see you have the good grace to be embarrassed!" she said, trying to be serious. "I should listen to my mother. She's warned me about boys like you!"

"Yeah well, quite right," Daniel said, slipping his arms around Bethany's waist and lifting her on to more solid ground.

"I could stay here *all* night," she said, snuggling into his arms.

"What? Sleep out on the cliffs?"

"Sure...with you. We could lie here and map out the moon, count the shooting stars and listen to the sea pounding."

"Never tell me you're not a romantic!"

"It's not that," she said, gazing up into a sky that had dark clouds hanging over them. "It's dramatic, beautiful and frightening, all rolled into one."

"You've been reading Frankenstein...or Wuthering Heights, I bet."

"I have. I am...now, Wuthering Heights, I mean. I've got to the bit where Robert overhears -"

"Robert?" Daniel frowned. "You mean Heathcliff?"

"I do. Course I do!"

"I think you're losing it, Freckles; it must be my magnetism that's getting to you!" he said, standing up and pulling Bethany after him.

"Oh yeah, listen to the master of the overstatement!" she said, straightening her clothes.

"Allow me!"

"Hands off...I've told you -!"

By the time they had circumnavigated the lower slopes, the landscape had changed. Rock, scrub and gorse had given way to the odd tree and the ground had a sparse covering of grass.

"I bet we'll come out down by the Mariner's Arms. You know, the tiny pub amongst all those narrow alleyways."

"Hopefully!" Daniel's grin broadened. "I could do with a pint!"

"Yeah, well dream on! With a baby face like yours, they'd never let you in!" she said, ducking out of the way of the mock backhander she knew would come. "Anyway Daniel, it's just occurred to me!"

"What?"

"Well, think about it. Who from the castle would want to come down to share in the low life even if they were prepared to risk life and limb getting there? I've certainly no intention of doing that again."

"Conversely. Who would be mad enough to climb up there, and why for that matter?"

"Exactly...who but someone keeping a secret assignation," Bethany said with a whimsical raising of her eye-brows.

"Neat theory. But no. It's too unrealistic."

"Stranger things can happen."

"I know, but no. I don't buy it!" he said, looking across the roof tops to the bay beyond.

When the going became easier they ambled their way towards the sound of traffic, the arcade pop music and squealing children playing on the sands. Daniel estimated the height of the wall that formed part of the day tripper's car park, hurdled it, rubbed his gravelly hands and reached up to help Bethany. Unfazed, she jumped, using his shoulders to break her landing.

"Thank God we've made it!" he said, looking back and upward to the castle ramparts. "I can hardly believe it. I tell you what, you've got a hell of a lot of spirit."

"Mm, praise indeed!" she said, heading into the ginnel. Daniel followed the weak shaft of sunlight along the wall. It was like an eclipse with none of the grandeur, none of the awe.

Daniel shuddered. "Do we really need to do this?" he said.

"We do. It's a short cut."

"It's a dump," he said, scanning the old brick walls that ran with damp. "What's the matter?"

"Water. I can hear running water..." Bethany swivelled round. "I can't see any water," she said, "or hear it."

"And that smell. Urine, stale urine and shit," he said, wrinkling his nose.

"More than likely; it's probably used as an after hours latrine!"

"It's fetid. It's...it's disgusting," but before Bethany could reply Daniel had turned toward the wall and retched. "Ugh God! Sorry Beth," he said, rooting in his pocket for a handkerchief. "How do we get out of here? It's gross!"

"OK. This way," she said.

Daniel marvelled at her calmness. Girls were supposed to be squeamish but she was totally unruffled while he was a trembling wreck.

Emerging from the narrow alley to face the sea, he breathed in the salty air. "That's better! Sorry about that Freckles. Have we time to walk along the beach for a bit?" he said.

"If you need to. We can grab a hamburger instead of having a sit down fish and chip tea if you like."

"Not for me, but I'll get you one."

Bethany slipped her hand into his, "Are you all right? You look awful."

"I'll be fine." But Bethany was not convinced.

"Your hands are all clammy. Look, just walk me to meet mum. Let's skip the meal and have a coffee in the town. I can make do with a sarni."

"Sure, but a walk on the sands first, hey?"

It wasn't until they were back home having tea that her mother gave Bethany the present.

"Oh, mum! These are fantastic, just right," she said, slipping the power bracelets on to her wrist and admiring their colours. "Sapphire and Jade beads - my star sign gems. Mum, you never cease to surprise me. Just when I think you're all traditional and that, you go all hip on me! How did you know which -?"

"Gracious me, Bethany. I know your birth date, don't I and I have a tongue in my head. Besides the young lady in the boutique was very helpful." Bethany gasped..."Mum you didn't go into Queen Mab's?"

"I did indeed and why not?"

"No reason. But I didn't bring you a pressi..."

"No but you gave me one all the same. I've had a lovely day and it began with you and me..." she said, clearly embarrassed by the show of feeling. "Yes, a lovely day, but a tiring one. Much as I love your aunty Barbara, she does chatter on!"

Chapter 29

Bethany had no idea why she had woken so suddenly. There had been no disturbing dream and the house was wrapped in silence. Perhaps it was the cold seeping into her consciousness. Turning over, she pulled the duvet after her. She must have crashed out on top of the bed, the moisturising routine, the diary writing and the ritual of looking over the roof tops to contemplate the night sky, simply hadn't happened. Curling up, Bethany sought the warmth but the cold hung around so that she tossed and turned until the first light teamed up with her restlessness. Swinging her legs over the edge of the bed she reached for her dressing gown. Taking a shower was a non starter; the plumbing in the cottage would slurp and clang to its own agenda and it was far too early to wake her mum. Pulling on her gaudy red and yellow pop socks, she knelt beside the bed and delved under the mattress for her diary.

Dear diary,

I shouldn't have to hide you away like this, I know. Mum has always respected my privacy, but if I'm to carry on writing to you, I'll have to. I mean, the subject matter has changed slightly! I can't believe it. One minute I'm the goody two shoes of Appleby High and now- oh my God, I'm blushing at the thought. And I swore I'd get a grip on myself didn't I? Well, talk about 'the best laid plans of mice and men' as dad would have said. Oh dad, dear dad... wherever you are...Perhaps I should be writing to you instead. If only. Not that you'd approve either, I know that, but we could always talk couldn't we and I know you would at least understand. I mean, you and mum didn't exactly find me under a gooseberry bush did you? And mum, you must have felt like me...all weak at the knees and so sensitive...I mean, every time he touches me I turn to jelly. But I wasn't born out of wedlock so how could you wait? How could you fight it? Why fight it? Oh I know you'd say there's a time and a place and that anything worth having is worth waiting for, but dad...I really want to and times have changed. If Daniel wears a condom or I get on the pill, wouldn't that make it OK? I'm nearly sixteen after all...and yet, deep down in the heart of me I'm scared and I don't want to feel guilty...but I do! Or is it that I don't want you to be disappointed in me...? The PSE teacher told us all about the mechanics of sex, but nothing about feelings...oh, dad...mum...help!

By now the light was stealing into the room. Bethany sighed, snapped her diary shut, locked it and drew the curtains back. The deep blush of sunrise was foreboding. 'Well, rain or shine, tired or not she would have to get back to see the curator. In the afternoon. Yes, that's it. In the morning she'd help her mum,' Bethany thought as she snuggled back under the duvet. This time she slept.

Her mother's shrill call jarred Bethany out of her deep sleep. She stirred, resentful of the intrusion. Again it came.

"Come on now, Bethany, the morning's half over!"

Bethany stretched, her toes reaching the bottom of the mattress, her arms doubling back to grip the bed head. "Coming mum! Just give me five!"

"God preserve me, there you go again. Five what? For goodness sake say what you mean, Bethany. Besides, I thought you were seeing Veronica today." She was. The thought galvanized her into action. Bethany drew her legs up from beneath the duvet, lifted them high into the air, raised her buttocks off the bed spreading her fingers wide and began her cycling exercises. She would do as many revolutions as there were gold studded florets around the mirror. Too many though and 'thunder thighs' would take on a whole new meaning!

When she finally made it downstairs, the table had been cleared of the breakfast dishes and the wicker fruit basket returned to the table, another symbol of order, time and place.

"Your breakfast's in the oven but the tea's luke warm; you might want to make another pot." Bethany reached up for the green padded oven glove. This sudden expectation that she should want to be independent was a sure sign that her mother was annoyed. "I'm off to help with the flowers in church and then to the shop," she said, rummaging about in her purse. Oh - and Veronica rang."

"Well why didn't you call me!"

"Tst! Five minutes was what you wanted, Bethany - half an hour ago. Anyway, she said she was going into Appleby; she'd meet you between two and two-thirty under the clock tower if you were interested. Said she wouldn't wait though, and I should think not either!" Bethany tried to control the wave of anger that swept over her. One, she was annoyed that Veronica should take that attitude. Two, she resented her mother taking sides.

"I'll be there," she said, scrolling her bracelets over her wrist.

"Aren't you going to wear them today?" Bethany looked up. Her mother's tone, suddenly softer. 'What was it with her mother, pleasant one minute, miserable the next? Only teenagers were supposed to behave like a first rate twit and she was definitely too old to pin it on the menopause.'

"Not today." Bethany lied, inwardly ashamed of her peevishness. "I'd hate to lose them. And mum, can I have the key to the cabinet? I need to take some photos of the barrel. Black and white ones. I need to enlarge them for the detail. I need to see the detail," she said again for no other reason than to ease the stress she always felt when the subject was mentioned. This time her mother didn't argue. She sauntered into the kitchen, returning with the key.

"I thought you kept it under the vase, mum. I looked for it the other day."

"Well, yes...but it's best with me. You only have to ask. Just be careful with it and put it back safely that's all."

"OK. And I'll leave the back door key in the usual place when I go out. I won't be home late."

"Are you seeing Daniel?"

"No, not for a few days, but Veronica'll have a lot to tell me and afterwards I'm going back to the castle so don't worry."

"No. I've to let you have some space, remember! she said. Then, opening the door, she paused to button up her cardigan against the chill morning. "Still, wherever you go, whatever you do, just take care."

"I will mum." But Bethany's softly spoken reply died on a disturbing draught of resentment.

The warmth between the two girls showed in their Rastafarian greeting. They had waved and grinned at one another from a distance but a physical show of affection was always necessary.

"The sun shone in the Somme then!" Bethany said, admiring Veronica's tan.

"You bet. It was great. Too hot for mum though. She was having trouble with her varicose veins again and kept chickening out of the trips dad had planned. I went though. It was OK. Dad's grandad fell in the Battle of Mons. It took a while but we finally found his grave, one of thousands of course. You'll have to go. It's special...moving," she said more quietly than Bethany had ever known.

"I will. It's something I've wanted to do," Bethany said, indicating a move in the direction of a sandwich and soft drinks bar down the street. "Look, let's get a coke and a sarni. We can sit on the sands for a bit - give you a chance to get some real air in your lungs! Besides, you'll need it. I want you to tell me everything!"

"That usually means *you* can't wait to tell *me* everything! OK then, let's have a paddle. And have you brought your bucket and spade!" Bethany retaliated with a grin.

"No, but I've raided my piggy bank and because you're my bestest friend I'll let you have a lick of my ice cream!"

"Done, but it had better be a Knickerbocker glory! My favourite! I haven't got long though." Veronica added between fits of giggling. "An hour maybe. I've promised mum I'd do some jobs in town. How's your mum by the way?"

"She's..." Bethany struggled to find the words. Veronica waited. "She's..."

"Maungy, miffed and misunderstood, or is that a fairer description of you!"

"Hey, Ron! Why is it you always take mum's part?"

"I like her, that's why." Veronica's straight talking always got Bethany riled.

"Yeah, and you're supposed to like me."

"Ah but..." Veronica's 'but' hung in the air and she smiled.

"But what?"

"Well, you can hack a bit of aggro. For all your mum's a bit strict and straight-faced she's an OK sort of person. I also happen to think she's a bit vulnerable."

"She likes you too" Bethany conceded, "Come to think of it you can't put a foot wrong!"

"That's because I don't live with her. I mean, for starters, how would she take to my fag addiction? If she saw smoke rising from our place, she'd happily convince herself the chimney was on fire. It wouldn't occur to her that it was me puffing at a fag as if there was no tomorrow! It's all image with your mum but for all that, I like her. Underneath that hard exterior, it's my guess she's as soft as putty and she cares. Anyway, tell me about Daniel! Have you finally figured out why he isn't a schmuck?"

"Ron you are amazing, always wanting to know what makes people tick."

"Yeah. That's why I want to do Psychiatry."

"You're that sure?"

"I'm sure," she said with an emphatic nod.

"I wish I could be. I've absolutely no idea what I want to do. No direction. No ambitions, no focus!"

"Well, that's not exactly true. From where I'm standing you're focused on Daniel well enough!" Bethany pursed her lips and nodded.

"True," she said, smiling "and the English assignment -"

"There you are then. I haven't even started mine! So what are you doing?"

"Well, we have a sort of barrel in our cabinet. It's a family heirloom; it's engraved and it's got the Rossitor monogram on it."

"What? *The* Rossitor monogram?"

"The very one." Bethany looked across at her friend, surprised at her reaction.

"So where did it come from? I mean how come the Mallinson's have it?"

"Ask me another. I only know I can't get it out of my mind. To be honest, I'll be glad when I've finished the project. It's driving me nuts. Anyway how do you know about the Rossitors?"

"Oh everybody knows about them. I'm surprised you didn't. Still, I only know because of my Nan. She was really lonely when Pops died. I ended up walking around the castle grounds with her every Sunday afternoon. I can remember moaning on to her about dad grounding me every time I did something wrong. Then she told me about Lord Rossitor 'so called' and what an evil man he was supposed to have been, shutting his daughter out of his life and sending her away because she'd done something bad."

"Like what?"

"Like being born. Her mother died giving birth to her. Rossitor never forgave the little girl. Apparently theirs was the grandest passion of all time. He turned to drink and gambling and died a bitter, twisted old man, or so they say."

"That's awful. A nasty piece of work, hey?"

"I'll say. Some of it may have been exaggerated though." Bethany was intrigued.

"So what happened to the daughter?"

"Now there the story dies. No one seems to know."

"Well I'm going up to the castle in a bit. I'll ask the curator. He's very dishy I might tell you. But then, yeah, you're all fixed up dating Trevor! You wouldn't be interested in a handsome, casual, down to earth history buff!"

"Don't tempt me. And yes, I am dating Trev and yes, I do have to go," she said, standing up and slinging her weave bag over her shoulders.

"Oh come on! Stay and tell all, Ron!"

"Next week. Same time, same place. I've got an essay to write, remember!"

"You really mean to give up your sloppy life style then!"

"Watch this space!" she said, a hyena grin crossing her face. Then, the Rastafarian goodbye said, she walked away, her lolloping, undignified gait apparently a thing of the past. Tripping across the soft sand Ron blended in amongst the holiday makers. So many dads, mules all of them, lumbered with hired deck chairs and windbreaks. Then there were the mums, in meerkat stance, alert and anxious, their broods in disarray, full of mad-cap excitement. Bethany wondered at her friend and suddenly felt a moment of panic. Things were changing, perhaps forever. She sighed. She wanted so much to hang on to the safe world she understood with its dos and donts set down in tablets of stone. The problem was that she couldn't just accept the rules anymore. She had other ideas, half-formed maybe, untried and untested, but they were there all the same. A new world beckoned. Every now and then, terrapin-like, she would emerge from the old, test the air and withdraw into her shell again. A certain nervousness would win the day, but not for long. Bethany looked up to see the young gulls already competent and flying free. She remembered then the dusky pink dawn. Red sky in the morning, sailor's warning! If she was to go up to the castle she had better be on her way; there could be no doubt that it would rain.

The curator looked up from his paperwork when she opened the door to the museum. His interest was immediate and his smile, warm. "Hi there!" Bethany blushed.

"Lord Rossitor, wasn't it?"

"That's right. A friend just told me he was a gambler and a drunk."

"So the locals would have us believe. Certainly he let the castle go to wrack, if not ruin. After he died, a lot of work had to be done on it. The inventory records confirm that. It was used as a prison for a bit then converted into a garrison. He had no male heir of course."

"But there was a daughter, wasn't there?"

"True. Her baptism *was* recorded. She was christened 'Elizabeth' after her mother; at least he did that for her. Oh and she was confirmed. That's recorded as well."

"So what happened to her? Did she marry?"

"That's the thing. After her confirmation it's as if she ceased to exist. If we're to believe local tittle-tattle and they say there's no smoke without fire, Rossitor blamed her for the death of his wife. She died giving birth. The poor fellow went into shock and neglected the little girl. Perhaps she died, so many did."

"But wouldn't there be a grave?"

"Sure! And the death would have been recorded. Then again, the story goes that he turned her out."

"What for?"

"Who knows? In any event, it seems she was never heard of again and the old boy went mad...with grief I suppose." Bethany couldn't help herself:

"Grief? More like guilt if you ask me! Well, thanks anyway," she said and stepped out onto the cobbled way.

A cold breeze had sprung up. All the same she would wander around the castle grounds. She had promised herself that, and set off briskly, buoyant at the idea of walking along the cliff edge as far as the promontory. 'And no sour faced, pot-bellied, bald-headed little man is going to stop me,' she thought when, at the gate kiosk, the apparently bored ticket collector stamped her student card without a trace of a smile.

The castle grounds were extensive. What remained of the curtain wall plunged the smooth green turf into darkness. Bethany headed off across the sweep of tended lawn, past the keep, past the great hall, past the well, (mute guardian of dreamers) till she came to the foundation stones of the tower. Once it had held prisoners, she knew that much, but the elements had claimed it. Little remained to suggest the cruel justice of times past, but it was said that on a still, dark night, the dragging sound of leg irons and a crescendo of collective moans are carried in the wind. Bethany shivered. She wished Daniel had been with her and cursed herself for running off that time. Squeezing through the gap in the castle wall again, she had to admit he knew how to pick a good spot. Nestling in the natural hollow between tufted mounds of coarse grass was like being in a hammock. She was safe and at ease with herself. It was ten minutes to one. She had time to spare, an hour perhaps to look out across the sea that might have been an ocean, to feel the sharpness of the wind that would bring a tell-tale colour to her face, and to taste the salt on her lips.

But the dark clouds began to settle making it appear late afternoon. She closed her eyes. It was easier to think that way, easier to use that self-imposed darkness to cut out the sight of time-worn rocks, the expanse of sea and sky that seemed, unusually, to accentuate a sudden feeling of loneliness. It was a new phenomenon. She had wanted to think about Daniel, about the boy who would become a man. She could not. She had wanted to imagine a future, her future with him but could not. Some deep emptiness had invaded her thoughts and stolen her mind. Bethany felt her chest tighten. She stirred uneasily. A sudden, cold, unearthly breeze swept over her. She opened her eyes to see the bright edge of the sun disappearing behind a black cloud. Eerie rays and folds of light writhed about on the blustery cliff edge. Behind it, the white spectre. "I'm here… listening…waiting...!" but Bethany's cry was lost to the sound of the raucous gulls gathering above. Blending in with the unreal curtain of light, the ghostly form of the woman drifted away. Only one certainty remained...the sorrowful cry, that came like an echo of Bethany's own, dying…dying into silence. Then the gusty wind eased and the sun shone.

Sure now that she must follow her instincts, sure that they never lied, Bethany looked up. The seagulls had gone. Only one remained. Wings outstretched, it seemed for a moment to hang there before floating in to settle on a rock close by. She turned to go. Behind her, the hiss of sea spray waged war on the rocks. Before her, the defiant, jagged masonry made long, finger-pointing shadows that stretched across the castle grounds while above, the seagull wove figures of eight around her…

Chapter 30

"Really?" Bethany swapped the receiver over and rearranged herself on the settee. She had waited ages for Daniel to phone. "Let me get this right. Your dad will run us up to The Cod on Saturday?"

"Yep, that's the idea. I took him up on it. I hope I did right."

"You did; that's great. Besides, it's a long haul up there and you know my legs! Well, that's good of him!"

"It's no big deal!"

"It certainly is. You should be grateful!"

"Yeah. OK Freckles, but it's too early in the morning for a lecture. He's going in that direction anyway." Unfazed by the put-down, she continued,

"All the same! So how do we get back? Tell you what, we'll hitch-hike. I'll flaunt my charms on the roadside whilst you lie low amongst the heather! Then just when the driver thinks he's onto a good thing, you can leap up, take him by surprise and jump in the back!"

"Well, how original! Anyway, dad's got all that arranged too."

"So that's what's bugging you!" she said, picking up his resentful tone.

"I don't like people arranging things over my head I suppose."

"He's not 'people' - he's your dad for goodness sake! Anyway it was your choice in the end; you could have refused!"

"I know."

"So what else has he decided?"

"To use the bike rack. Then we can cycle home."

"Even better," Bethany said, trying not to sound as if she was bumping up his father again. "Shall I make another picnic?"

"No, since we're arriving in style we may as well have a bar meal. My treat!"

"That's if they do bar meals. Not many people get up there!"

"Yeah, but when they do, they're ravenous: walkers, twitchers - great outdoor types like me. Tell you what though; bring a survival pack, a few sarnies, chocolate and stuff."

"OK."

"Anyway look, Bethany I've got to go.' Yer don't get owt for nowt in our 'ouse, yer know!" There it was again, the edge of resentment. "I've got to wash and polish the car. That's the deal. It's called using a sprat to catch a mackerel! So I'll see you on Saturday morning. On the dot, 9.30. Dad's got this appointment."

"OK. Tarra then!"

"Cheers!" The phone clicked in a too-business-like way. Bethany put the receiver back on its cradle thinking that she really should try to bottom the problem Daniel seemed to have with his dad. It kept resurfacing and all the while she'd expected him to share her own preoccupations. That would have to change.

"You'll like Mr. Foster, mum. He's OK," Bethany said, trying to ease the underlying tension in her mum. As usual, she hated the idea of being coerced into meeting people she didn't know.

"Will I now?" she said, indicating the Mercedes drawing up, "but I can't see what we could possibly have in common with a family like that!" she said, making for the kitchen.

"Oh no you don't! This way, mum," Bethany said, leading her back. "No sneaking off!" Her mother sniffed a disapproving acceptance, took off her pinny and opened the door.

"Ah...we meet at last, Mrs. Mallinson!"

"Indeed. How do you do?" she said, taking his outstretched hand.

"I'm fine, now that I'm getting shot of this one for the day!" Mr. Foster slammed his hand down on his son's shoulder. "I warn you, this little lady doesn't know what she's taking on! Isn't that right, Danny Boy!" Daniel shrugged his father off, but his anger was masked in the simultaneous task of lifting and securing Bethany's bike on the rack. Bethany forced a smile but it was her mother who broke the awkward silence.

"Oh I don't know," she said, "he looks after Bethany right enough!" Grateful and surprised that her mother was defending Daniel, Bethany's forced smile broadened.

"And I should hope so. Never let it be said that a son of mine doesn't know how to treat a lady. Ready, sunshine?"

"Yes, dad."

"We'll be on our way then," Mr. Foster said, ignoring the resentment in Daniel's tone. "I hope it won't be too long before we meet again, Mrs. Mallinson. You must come over for a meal. Daniel will make the arrangements, won't you, son?" Daniel nodded and, smiling a goodbye, saw Bethany into the back seat.

"Bye, mum!"

Relieved to see them round the corner, Mrs. Mallinson latched the garden gate behind her.

"By crickey, Lisa, you'll have t' queen's very own 'oss and carriage tonning up afore long!"

Mrs. Mallinson looked up to see her neighbour shaking a mat at the upstairs window.

"At the very least, Mrs. Crooks," she said, whilst wondering what had possessed her to give the woman leave to call her Lisa. "The cheeky faggot!" but her words were muttered rather than spoken. She had no mind to argue. A cup of tea was what she really needed.

From a distance 'The Cod' seemed to sit precariously on the cliff edge as if an unexpected sneeze from a lonely traveller would be enough to topple it. But not so; by the time the car had pulled into the gravelled parking area, the sweep of open moor between it and the coast was obvious

"OK you two!" Mr. Foster was in a hurry. He helped Daniel with the bikes, propping them up against the dry-stone wall that marked the perimeter. "No need to secure them here!" he said with a grin. "The only other life form you're likely to see are sheep. Well, have a good time and I hope you find what you're looking for! Bye, son; bye, Bethany."

Mr. Foster sped away leaving skid marks on the gravel.

"0 to 60 in five seconds, that's dad all right." Bethany linked arms. "You told him about our mission then?"

"Oh yeah. Shouldn't I have?" Bethany shrugged.

"That cod won't have a fish in its gills much longer. It's a bit run down," he said, trying the elderly door beneath the lob-sided pub sign hanging on one hinge. "The dry stone walls will be around for ever though. The bad weather cuts everything down to size up here- except for those and the sheep of course."

Daniel tried the door again, this time putting his shoulder to it. It creaked defiantly. The owner of this last refuge for lost souls looked up from his seat behind the bar, a vacant expression on his face. Neither Daniel's impromptu arrival, Bethany's giggling, nor the latch clanking behind them made any impression.

"Morning!" At last, through the darkness, a mumble of acknowledgement. "Beer?"

"Meet the master of monosyllabic speech!" Daniel whispered. "It's hob- nobbing with the sheep that does it! Never get too chummy with them say I!"

Bethany's, "Sh!" was delivered with a sharp elbow dig.

"So what will you have, Freckles...a shandy?"

"Why not? Yes, thanks."

"A beer and a shandy please, mate!" Into this picture a woman loomed. Rotund, very rotund and rolling. Even in the semi darkness her red, veined cheeks shone beacon-bright. Daniel thought they could as soon have set her up on the roof than rely on the dangling pub sign outside. He grinned.

"Come on our Albert," she said, "shake a leg. Yon couple 'ave better things ter do than watch thee reading t' paper! And mind yer face don't crack while yer at it!" she added under her breath. "Now, how d' yer like yer shandy, sweetheart?" she said, pausing at the tap and looking over the counter at Bethany.

"Er..., not too strong, thanks."

"And any chance of a pub lunch later on?" Daniel asked?

"Don't do 'em!" Albert had resurfaced.

175

"Aw, shut up and get back ter t' paper. If yer could read, it would 'elp. But that way yer might 'ave ter buy two a year, you old skin flint! As a rule we don't, luvvie" she said, glaring at her husband, "but I'll see what we've got." Then she ambled off, Albert tutting and moaning in her wake.

"Oh... er...!"

"Yes luv?" Turning back she collided headlong into her husband. "Tst! I wish thoo'ld get out from under me feet! Yes luv?" she said again.

"The snug. Which part of the pub is the snug, the old snug that is?"

"Eh, our Albert, listen ter this! Young man's on about t' old snug!" But there was no reply. "It is old an all," she said, leaving a look of impatience behind her and it's pokey. Most that cum 'ere prefer open spaces like. But I'll tell yer what, I'll get our Albert ter mek yer a bit o' fire up. Any road, this way me loves."

Half an hour later, the "bit of fire" had taken hold, warming the little room and helping to bring the surroundings into focus. Dull red and black diamond shaped tiles, many now cracked, made the floor uneven. Daniel reached over, picked out a log from those stacked in the recess and settled it on the pyramid of coals. It was tinder dry. Straight away the flames lapped around it. The sparks spat and crackled. Little puffs of black smoke curled upwards into the chimney, a few straying out and upwards to meet the stained front of the mantle piece. There was no fender to keep the embers in check. Bethany sat back in the wooden settle with its panelled back. She ran her hands down its winged sides.

"So this is it! To think Lord Rossitor and the Lady Elizabeth might have sat in this very seat!"

"Yes, and came away with sore bums," he said, rubbing his backside. "I mean, a cushion wouldn't come amiss."

"Oh Daniel! Don't spoil it. Use your imagination! We could be in a time warp!"

"Sorry!" The tone was critical. Bethany picked up on it. She leaned against him, stroking his thigh. "Come on, Daniel," she encouraged. "How can you not be moved by -?"

"Oh I'm moved all right," he said, unconsciously spreading his legs wider and grinning lasciviously.

"Daniel Foster!" Bethany lent back and took her hand away. "I mean, look at all these," she said, fingering the pewter jugs and candlesticks. "And look, a musket. It's another world even down to the clay pipes. I mean, who would have used the snug all those years ago? Why would they come to such a forsaken place anyway?"

"People wanting anonymity I suppose. Wheelers, dealers...lovers. Look, I was saving this up till later, but as it's your number one priority -." Daniel reached into his back pocket and pulled out an envelope.

"That's not fair, Daniel!" she said, but in her heart she knew he was right. The barrel was the only thing she could think about, yet in some strange way she knew he was part of it. "I'm preoccupied, I suppose. Yes, I admit it," she said "but I think about you all the time."

"Well, thanks. Talk about being an also ran!"

"There you go again. You sound as if you're jealous. How can you be jealous of a story, Daniel! You'd have a right to moan if I was chasing after the curator for God's sake!"

"That's -"

"I know," she cut in, "definitely out of order and unfair. "Come on Daniel, let's not row. We don't spend that much time together and I might never get the chance to come up here again."

"But that's the only reason we're here and you know it!!" Bethany's eyes filmed over. "I have to be, I told you that," she said, "but back at the castle that day you said you understood."

"I said I was trying to and that I'd find a way, but not this way. I'm being manipulated and I don't like it."

"Well, you're wrong. Believe me, I know what it is to be manipulated. Ever since I started on this business I've been compelled to -"

"To what?"

Bethany groaned. "Honestly Daniel, you sound just like my mum!"

"And I'm beginning to feel like her! You need to take time for people, Bethany!"

"Really!" Bethany pouted. "Look, Daniel," she said after a pause, "don't you see, I've got to find out about the ghost. She can't rest. She needs to know! Oh God, I don't know what she needs to know, but something. And she won't rest until she finds what she's looking for and -" Bethany stopped short, suddenly drained of energy. Her shoulders sagged and her deep sigh seemed to fill the little room with its tea chest, coils of rope, fish nets. "Look," she said, "there, there between the rings on the beer barrel...the one in the corner, can't you see, it's the monogram, just as Walt said: R & E - Robert and Elizabeth."

"Robert? Not Richard? Rossitor's Christian name was Richard, remember?"

"Yes...but no, it's definitely Robert; it has to be. I heard it, *that* name. That's what I wanted to tell you. The last time I saw...you know, I heard her calling out. I wish you could understand. I wish...I mean...it's that name that keeps coming into my mind all the time."

"OK," he said, cupping his hand over hers. "Stop talking and read this," he said, handing over the letter "and just for the record, I'm a converted man. I believe you."

"You do? What is it?" she said, hardly able to contain her curiosity. Bethany's smile and look of incredulity warmed him. "But why... I...?"

"Read it! It came in the post yesterday. It's from Lloyd's, the shipping people."

Dear Mr. Foster,

Further to your recent inquiry regarding the luggers operating on the east coast in 1776, my secretary informs me that you subsequently telephoned the office with a view to locating the names of the crew who were assigned to what we can confirm was The Juniper. For your interest I also enclose a photo copy of the manifest which indicates the cargo carried and the destinations involved...

Bethany was riveted. "So it's The Juniper," she said at last.

"It has to be." Daniel handed the list over. "Nothing else even vaguely links to the letters on the barrel.

"And the crew?"

"Well look." Daniel lay the inventory down on the table, smoothing the creases out with the heel of his hand. "Here's the scoop!" Running his index finger down the surnames, he stopped at Granby and slowly worked his way across:

Name	Date of Birth	Place of birth	Trade
Granby Robert	24-3-1758	Penhill Bay	Carpenter

Bethany sank back into her chair.

"So it's true. A Robert did live in Penhill Bay. And these carvings! Robert might have done them and maybe they're not referring to Lord Rossitor and his wife. Maybe they're referring to the daughter. Unless...unless the Lady Elizabeth was having a relationship with this Robert. Maybe the daughter wasn't even Lord Rossitor's and that's why he...oh God..."

Daniel grinned. "Unlikely," he said. Bethany ran her fingers through her hair. Interlocking them behind her head she sat, mesmerized, staring at the document. "Well anyway, he's the one,

I'm sure. I'm sure!" she said, the repetition strengthening her conviction. "Once I got it mixed up with Heathcliff, remember? And at the castle when the voice came to me, that's what I heard...Robert. But it was awesome...really weird. I knew it was the ghost, my ghost...calling out for her Robert. Her cry was so despairing Daniel, and I knew what she was feeling. I mean her loss was my loss and she was frightened...and so desperately alone."

"Hey, come on, Freckles!" he said when he felt her self control break and the tears brim over. "I've told you before, you can't let yourself be eaten up by all this, it's tearing you apart. Look," he said, squeezing her arm, "let's get some fresh air. You'll feel better out in the open and -" The snug door suddenly clicked open and the corner of a tray appeared. Daniel jumped to his feet.

"Now then me luvs. 'ere's a bite to eat. Oh I'm sorry!" The landlady's smile faded.

"That's OK. She's just a bit upset," Daniel said, moving the large, heavy glass ashtray aside and taking some of the weight from the tray.

"Well, I'll leave yer to it then," she said. "None o' me business like, but if ye need an 'elping 'and, son, I'm just in t' back kitchen." Bethany looked up at the kindly face and smiled. "Don't cry, lass. Yer 'll spoil yer bonny face. And try ter eat summat afore ye go out. It's bright enough now but along the coast t' weather can change in a flash," she said, snapping her fingers. "So when yer go out, you'd be best wrapping up. The chill wind can sneak up on yer, specially when yer a bit down in t' dumps like. So sup up, it 'll warm t' cockles of your 'eart!" and with an encouraging wink she turned tail and closed the door quietly behind her.

Chapter 31

Daniel and Bethany scanned the frilled coast line. Sunlight and shadows were playing hide and seek amongst the blue and purple hollows of the cliff face and the slopes that ran down to meet the sea, itself a shifting spectrum of blue and green.

"Feeling better?"

"Much, thanks," she said, squeezing his hand. "I'm an emotional wreck I know, but out here, well everything's different, easier somehow."

"Come on then. Let's climb down to the cove. It'll be sheltered there and you know what Runti-tunty said about not catching a chill!"

"Daniel, you are so disrespectful!"

"No I'm not! Runti-tunty? It's an affectionate nick-name, that's all. And when I get to know her better I'll use it to her face. In my book she's an OK kind of person so she gets a nick name. She'd be honoured if she knew. Anyway, come on...follow me and you won't go wrong!"

Bethany raised her eyes to heaven. "And you have the gall to say your father's controlling. Mum always says the apple doesn't fall too far away from the tree. Like father, like son if you ask me!"

"Who's asking!" Daniel ducked in the expectation of a back-hander. Bethany stuck her tongue out at him instead. "Well, just so long as you know there's only one chief up here, Freckles! And like I said before, do yourself a favour: stop chattering and you might make it in one piece!"

"Yes Sir! But don't push it!" she said, her stupid grin matching her even more stupid salute. Secretly though, she was pleased at Daniel's concern. In the normal way she'd have sallied forth, oblivious of the dangers. Now, she slithered down the slope in an undignified squat.

"Use the scrub to steady yourself, but be careful and watch the broom, it's prickly," he said, stifling a grin. "We don't want an action replay!" Bethany gave him the dead eye. "Don't even go there! You know, it's hard to believe the fishermen used to land cod here. And what did Runty-Tunty say about the boats beaching themselves?"

"Just that. Then they'd unload the cod, rope the boxes and yank them up. There'd be a pony and trap waiting at the top. Not easy!"

"They'd be tired out!"

"Understatement. They'd be knackered." Bethany nodded. She looked about her, the only sound that of the sea. Even the gulls apparently preferred the harbour with its comings and goings and rich pickings.

"It's in the back o'beyond! Whatever did they do for a bit of excitement?"

"Smuggle. Brandy and gin -" Daniel had stopped in mid sentence.

"What's the matter?"

"I've just had a thought -"

"Careful, you'll get brain fever!"

"Watch it, Freckles! It's just that Dad told me they used Juniper berries to make gin. Do you think there might be a link?"

"You mean our ship smuggled gin?"

"Whatever. It's a bit far-fetched I suppose, but you never know. Tell you what though, I can imagine them signalling the OK for it to be landed. Think about that for a bit of excitement. A night full of tension and uncertainty, the promise of a bit of dosh and never knowing where or when the Excise blokes might turn up. And if they did, making a bolt for it along the beach or across the moors," he said, rolling his eyes till only the whites showed, "they'd bring in the dogs and they'd tear them -"

"All right, Daniel. I get the gist!"

"Well you wanted to know what they did for a bit of excitement!"

"Yes, I did...and now you've told me, so skip the graphics!"

"How about a paddle then?"

"Now you're talking!"

With the tide down it was possible to walk to the inlet. Where it met the sea it was salt white and ridged as if by an artist's hand and beneath the mass of rock, the soft sand beckoned. Daniel had read Bethany's thoughts.

"We'll have to be careful!" He had spoken conspiratorially. "The tide might just sneak in and cut us off."

"We will," she replied and her eyes sparkled with the glee of a mischievous child.

It was good to leave the pebble beach behind and the sun trap was as secret a place as they could wish to find. "It's our very own!" Bethany twirled around like a dervish in a trance till she collapsed in a heap. "If it was for sale and I had the money, I'd buy it; it's perfect," she said, eventually lying down to share the sand pillow Daniel had made for them.

"Close your eyes, Daniel. Tell me, what can you hear? What can you feel?" For a minute neither of them spoke.

"The surf breaking," he said "and the sea lapping around the rocks."

"And the froth coating the edge of the shallows. Fizzy and sparkling like champagne."

"Very poetic, Freckles, albeit over the top!"

"Cheeky! The breeze lifting the strands of my hair then."

"And the passionate beat of your little heart because you can't wait for me to ravish you!" he said, sitting up and resting on one elbow. Bethany opened her eyes. "But I think," he said, lifting each stray strand of her hair from her forehead with a gentleness that both pleased and frightened her, "I think I'll make you wait!"

Bethany made to push him away. "Behave yourself!" she said, trying to regain her diminishing composure.

"But then again..." Daniel lent across her, brushing the tip of his nose with her own... "I can feel the warmth of your breath and -"

"...and?"

"And I... I..."Daniel's mouth played around her own, softly, at times barely touching, capriciously lowering her resistance so that she parted her lips and drew him close...

Perhaps it was a gradual awareness of the sky clouding over, snatching away the gentle warmth of the sun and the barely perceptible fine drizzle that interrupted their intimacy, but Bethany wasn't so sure. Daniel felt her unease, "What's up this time?" he said.

Bethany knelt up turning her back to the sea. She felt exposed and began to straighten her clothing. "I don't think we're alone!" Daniel scanned the area, this way and that, his eyes darting between the rock crevices along the beach and up to the cliff face. "There's no one about. Anyway we couldn't have...you know, not here, not now and the weather's changing. We're in for a downpour!"

"Maybe it's just as well!" she said, bending down to tie her laces. Daniel turned toward her, surprised.

"I thought you were definitely up for it?"

"God, yes. How can you think...God yes," she said, grinning with embarrassment.

"I'll take a rain check on that one then!" he said, helping her to her feet and drawing her close.

"Yes but..." Bethany kissed his neck and nuzzled his ear lobe "I think I might just keep you waiting next time!"

"Yeah! Course you will. After that display of - "

"Yeah, all right!"

"No need to be embarrassed," he said. "I know you can't help it. You obviously fancy me like crazy!"

"Tst!"

"Better get this on, Freckles. Come on, chop chop!" he said, pulling her orange fleece over her head. "I mean, think about it...if Runti-tunty's been playing gooseberry, with this on, she might think it was someone else thrashing about -!"

"All right Daniel! Stop embarrassing me. I'd be so ashamed! She would think I'm a trollop!"

"And so you are!" Bethany made a dive for him. Taken by surprise, he lost his balance and fell to the ground, pulling her after him. "A fiery trollop at that," he said, laughing loudly while trying to ward off her slaps and blows, "but also…"Daniel rolled over, regaining the advantage, "you're my very own beautiful trollop! All right, Freckles?"

"Ah well, that's different," she said. "I can go along with that!"

"Great. So it's pax then?"

"I guess."

"That's good," he said, "cause a trollop is a trollop is a trollop if you get my meaning!" This time Daniel was ready for her. Releasing her hands from above her head, he sprang to his feet, snatched up his socks and trainers and set off along the beach. He hadn't, of course, reckoned on the pebbles or Bethany catching up with him.

"You'd 't same idea then," Runty tunty said as she ambled toward the back door of the pub, her arms full of washing. She sniffed the air. "The weather 'asn't known what ter do these past few days. Still you've managed to get a good colour; it's a face like the rising sun you've got!" Bethany felt her blush rising. She smiled and lowered her eye-lids. "I expect yer young man's done that for thee!" she added with a giggle. "Ah, what it is to be a spring chicken!" but her half smile bore more than a trace of regret. "Well, you can't be off gallivanting without summat inside yer. Od on and I'll mek a luvely cup of 'ot soup. Besides our Alf did t' fire up. It' ud be a shame to waste it! There y 'are," she said, opening the door to the snug. "Get yerselves warmed up afore yer go!"

An hour later, Daniel and Bethany pitched their bikes northwards. "There's nowt up that way sweet heart! Just a few old ruins, no shelter, nowt. Yer don't want ter be caught up there if t ' weather wossens!"

"My thoughts precisely," Daniel said, glaring at Bethany.

Again she shouted after them. "There's allus another day yer know!"

Daniel responded in the best Yorkshire accent he could muster, "Aye, tha's not wrong! Dinner worry though, we'll be right enough but thanks any road!" and as if to prove a point, pushed hard down on the pedals leaving Bethany to say her own goodbye.

"A rare one, that un! What do you say, son?" she said when Graham Smithard appeared in the doorway armed with a sanding machine and a worn- down expression. Smithard muttered into his boots. "Dunno!" he said. Bethany's mind began to spin. 'What's he doing here?' she thought.

Then, running his hand up and down the side of the door frame, he turned his head toward her, narrowed his eyes and smirked. That was the Smithard she loathed. Responding to the shiver that seemed to engulf her and to the blush rising on her cheeks she turned to go.

"There you go, girl! P'raps you'll come this way again luv, but the next time you won't have to give the door a heave-ho! It'll work a treat by the time Graham's done with it...a good lad is our Graham." Bethany nodded, but her cheerful goodbye was a contradiction, an automatic gesture of politeness and she pedalled hard to catch up with Daniel.

Chapter 32

The ride up to Little Penhill wasn't easy. The vapour clung to their faces, and the wind, albeit subsiding, had protested its growing impotence, gusting like a bucking bronco. Bethany had been happy to follow Daniel's lead. He stopped just beyond the crest of a hill.

"This must be where we turn off," he said, indicating the rough outline of a track. Giving him a terrapin-like smile, Bethany emerged from the hood of her cagoule. With her arms resting on the handlebars, she looked towards the coast line expecting to see clear indications of dwelling houses. There were none. Daniel reached over and squeezed her arm. "You're disappointed. But the village did fall into the sea, remember."

"Hm!" she said, knowing she ought to believe what she knew to be true. "All the same. I need to go."

"It's a good way," he said, hoping her common sense would prevail.

Bethany picked up on his reluctance. "You'll wait here for me then?"

"Oh sure!" Daniel's sarcasm brought a silent response but her glance was shot through with accusation. "And you needn't look at me like that, Freckles. You're amazing. I mean, you really think its OK for me to sit here on my backside, a virtual comatose, whilst you go gallivanting off. You just don't get it, do you? Read my lips, Bethany. That part of the coast line is eroding. It's dangerous!"

"I know," she conceded.

"Well then!" Daniel regretted his self righteous tone, but her quiet, uncharacteristic reply had thrown him off guard.

"I thought we had a deal, that's all," she said.

"Here we go again. Bethany." This time he spoke quietly. "I said I'd take you. It's just that, well, look at the weather. It's changing by the minute, for the worse and it's nearly a quarter to four," he said, glancing at his watch. It' ll take us a good twenty minutes to cut through all this rough ground. We'd have to walk our bikes across and -"

"I know," she said again.

"But you still want to go!" There was no reply.

In the normal way, when she was being stubborn and unreasonable, Daniel would have put up a fight but in the ensuing silence he could only follow the intensity of her gaze toward the cliffs. It seemed then that she was other worldly. He would have to wait for her to come back to him, contenting himself with looking at her eyelashes, dewy with the mist. She could have been crying but no, her concentration was fixed outside her own sphere of hurt or disappointment. Daniel looked at the rosy glow of her complexion beneath the fine rain that had settled like tiny beads of perspiration on her face. He knew he was beaten.

"OK, I've done arguing the toss, but you're not going on your own!" he said, cutting into her thoughtfulness.

"All right! But there's no need to growl or stare at me like that!"

"No? Well, anyway...just...just come on," he said. He wanted to tell her how sexy she looked with her face all shiny and wet. He could not. He wanted to tell her how her vulnerability concerned him, but could not. Daniel gripped the centre of his handlebars and set off.

Little Penhill could only have been a tiny settlement. The track led all the way to the cliff edge; it appeared to be the only one.

"That's far enough, Bethany!" Daniel shouted after they had laid their bikes down and she had wandered off. She complied and meandered back where they sat together on a pile of fallen stones, left overs, used for repairing the dry stone walls, he suspected. Putting his arm around her he said as much. He could see that she felt let down.

"What did you expect to see, Beth?" His tone was sympathetic. She turned to him and smiled.

"Signs...signs of order, boundaries. Signs of ordinary people living ordinary lives, I suppose. There's only a few foundation stones to mark where the odd cottage might have been. You don't get the sense that it was once bustling with life -"

"Oh come on, Freckles. It was never a metropolis."

"You know what I mean," she said, looking across the expanse of gorse and maverick tufts of heather. "There's hardly anything left and people lived here once."

"There's the wall - and look, a Juniper tree!" His optimism kicked in. "Maybe that was a meeting place...a land mark and shelter for travellers. Anyway, it's a survivor."

"Big deal! Come on then. Let's explore!" she said, suddenly scrambling off the pile of stones and reaching for Daniel's outstretched hand, "Let's check *the* wall out!"

"We won't have to be long. The wind has dropped and the sea's too still for my liking." Bethany scanned the ocean, still and slate grey beneath a sombre sky.

"OK - race you!" she shouted, suddenly animated. Springing from tuft to tuft, she left Daniel behind. He took up the challenge. "All right clever clogs!" Darting this way and that he sprinted after her. "I'm coming!" he sang in true pantomime style. "I'm behind you!"

"Well, catch me if you can!"

But in the moment Bethany turned round to see just how far he had caught up, she fell. Daniel collapsed in a heap beside her. "Gotcha!" he said "and it serves you right!" But Bethany wasn't smiling. Her face was contorted with pain.

"Aw God," she moaned. "My ankle!" Daniel attempted to rub it. "Ouch! Oh don't, it hurts!"

"Well I'm going to have to get your trainer off or at least loosen the laces."

"OK, but be careful!"

"'course! God, this is all we need!"

"Well, thanks for the show of sympathy," she said, holding back the tears.

"I'm sorry! But if you'd -"

"Go on. Why don't you say it! If I'd listened to you -"

"Yeah, something like that! Anyway, let's get you over to the wall. It's a bit more sheltered. You'll have to clench your hands together around my neck and I'll ease you up, but let me take all the strain. And this time you'll do exactly as I say, right?" Daniel looked directly into her eyes but he had to wait for a response. "Hello...is there anybody there?"

"Yes boss," she said. "But there's no need to be rude. I don't know why I bother with you!" Daniel raised his eyes to heaven. But the pain seemed to subdue Bethany's banter and Daniel was worried.

By the time he had resettled her beside the wall and used the stray stones to build another at right angles to it, the breeze that always came off the sea had stilled. Daniel looked out across the slate grey, untroubled water. A moist haze was rising. He recognized the beginnings of a sea fret. He had been caught out in one before, but then he had been in a tent on the cliff top with the scout troop, just a couple of miles from home. But now. Not funny! Daniel sighed, cursing himself for the predicament they were in. He reached into his pocket for his mobile. It wasn't there. He checked again. Nothing. "What a mutt...what a bloody stupid mutt!"

"What's up?"

"Left my mobile in the back of dad's car, didn't I! Bloody fool that I am. Well, brace yourself, Freckles, it'll be a long night."

"I know. We're in trouble and it's all my fault."

"No point in apportioning blame!" he said, feeling like a hypocrite. "We'll just have to sit it out." Pulling a ground sheet from his ruck sack, he weighted it down on the wall with heavy stones and spread it across to the lower one making a lean-to. His cagoule became their ground sheet. "I always knew my boy scout days would come in useful," he said with a wry smile. Bethany grimaced. "Is it still hurting?"

"Big time!" Bethany shifted her bottom for comfort.

"Well, hang in there girl...we'll be all right," he said with false cheerfulness. He was of course lying. He hoped they would be OK, hyperthermia notwithstanding, because he also knew that the fog bank might hang over them all night.

"The light will go soon," Bethany said, "let's get our sarnies out. It'll save rummaging about later on."

"What a star! So you do have a practical side after all!"

"No, you know mum, she shoved this lot into my bag just as we were leaving."

"I always knew your mum was OK. I'll have to find her a nick-name!" he said, unfolding the silver foil. "Cheese and tomato. Great!"

"Yes, well she'll cheese and tomato us both about our lug 'oles if we ever get out of this one!" Bethany checked the flask. "Half empty!" she said with a defeated shrug of her shoulders.

"Half full you mean! Think positively at a time like this, Freckles!"

"OK," she said. "I'd like a wee."

Daniel bounced the heel of his hand off his forehead. "You'd like a pee! Of course you would. And now you tell me! Great timing, Freckles!"

"Sorree! But practically speaking I'd rather not wet myself!"

"And I thought we were home and dry for the night," he said, scrambling to his feet, "if you'll excuse the pun. OK then, let's do it!" Daniel opened the flap of the lean to. "But how...you can't squat, not with your foot...!"

"Never mind how. Just help me to the other side of the wall." Daniel obliged.

"Now what?"

"Now get two big stones. Put them more or less side by side resting against the wall. Then I won't have to squat so far down and I can lean back against the wall."

"Done, me lady," he said, edging them in place. "What now?"

"Now you'll have to turn your back and don't look!"

"Well, it's not as if we've only just met..."

"Maybe...but this is different!" she said, struggling to lower her jeans

Daniel clicked his tongue.

"Now what's the matter?" she said.

"You! This is hardly the time for false modesty! I mean, I don't know too much about these things, but I think you might need this!" he said, handing her a serviette. Her colour rising, Bethany snatched it out of his hand.

"Right. Now lower me down...but no looking!" she warned. "And God knows how I'm going to explain this one to my mum!"

Ten minutes later, they had resettled. Daniel pulled the bikes across the entrance. "Just in case we have visitors!" he warned. A look of dismay crossed Bethany's face. "Only joking, Freckles! Come on, who in their right mind would come out in this... no, I was thinking about -"

"Doolally folks, tramps, you know...losers, people like that you mean!"

"Aah, now then!" Daniel had been inspired. "It's true there be sum strange folks 'ere abouts..." Bethany smiled at his attempt at a West Country accent.

"Go on!" she said, humouring his need to tease.

"...Well there be one; but 'e be 'ardly 'uman. 'e be an old Spanish sailor, loike. Alphonse they call 'im. He's bin around 'ere since 'is ship foundered. Jumped ship 'e did when that there Spanish Armada sailed up that there coast trying ter escape our fleet loike. He 'ad ter wander the moors 'cause 'is eyes be torn out of 'is 'ead by one o' them there 'awks. He lost 'iself see. Folks say 'ees never slept since. For 'undreds o' years he's bin roaming round 'ere just 'oping some kind folk'd take 'im in. But they be affeared see 'cause 'is eye sockets be full o' maggots now loike and 'is flesh be 'anging off in tatters -"

"Yeah, OK. I get the gist," Bethany said, cutting him short and peering through the bicycle frames to catch the last of the fading light. "Want another sarni?"

"Later. We'd better hang on to the few we have left."

Their simultaneous lapse into silence seemed almost uncanny, both perhaps realising the remoteness of their hideaway, both listening for the roar of the shingle rushing into the inlets carved out by the wind and rain. It wasn't there. It was as if all that was natural had passed away. There was no midnight, star-spangled sky causing them to wonder at the birth of the universe or the concept of infinity, only a ghostly, grey canopy. There were no fleeting shadows caused by the interplay of wind and moon; only the heavy dank air and the infinite possibility of a faceless, formless listener, mission unknown. The fox did not cough nor the sheep bleat. There was no scurry or scuttle, no frightened cries of hunted night creatures, only a huge emptiness, an unearthly silence and unspoken fears.

"I'm not sure about all this, Freckles. Perhaps I should try and get some help!"

"Don't be daft!" Bethany said. She had drifted back to thoughts of her mother going berserk with worry and of the explanation that would cut no ice. "Penny for them?" he said, putting his arm around her and drawing her close. "Don't tell me. I can guess: your mother, your ghost or both!" In the half light Bethany smiled.

"No. Elizabeth, Rossitor's daughter, rejected by that moron of a father! I know she's the reason we're here though. I can feel it in my bones. And no, I don't want you to go for help. I don't ever want you to leave me, Daniel. Not ever."

"Not ever is a long time, Freckles," he said, noting the desperation in her voice. Bethany snuggled closer and in the encroaching darkness he responded. Tilting her chin he kissed her, gently coaxing her lips apart. "Do I love you? I guess," he murmured and his tenderness compelled her to enjoy the touch of his hands feeling their way around her body, tightly clothed and inaccessible.

"One day...one day soon we will...we..."

"Sh. It's OK. We can wait," he whispered. But Bethany was not comforted, nor was her own need of him stilled.

"Mm," she said, drawing him closer...

When Daniel woke Bethany was lying across his chest. His right arm was tingling and his hand already numb. He clenched his fingers and spread them wide, again and again, until the circulation came back. Gently, he moved her aside, rubbed his arms and scrambled to the entrance of the lean-to. The longest part of the night had passed. The illuminated face of his watch shone bright. Three o'clock. Peering between the spokes of the bicycle wheels, he could just make out the ragged outline of the Juniper tree and he could feel the faintest breath of air on his face. With a bit of luck daybreak might even be worth watching.

Bethany stirred. He turned to her. The silver foil he had wrapped around her swollen ankle was still in place. Daniel lay back against the cold stone wall. He was positioned awkwardly. Unless he disturbed her, that's how it would have to be. So be it. She had at least slept, though fitfully at first. Soon the gnawing ache in her foot would register. He would let her sleep on, oblivious to the daytime demons; time enough to think about reality, but -

Hearing the distant hum of a motor he eased her to one side. Regardless of the weather conditions, he knew someone would be searching for them. He had no doubt about that. The dull sound came again. Daniel thought it might be his father driving up and down the road, but no, even in all this dampness, the Merc would never sound like that! Well, Runti-tunty's misery of a husband then, out on that clapped-out motorbike he'd seen stashed away. His dad would certainly have been in contact with them- and Bethany's mother. Oh my God! One way or another, he knew he'd never be allowed to live this one down. He envisaged the, "In the study, boy!" directive and his mother's helplessness watching the door close behind them. He envisaged and he shuddered. He wondered what his parents had ever seen in one another. He with his exhibitionist, verbal bullying; she with her submissive acceptance. Well the gene blueprint would leave him somewhere in between he supposed. Daniel looked across at Bethany curled up in the foetal position. Her mouth was slightly open, her breathing light. She was the one person he could not take or leave. She had become the cornerstone of his life and he wondered how and where that had happened. In just one month his whole focus had changed. And now he had duffed it. Her mother would never agree to him seeing Bethany again. Well, he'd meet that problem when he came to it.

The insistent slap of the rotor blades reached into Bethany's consciousness.

"What's that?" she said, easing herself into a sitting position and rubbing her eyes with her knuckles.

"It's been around for a bit." Daniel shifted to listen more intently. "It's a helicopter I think."

"A helicopter? What, looking for us, in this weather!" Her disbelief was palpable. Her worries were surfacing.

"Mebbe...it was a pea-souper but it's letting up a bit. We'll just have to sit it out. If dad hasn't turned up by first light I'll head off back to the Cod."

"No Daniel. You promised you wouldn't leave me!"

"I know I did." Daniel began to massage the back of her neck "But it's been a long night Beth and the cold's got into you," he said, rubbing her forearms. "You're trembling like one of those shiver mice! Anyway, how's the ankle? Throbbing?"

"Pretty much!"

"There you are then. I have to get help...you know that."

Chapter 33

The glow from the luminous strips on his anorak was the last she saw of Daniel though the sound of his bike rattling across the rough ground hung around a little longer. Once, she swore he had stopped to turn and wave. The action, in slow time, had seemed almost spectral and when, instead of the clatter of bicycle chain, she thought she heard the echoing clang of leg irons, Bethany shrank back into the gloom. She was cold. She was hungry, yet her greater instinct was to sleep. 'Time enough to face the day.' Taking care not to catch her foot, she lay down. In another hour or so, dawn would break. Curling up, she tried to imagine herself back in her own bed with the duvet pulled up to her chin, tried to rekindle the comfort zone of a warm Sunday morning lie-in and the drift into sleep for an indulgent extra half an hour. It was not to be.

Daniel's stubbornness still rankled. She had begged him to stay but he wouldn't listen. His argument had been sensible enough. In her head she had agreed with him: another day in the open with no food or drink and her foot giving her gyp was not really an option. Why then, when he had told her to use her common sense, had she got so upset? There was no real answer, at least not one she could rationalise. What if he didn't come back? What if some harm might come to him? Then she could only wait up on the cliff top, alone and desperate in her longing to feel the warmth of his arms around her, to hear his comforting words. Bethany stirred. She wanted to stay with thoughts of Daniel, to be alive to her own senses, to enjoy the fact and the fiction of him, but she could not. The drowsy veil of sleep was distorting his image. Something else was pulling so that she found herself embroiled in a half perceived war of opposites where sleep and wakefulness tussled for dominance, where the past and the present grappled for her consciousness. Bethany reached out, like a blind-folded child, desperate and uncertain, but Daniel was drifting away and with him the comforting smell of sawdust that was his alone...

"Robert...Robert! Don't leave me, please don't..."

But she must not worry. He'd be back, to sit astride the stool in his favourite spot. With his back to the south-facing cottage wall, he could catch the light. Sometimes he would sit, fashioning his wood till the shavings buried his feet. Then, when the sun began to wane, he would harness the old mare and ride off to market on the far side of the moor; that's when and where the bargains were to be had so that he never failed to bring something back for the pot. At other times he would stride off to the cliff edge. In the distance she would watch him still chipping away on his wood. But when he gazed out to sea she knew he was remembering his other life aboard his beloved Juniper, so heavily laden that she rode heavy in the water; she knew that he missed the life of a seaman. Yet still he worked, shaving and sanding, fashioning the smaller items he made as a surprise - yet another toy for the unborn child. This time, though, he'd kept it secret so that she knew the gift would be for her. Then when he strode back from the cliff top with a silly grin on his face and told her to close her eyes and open her hands, she had to feign surprise. This time it was a barrel. Elizabeth turned it around and around, marvelling at the embossed carvings and her family monogram. Then she had cried, burying her head into his jerkin to hide the sadness of the life she had also left behind and to black out her pain, a pain that might last forever. And forever was a long, long time...

Now, the thought of absolute blackness filled her with terror. Wrestling with the cold, she rubbed her arms and thighs; the friction would warm her. But what if her arms were raised, roped at the wrist and shackled to the wall, what then? Then the blood would drain from them and with it, strength. She would feel their weight, the tingling and the numbness that followed. Here in her own hideaway the dampness was a fleeting thing, even now there was promise of sweeter, cleaner air. What would it be like then to be entombed in a stagnant, suffocating space where the only sounds were of water trickling through the rocks; water you could not taste though your thirst raged, the weakening groans of other prisoners and the beating of your own heart. Then, what of fear, fear of a slow, lonely death from starvation. Fear of the unknown. What of memory too? The agony and the joy of recalling unrealised hopes and dreams. Wouldn't she want to cry out, wouldn't she want to be heard?

Bethany wiped her eyes with the back of her sleeve. She was shivering. Stifling her sobs, she crawled toward the entrance and wedged herself against the wall. Her retreat was still shrouded in mist; she could only imagine the beauty of the moors she knew so well. Bethany listened for the whirring sound of the helicopter but the larger sound of silence had settled all around. Comfort food was what she wanted. She reached over for the sandwich box. In it was the last packet of crisps. She pulled the bag apart. The familiar crinkle made her feel less lonely, less isolated and she lay back. She wondered just how long she could make each crisp last, like the child she used to be, waiting for a sweet to dissolve on her tongue, forcing herself not to bite. And like that child she would eat them slowly until the very last one. That would be the moment when Daniel would come back. She would have another crisp every ten minutes.

Laying her head against the wall she closed her eyes, savouring the salty taste, till the crisp lay on her tongue like a Communion wafer, tasteless yet strangely nourishing. Then, through the acute silence, squelchy footsteps came toward her - "Daniel!" she whispered and lent expectantly toward the entrance. But no, he would have called out. He would know that she would be frightened and suddenly she was frightened. Bethany shrank back into the shadows, her hopes dashed, her adrenalin rushing. With one hand clapped over her mouth she tried desperately to still her breathing. Watching through a small gap in the lean-to covering, she waited. The mist parted. A headless body strode towards her, filling the entrance. Terrified, Bethany sank back into the corner. Her heart raced. Wrapping her arms around herself she squeezed her eyes tight shut. Waiting…waiting…

"Anybody about!"

Bethany caught her breath. This was a catch 22 then? Answer and she would be discovered. Keep quiet and -. Suddenly the bicycle was moved aside. The heavy booted, corduroy legs bent low. The lean-to cover shot back. An arm swung forward and a bunch of rabbits was dumped on her lap. Bethany shrieked. She wanted to scramble to her knees, to rid herself of the limp, still warm softness she could feel through her jeans. Shuddering with fear and disgust, she clenched her fists, unconscious even of her nails cutting deep into her palms.

"Get them - get them off me!" she screamed, but even when she felt them slithering away, the image of the unwelcome bouquet would not leave her: the posy of grey-brown fur tied at the neck with a love knot of silver wire nudged her sense of revulsion: three blooms, wilting: six petals drooping and six flower centres, glass-eyed and chillingly cold. "That's disgusting! How could you!" she said when Albert's red face appeared in the torch light. The landlord picked up on the accusation. Glaring at Bethany, he wiped the dew drop hanging on the end of his nose with the back of his sleeve,

"Each to 'is own, girl!" His glare intensified and he frowned. "Any road, I'd 'ave thought thee'd be glad ter see me, lass. Most would!" he said, taking a flask from the old army kit bag he carried across his shoulder. It had shared the same space as his poaching paraphernalia. Bethany shuddered; the knife that had gutted the rabbits was still bloody and the flask was streaked with it too. She felt her anger rise again. Albert unscrewed the top of the flask. The steamy aroma of home made soup sharpened her taste buds. Bethany swallowed on her own saliva. "I am," she said. "'course I am. Thanks. It's just that you frightened me and…and I hate it when animals are trapped and hunted!"

"Frittened, yer say! You need be frittened 'cause if yer were mine I'd tan yer backside, big as y'are!" Bethany shifted uncomfortably.

"We weren't lost...we knew where we were," she said, lamely realising she was repeating herself..."it was the sea fret. We couldn't see our way home and..." Bethany's explanation fizzled out. Her waffling excuse was getting her nowhere. Albert's long drawn out, "Nooo!" hung in the air. "But if ye'd 'arkened to the bit of advice the Mrs gave yer, yer'd be wak'ning up in yer own beds bi now, instead o' worrying the insides out o' your poor mother all through t' neet." The landlord paused, sure he had made his point. "Any road, what 'ave yer dun ter yer foot?" he said, indicating the silver foil "and where's t' young fella? Don't tell me he's been out roaming t' moors all neet. Silly bugger! If 'e met up with Alphonse he'd a known about it all right!"

Bethany's eyes widened. She had thought Daniel had made the story up. "No. He waited till early morning and set off to your place to get help," she said quick to defend him. "I've sprained my ankle."

"We've missed one another then. Well t' Mrs 'll see to 'im. Fog's lifting an' all," he said, "but that doesn't 'elp you, does it lass? All I can say is it's to be 'oped thars lont a lesson. Yer mam's 'alf mad wi worry -"

"How do you...did mum -?"

"Aye, yer mam's been in touch all right. She's probably on ' er way t' Cod bi now. Yon fella's dad said he'd bring 'er over. It were too bad ter cum out last neet o' course."

"We heard the helicopter -"

"Aye. Well I 'ope yer didn't think it were out on your account! Aw no, girl. There were a cliff fall. 'arf o t' cliff face fell away from t' castle like. There's muck and boulders all across t' front. Some of 'em rolled in ter t' sea. 'elecopter were out soon as it were safe in case t' campers 'ad parked up thereabouts. It'll be in all t' papers o' course. These cliffs are allus eroding. This 'ere 'amlet went down an all. Any road, happen you'll 'av a bit a grov'lling ter do when yer see yer mam!"

"I know. Was she really mad?" Bethany said after a pause.

"More worried, tearful like! Well...ye'd be t' same wouldn't yer?"

"I suppose."

"There's no supposing about it, lass!" His voice had gone up an octave. "You youngsters are al t' same. Yer want ter grow up too soon if y' ask me, but you 'ave ter be responsible an' all. Listen ter a bit of advice like." Bethany buried her head into the folds of her anorak, desperately trying not to well up.

"Still, all's well that end's well. As I told yer mam, if you were still on t' moors I'd find yer. There in't a stone I don't know hereabouts. Lived 'ere ever since I were a lad, rabbit catching an" -. Albert stopped short. "In t' old days we'd ter poach ter feed us bellies then it became an 'abit I suppose," he said by way of half an apology.

"There's no supposing about it," Bethany said with a watery smile, "and times 'av changed like!"

"Ah! I'll 'av ter think on that then," he conceded with an uncharacteristic grin. "Still, its good ter be on't moors even if it's only ter get away from 't nagging wife!" Albert winked. It was the first sign of warmth that she had seen. Suddenly Bethany felt like a conspirator. "Any road, like I told yer mam, give 'em sum credit, Mrs. They'll use their common sense and stay put. And it's not as if it's winter. They're young and fit," says I, "and they'll 'av no trouble keeping one another warm...and so you 'ave," he said looking around and nodding his approval. "Yer mam can be right proud of yer!" Bethany's eyes brimmed. Albert had hit a chord. She began to sob.

"Ah, don't tek on now, lass," he said. "I tek it you've cum ter no 'arm, 'ave yer?" The pause was significant. Albert shuffled about clearly embarrassed by a question that might have been innocent enough had he not, even in the torch light, seen Bethany blushing. "Well, it's nowt ter do we me. I just thought...well, there y'are!"

Still snivelling, Bethany took the crumpled up piece of rag offered. "Don't worry, it's clean enough," he said, noting her hesitation. "Any road, yer mam 'll be that pleased ter see yer back safe and sound...whatever."

"I hope so...but I'm OK...I'm fine!"

"Well then, stop worriting! 'course some of us get a second chance ter do things proper, like, and some of us don't. You're lucky..." Albert suddenly became thoughtful. Looking up at him she waited for him to continue. "It might surprise yer ter know lass, me and the Mrs were young once. Impulsive, couldn't wait. Yer know 'ow it is I expect." Embarrassed, Bethany lowered her eyes but nodded all the same. "Yer don't think we've lived in t' back 'o beyond all these years for t' fun on it, do yer? By eck, nooo! In t' awd days, if yer made yer bed, yer'd ter lie in it. Put up and shut up like. Nobody in t' family 'd elp yer. When the Mrs told 'er mam she were four months gone, she threw 'er out. We'd shamed 'em like. My awld fella did same wi me, but I were a bloke. I could look after mesen. Still it were too late for tears; babby were a fact o' life. We 'ad ter shack up somewheres! Landlord at t' Cod were our saving grace. His Mrs were a good sort an all. They gave us a room and I did a few jobs fer 'em. It made us a few bob. But in t' depths o' winter, room were that cold. The bairn didn't stand a chance. Mrs 'ad an 'ard time an all. It were a breech birth and t' little un come early. There were no midwives in them days, well, not up 'ere any road. The babby clung on ter life fer a bit but the Mrs got mastitis bad and couldn't feed 'er. Yes," he murmured "it were a little lass, a bonny mite fer all 'er wrinkles! But she wouldn't tek ter t' bottle and pneumonia soon took 'old on 'er. She were all o' ten days old when she died and t' wife never could go full term after that. So yer see lass, p'raps it's best not to tek a chance. Things are different now I know, but t' bairns still need the best start they can get."

"Oh...but when I saw Graham at the Cod, I thought he was your son. He's in my class at school."

"Is ee now? And 'e is our son, adopted, like. You're not going ter believe it, but we found 'im wandering around outside. It were a

202

mystery 'ow he got there. We supposed he'd been abandoned 'cause nobody claimed him. The poor lad. He were only a toddler, didn't even know 'is name. They took 'im away o'course but the wife kept on at t' authorities and in t'end they let us adopt him. He's a funny un, I know. A loner. Never does have much ter say for 'imself but it's 'ardly surprising. Any road don't look so glum. That there tale 'ad an 'appy ending. Eh up!" Albert lent forward and poked his head out of the lean-to. "Thought so! This'll be yer mam so don't forget," he said with a friendly wink, "steady as yer go, girl!"

Chapter 34

The purr of an engine mingled with the crunch of tyres riding the loose stones was the first thing Bethany heard when Albert eased her out of the lean-to, shoulders first.

"It's good to be upright again!" she said, rubbing her bottom and thighs.

"Aye, it's bin a long night for thee, I expect!"

"Understatement, believe me Albert and it'll be an even longer day…!" In the distance twin, pale yellow lights broke through the diminishing mist. It was good to see the soft outlines of the material world again and hear the occasional hum of a passing car. Sighing, she lent against the stone wall.

"It'll be right, don't fret! It's yer mam. Mams always cum good in t' end!" Bethany looked at this man she had thought so strange. For one so uncommunicative, so cut off, he had a lot to say.

"Thanks, Albert!" she said, reaching up and pecking his cheek.

"All saints, girl! It mun be my lucky day. T' wife said it would be. Don't ask me why or ow she knows. I's think she must 'ave 'ad one o' them there visitations…insights. That's what she calls 'em," he said, chuckling to himself.

"Don't mock, Albert! I have them as well!" Bethany said with a quizzical raising of her eye brows and a secretive smile.

"Gerraway!"

"Yes. Well, there's nowt so funny as folk-!" she said in her best Yorkshire accent.

"Aye, you're not wrong, lass but oops, here's your fella!" Daniel leapt out of the car and sprinted across, a huge grin on his face.

"I told you I'd be back! Are you OK?" he said, putting a protective arm around her.

"Thanks to Albert...he's been looking after me, keeping me company." Nodding his thanks, Daniel grinned. "Good on yer, mate!"

"I just 'appened along."

"Oh yeah...like being out all night starting five minutes after dad rang!"

"Ah well, it teks me five minutes to gather me monkeys and parrots - and me wits o 'course!" he said, lifting his cap to scratch his head.

"Well, thanks anyway, mate. You'd best get in the car. We'll run you back."

"No fear! Get inter one o' them posh contraptions wi a string o' dead rabbits on me arm. I's think not," he said, holding them up like a trophy. Bethany flinched.

"Aw...sorry luv. I clean forgot! No. I'd best be on me way. The wife 'll think I've teken off. She might even 'av locked door on me agin bi now!" he said, replacing his cap. "Besides, yer mam's waited on yer long enough. Yer don't want me 'olding up t' proceedings!"

"We'll be back up to see you though, Albert!" Bethany said.

"Aye, right enough!" and he strode off, the sad and bedraggled bouquet slung over his shoulders.

"Come on then, son. Get this lean-to demolished. As for you young lady -" Bethany couldn't tell whether she was being admonished or sympathetically maneuvered toward the car.

"Hello, mum!" Bethany said when her mother got out of the car.

"Now then!" The greeting was typical enough but there was sadness in her tired eyes.

"It seems I'm always saying sorry these days, mum," she said, reaching for her.

"Yes, well...you're safe thank God...that's all that matters," her mother said, returning a hug. "I...I think Mr. Foster wants you in the back with me." Bethany sighed. Her mother's matter of factness was a screen she hid behind; personal matters could never be given a public airing. The telling off would come later.

"I do, Mrs. Mallinson. So if you could just settle your bottom on the seat Bethany, I'll ease you in from behind."

Five minutes later, Bethany was propped up against the door, her feet cushioned on her mother's lap.

"Comfortable?" The question was well meant.

"Mm, yes thanks, mum." It was a lie. For years there had been no warm, spontaneous contact with her mother. Ever since the day of the funeral she had been withdrawn. Bethany had desperately wanted to hug her, to see her lovely smile through the mask of sadness. But it was her uncle who had held her hand as they stood by the grave side and looked down into that yawning hole, her uncle who had put his arm around her as they walked down the churchyard path, their heads bent low. Bethany would never forget the darkness and the gloom of that rainy day and the even darker recesses beneath the yew trees. It marked the before and the after of her mother's life; it marked the time when the mask hardened. Now even this small intimacy embarrassed them both.

"I'm...I'm really glad to be coming home, mum."

"So you should be...and I'll be glad to have you home," she added almost as an after thought, but her eyes never left the window so that the drive home along the narrow, winding moorland road seemed as endless as the still, misty hills surrounding them.

The little conversation between father and son was barely audible. Daniel could not be reached. In the company of his father, he was subdued, turning only occasionally to smile and maybe encourage her. Least ways that was what she hoped and believed. Bethany settled down to accept the silence. Now and then the phantom of a petrified tree distracted her, its tortured and frenzied branches reaching out westward. Now and then the sad bleat of a sheep cut through the chill of recrimination. Both in a strange way disturbed her. Instead she tried to focus on the pale light of sunrise, flickering nervously between the dips and hollows of the moorland.

And so it was until she felt her mother fingering the travel rug that lay over her legs…in the thickness of her disapproval, she was tucking Bethany in.

Chapter 35

For two days her mother drifted in and out of the tiny sitting room, quietly fussing. Even so, a veiled awkwardness hung over the cottage. Bethany knew her mother would come round. She only had to wait. It was as if her worries had to be nurtured through a grand silence, like a cloistered nun, the coifs of habit denying a wider view. In the end her practical, common sense side would confront her stubbornness - and win. 'But God, what a waste of time!' Bethany thought as she sat in the fireside chair with a cushioned stool supporting her ankle.

"I can't sit here forever, mum," she said in an attempt to get her mother talking. "I've got to sort out my project."

"You'll do no such thing!"

"But Mum I -"

"You'll do no such thing!" she repeated, cutting Bethany off so that there was nothing to do but resign herself to the long haul. "And you can forget about school until that ankle's properly better!"

"Mum...I need to be there at the end of term!"

"No, Bethany. This time I'm going to have my way...besides we need to talk..." Turning to gaze out of the window, Mrs. Mallinson paused. Bethany's mind raced. 'Come on mum,' she thought...'why don't you ask me - get it over with... "Are you still intact...? Are you still a virgin... have you done it...can you still hold your head up when you bump into Mrs. Crooks!" Bethany winced.

"I was worried to death! My lass, out in sub zero temperatures and the worst sea fret we've had in a decade!"

"Sub-Zero, mum!! I was OK," she said, "most of the time Daniel was there anyway." Mistake...Big mistake.

"Exactly the point I'll be raising when I get back from the shops!" she said, looking Bethany in the eye. "Meanwhile, perhaps you'd like to make yourself useful and scrape the taties."

"Sure!" Bethany said, smoothing out the old tea towel her mother laid across her knee. A bowl of tepid water lurching to and fro followed. 'Just like my churning insides!' Bethany thought.

"And be sure to keep that leg up whilst I'm away. I don't want you gallivanting up and down those stairs." When her mother closed the door on the unsettling atmosphere, Bethany heaved a sigh of relief.

"Brrrrr....brrrrrr!" Bethany limped across to answer the phone.

"Ah, Ron! Thank God it's you," she said, sitting on one kitchen chair and resting her leg on another. "I've tried ringing you loads of times but there was no reply."

"Yeah, well, mum and dad have gone off on a celebratory weekend. It's their 25th anniversary."

"You're keeping house then? And whilst the cats are away..." Bethany's innuendo fell flat! 'The new Ron was getting far too serious!' she thought.

"Something like that. Trev's been teaching me the art of rigging up tents. We're planning a weekend to ourselves when mum and dad get back. He says it's time I learnt some survival techniques!" Bethany's sigh was clearly envious.

"And your mum and dad don't mind," she said, scratching her head in disbelief. "I mean, you've only been going with Trev for a bit. So where will you go? The remote jungles of Borneo or the Siberian wasteland?"

"The back garden!" Bethany tutted. Ron giggled. "Gotcha!" she said.

"Oh yeah...OK! So what else have you been doing?"

"Well, um...by all accounts certainly not what you two have been up to!"

Feeling a blush rise, Bethany cupped her cheek in her hand. "What's that supposed to mean?" she said.

"Rumour has it, well, put it this way...you and Daniel...on the beach? Does it ring a bell?" Silence. "Beth?"

"So, put it this way, since when did my best friend become a gossip monger?"

"No need to be tetchy, Beth. It's what's called loyalty. Better you hear it from me than someone else. You know, forewarned is forearmed."

"I suppose. Well, whatever people are thinking, they're wrong. We were... well...you know, just messing about!" Clearly exasperated Ron jumped in -

"For God's sake, Beth. Let's call a spade a spade, shall we! You were having a good old snog!"

"Yeah...all right, so what? It's not the crime of the century," she said. "And I knew someone was watching so we -"

"Stopped?"

"Something like that..." Bethany conceded.

"Just as well then!"

"Anyway, stop blabbering Ron and listen! It was Graham Smithard. I know it. We went up to the Cod, that pub up on the coast and well, as usual, he was hanging around. I always thought he was a bit of a perv, but the thing is he -"

"Maybe he's lonely, Beth, that's all. Probably can't get a girl of his own either and is nursing a grand passion for you, though I can't imagine why!"

Ignoring the insult, Bethany shuddered. "Yeah well your psychological assessment doesn't help me one bit, does it! He's weird, yes, but," Bethany sighed. Albert's story about him having been abandoned had been chasing around in her head. "The thing is -"

"Oh stop worrying. The gossip'll be a nine day wonder...just as long as it won't turn out to be a nine month, ' is she...or isn't she drama!"

"Ha ha! Well, there's nothing for it but to keep everybody's hopes up then, keep them guessing!"

"That's more like it, Beth! There's still a bit of an old fire brand left in you after all! Tell you what," she added with a mischievous giggle, "I'll do something uncharacteristically foolhardy just to spice things up! Distract them, you know. It'll take the heat out of it all. A bit of interesting graffiti maybe. Isn't it sad though when you think about it. I mean, people having to get their kicks out of other people's misfortune and if that doesn't work, they'll invent something or come up with a totally wrong conclusion."

Still thinking about Smithard, Bethany coloured up. "Yeah and sometimes they're way off the mark. But if mum gets word of it, I'm dead! As it is, she wants to have a talk and you know what that means!"

"Oh well, don't be too hard on her. You're her only daughter after all and with no husband around -"

"I seem to have heard that argument before!"

"Well, it's true. Think about it! Anyway, I'm sorry to have been the bearer of bad news but then, what are friends for? Are you coming back in time for the leaver's do?"

"I wish, but probably not."

"Right oh. Maybe just as well! Now I'm going...can't sit around chin wagging with you all day. I've got some serious thinking to do. How can I get Trev into a compromising position for starters!" she said, her cheerful banter making Bethany smile as usual. "But I'll pop across ASAP. We can have a long chat, maybe do some gossip mongering of our own! If I'm still your friend that is?"

"Don't be daft! Tarra, Ron and thanks for ringing."

"Hi, mum! Here, let me help," Bethany said when her mother plonked the shopping basket on the table.

"Thanks. I'm dying for a cuppa. Just pop the paper in the magazine rack, will you?" Bethany reached for her mother's outstretched hand. Stumbling awkwardly she almost lost her balance, the paper dropping to the floor. "Ouch!" In a moment her mother was by her side, but Bethany's attention was on the newspaper headline:

Shame on you, Lord Rossitor!

"Oh my God…look, mum!" Bethany said as she stooped to pick it up.

"Yes…yes, but are you all right!"

"Yes. Yes!" she snapped. She couldn't help it. "Sorry, mum but heck, here, you read it, read it out loud! I'm that excited my eyes won't focus."

Mrs. Mallinson rummaged around in her handbag for her spectacles and sidled over to the window. "Give it here then," she said.

On one of the quietest nights of the year with a sea fret hanging over the area, the earth moved. It should have been a noisy affair. Someone should have heard the shift of boulders and scrub; someone should have felt the tremors that come with a cliff fall. No one did. The rescue helicopter crew with an aerial photographer aboard was the first to witness the collapse of the castle face, the first to see the torn gaping hole that changed a landscape. Thankfully there were no casualties.

Yet, as we slept, a greater horror was being exposed. The skeletal remains of a man in leg irons were found in what appeared to be a roughly structured cave, sealed off it seems from the upper dungeons by an iron grid.

There's no doubt the engineers will have their work cut out securing the cliff face, but the local historians are bound to tease out the truth behind the grim discovery. If the writing scratched into the bare rock is to believed, the man died some time in the late 1700s.

The scrawl, probably that of a man who knew he was dying, gives us some insight into his life, if not his death. Clearly, his last thoughts were of his loved ones. An arrow is scored through a heart... "Oh no! Not that!" Mrs. Mallinson stopped short, the colour draining from her face.

Bethany scrambled over, "What's the matter, mum?" she said, helping her mother into a chair. "What is it?" Bethany snatched the paper out of her mother's hands: The inscription reads, R G loves E. Rossitor and Eliza –

And amongst the tattered remains of his leather jerkin lay a small chisel, a carpenter's tool, perhaps indicating his trade.

We can only guess at his suffering. His scrawl may have been his final act of defiance and of longing in a place that revealed no water source, only the scoured out trench that carried human waste from the castle. We may never know the story that lies behind his entombment. What we do know is that this is the first record we have of Lord Rossitor's daughter since her confirmation records came to light. What happened to her remains a mystery but we know that she was loved. As for Eliza? Who was she? Who indeed! Well, the mystery deepens and we look forward to unravelling the story that is already beginning to resemble a saga. Meanwhile, we do know that the man known as R G died in a dark, secret place, but, in speaking to us from the past, he has defied his lonely, ignoble end.

"I knew it! I knew it," Bethany said, "all the while…"

Bethany glanced at her mother bathed now in a shaft of sunlight and dust particles. And the silence grew. But for the tremor in her hand her mother could have been a marble statue. She was so pale and still. Bethany bent down and took her arm.

"Are you all right, mum!"

"Yes...I'm...these. Oh dear...!" Mrs. Mallinson rummaged around in her cardigan sleeve ends. Bethany forestalled her.

"Here," she said, reaching over to the box of tissues on the window sill. "What is it mum...it's not like you to cry over other people's problems...and hey," Bethany encouraged, "who is it that always tells me not to get too involved in the past!" Trying to compose herself, Mrs. Mallinson snuffled into the tissue. "I know...it's just that...well..." With a sigh that could have launched a sailing ship and a pause that seemed to go on for ever, she reached into her apron pocket. "Here," she said, pressing the cabinet key into Bethany's hand. "Fetch me the barrel."

"Sure...but why?" Bethany frowned. For once she was speechless.

"It's time," her mother said, her tone one of resignation. "This is all we have to remind us that these two young people ever existed," she said, taking and caressing the barrel as if it were an object of love and respect. Bethany edged closer to her mother, her excitement almost too much to bear.

"It's awesome isn't it, mum!" she said.

"Awesome?" Mrs. Mallinson smiled. "Well if you mean it makes your blood run cold, you'd be on the right lines. That Lord Rossitor!" The name clearly stuck in her gullet. "Some Lord! He was vile...but then," she said, tracing her fingers across the engravings, "I know how grief can change a person…It seems after he lost his wife in childbirth, he went to pieces and took to smuggling."

"Would that be gin, mum?" Surprised, Mrs. Mallinson turned to her daughter.

"Yes," she said, "but how would you know that?"

"The ship...here," Bethany said. The barrel gives us a date so Daniel wrote to the Lloyds shipping. They gave us the name of the ship Robert Granby had served on. And look, those same initials were on the dungeon wall!" she said pushing the newspaper towards her mother. "And the ship...it was the Juniper, not the Jupiter as we thought at first...and then we discovered they made gin out of the Juniper berries. All the pieces fitted in our jigsaw, don't you see, mum?"

"Yes, Bethany, I...I...suppose I always did -"

"So...why didn't you tell me? Why wouldn't you talk about it?" Bethany's interest was beginning to spill over.

"Because...well, you know what I'm like! I don't like airing -"

Bethany smiled, "I know mum, your washing, dirty or otherwise in public. And I was probing...always pushing, trying to get at the truth...but," Bethany frowned, "but what had all this to do with us, our family I mean. It's only a story."

"I saw the similarity between you and Daniel in it, I suppose, he coming from such a well-to-do background and...well, it was frightening. You're both so young and becoming too close too quickly it seemed to me. I didn't want it to end in a tragedy, you unwed, bringing a child into the world! It was foolish. I realise that now."

"Oh, mum! I know you've been worrying about that. But there's no need!"

"Really?" Bethany reached out to squeeze her mother's hand.

"Yes, so settle yourself, mum and come on, tell me what happened."

"Well, this R G," she said, glancing at the newspaper article, "obviously ended up in a dungeon, an oubliette. They used them to put prisoners they prefer to forget about. Why, and what led up to it, who knows, but there's something here you'll have to read if you're going to make any sense of it at all."

Mrs. Mallinson ran her fingers across the engraving on the barrel. Bethany leaned forward, too amazed to speak. "Robert was a fine carpenter! Look," she said, "you have to let your finger tips wander across. You'll feel a slight depression. See here, it's just where you'd expect it to be really. I mean, the sails would billow out on a high sea, wouldn't they?" Mrs. Mallinson passed the barrel over. "Well, try it. Press it," she said, "it won't bite!" But it might as well have done. The lid shot open.

"Oh!" Bethany sank back, the adrenalin rush almost too much to bear. She looked inside.

"Be careful with it now...!" Bethany reached into the barrel. She felt the parchment, felt it and lifted it out, gently, watchful of every crinkle and crease. "Mum, this is amazing, and to think you knew about it all the time. No wonder you've been so prickly! But wh..." Held by the writing, Bethany's voice trailed off...

My love,

I leave this letter in case you should return and find me gone, for without you to protect me, I must find safe lodging for the child. It has been eight days since you took to your horse and rode off so defiantly. Had I not bewailed the fact that father neither knew nor cared for his granddaughter, you might still be here...had I not wept so woefully but kept faith only with you. Oh Robert, dear Robert, where art thou? I cannot believe you wouldst knowingly desert us, you who nightly climbed the treacherous castle cliff face to meet me. When I think about the risk you took avoiding the guards and certain reprisal or even death had you been discovered, I shudder. When I think about how my father used you to his own ends...well, turncoat that he was, I feel so ashamed. But no, the devil himself could not tempt you away...not by dint of advancement, money or selfish desire.

Since you left, my bonnet has not left my head. I have searched and called out, fearing you have befallen some dreadful accident. And I have waited under the Juniper tree, but all in vain...in vain. Good swordsman though I know thou art, I pray thou hast not been set upon by vagabonds. Perchance you sallied forth too full of pride and hope that our little Eliza might at last meet her grandfather. Perchance he set the guards upon you, unmoved, as well I feared he might be. Perchance he threatened you, disowning us again and sent you whipped, penniless and horseless on your way. If this be so, just find your way back to us, my love.

For sure neither I nor our child will ever look out across the sea from those castle turrets that grace my childhood home. That which was my birthright is no more. Well-a-day! I think not of feather beds now. It is enough to lay our heads on the soft turf, to speak of love and make an honest life, but soon I must don my cloak, wrap the child well and leave this place, for our meager rations are almost gone.

So take heart, Robert, my love. You know the manner of the fisher folk in Penhill Bay. They are simple, open people. Oft have I watched them casting nets even in heavy seas and they have seen me heavy with child looking out across the ocean. Yesterday I ventured out. I stood upon the cliff edge which is my joy and held our child aloft for them to see. Except that you are gone from us forever, I have not a single fear. For certain, the fisher folk will not spurn me. When next the sea is becalmed with a fair wind to carry my words, I will holler out and seek their help, unless my dearest love, thou hast returned to kindle a fire, to scour the moors for rabbit or grouse and to take us in your arms once more. Well, you said I was your fair mistress and now you have two! Our little Eliza gave me her first smile today, she has your laughing eyes Robert; but alas, she wears a frown. So, find your way back to us my love for it is to Penhill Bay we will go. There, please God, you will find us waiting.

Meanwhile, as God is my witness, each day...each night, I will call to thee my love. When the sea is like a mill pond, listen. Listen well when the leaves stir through the juniper tree. And in the quiet and fearful moments as you walk the cliffs, listen to your heart, for there will I be. Listen well....for I will not rest in my grave until we meet again.

Godspeed,

Elizabeth

Chapter 36

Bethany stepped under the shower. 'Hm...great!' she thought as the water sought out every contour of her body. It had been a warm day so that when at last she collapsed on top of the bed her senses woke to the cool, salty breeze drifting in through the open window. Sighing, she closed her eyes and hugged the pillow. Had she been a cat she would have purred with pleasure. But her mind was not so easily soothed. True, the upturn of a smile on her mother's face and the taut lines giving way to the softer ones had warmed her heart. True, they had found a new understanding, a new openness so that the closed years were almost behind them. Bethany pinched the top of her nose to stem her tears. She got up. The early evening air was giving her goose pimples. Rubbing her arms, the friction warmed her. She turned to face the window. Watching the golden glow of sunset she wished her unanswered questions would disappear with it. So Elizabeth, pregnant and ostracised ran away with her lover. Without the support of her father and despite Robert's best efforts they had lived a hand to mouth existence. All facts, unwelcome certainly, but as her mother had said, all facts...merely historical facts. 'Yes...yes... but...'

Hearing her mother climbing the stairs and the rattle of crockery, Bethany anticipated the tap on the door. Readjusting the bath towel she secured it, sarong style.

"Can I come in?" her mother said, opening the door a tad.

"'course! Ah, good one, mum," Bethany said, eyeing the cups of cocoa and plate of digestives. Relieving her mother of the tray, she set it on the dressing table. Sit on the window seat, mum. I'll close the window. It's drafty, and..."

"And what?" Mrs. Mallinson reached over for her cocoa, looked up and waited for an answer.

"Ah w...w...well," Bethany stuttered. "We might have visitors, you know: moths and long leggedy beasties, ghosties and things that go bump in the night!" she said, avoiding her mother's fixed gaze.

"Nonsense!" Bethany breathed in deeply. Her mother's matter of factness was back and it would be a long time before she would be able to confide in her about the ghost. She wouldn't be able to get past the first sentence without being shot down. "Tell you what though, mum," she said, changing the subject, "it isn't every night we have a nightcap together so let's make it a celebration! Let's go mad, let's have a dunking session!"

"Oh, Bethany. Well, you dunk if you must, but whilst I still have some teeth I'll let them do the munching! Besides, somebody's got to show a bit of decorum!" Daintily nibbling away, with her little finger posed for effect, Mrs. Mallinson grinned. Bethany giggled and switched on the dressing table light.

"This is great, mum, and it's good to see you smiling again..."

"Has it really been that bad?" she said, reaching over to squeeze Bethany's arm. "I'm sorry. Ever since your dad died it's been...well, what a waste of time. He wouldn't have wanted me to grieve, I know that, but how I've missed him."

"Me too," Bethany said, "but Dad would have wanted us to move on. Perhaps you should have taken a little job or even married again!"

"Good gracious, lass...how fanciful can you get! No, I don't think so, besides who would have me?"

"Walter would!"

"Would he now!" Beneath her soft smile, Mrs. Mallinson blushed!

"So there *was* something between the two of you?" Bethany teased.

"He was wonderful, Bethany. After your dad died he was so attentive, such a support, and I know he had a soft spot for me!"

"Understatement of the year, mum. The last time I saw him he was all coy when he asked about you. Sort of suggested I was a bit of all right but not a patch on you. Then he clammed up but it's obvious he's still carrying a torch!" Mrs. Mallinson grinned.

"After all this time? Well I never!"

"So what went wrong, mum? He's great. I like him, he's like a second dad really! Tells me off and sort of watches out for me!"

"More like a grandad I should think. He's getting on now, there were a few years between us and retirement doesn't seem to have suited him; he's aged a lot lately." Mrs. Mallinson paused. "No, Bethany, it wasn't meant to be. Besides," her mother said, "we're distant cousins."

"*What?*" Bethany asked, her voice rising an octave. "Why didn't you tell me?"

"Hey, calm down, lass! It wasn't meant to be a secret. It just didn't come up. But apart from that," she said, referring back to their friendship, "lovely man though he is, our backgrounds are like chalk and cheese."

"You make a lot of that, mum!"

"I do, well I did, but I've had big thinks and I'm taking your advice. I'm learning how to chill!"

"Oh, mum!" It was so strange to hear her mother using teen speak.

"And it's not before time," she added. "With all that's happened I feel drained and somehow I don't think it's over yet."

"No, not quite," Bethany said, the ghost uppermost in her mind. "I'm still in a turmoil about Elizabeth...can't seem to get her out of my mind. I mean, what could have happened to her? Did she go to Penhill and live with the fisher folk? Did she settle down and bring up the baby? Maybe she met someone else...?"

Mrs. Mallinson shrank back against the cushioning on the window seat, her face in the shadows. For a while she remained silent, the only sound the tinkle of the spoon as she stirred her cocoa. Round and around; again and again.

Bethany reached over to take the cup and saucer from her. "You'll be spilling it if you're not careful," she said, settling beside her. "What's eating you, mum? Come on! Spit it out; it doesn't do any good bottling things up!" Mrs. Mallinson looked up at her daughter and smiled. "Since when did you become so wise?" she said. In the half light, Bethany could see her eyes beginning to well and sparkle.

"I don't know about that, mum. Ron would say I'm just down right nosy!"

"Hm, well you get that from your father," she said between sniffles. "He never could rest until he'd followed every by-way looking for answers, pitfall or no pitfall. Like a pointer he was. Still…" a wistful smile crossed her face, "I wish he was here…"

"He's around, mum; I'm sure of it. When I'm miserable I always sit in his chair and you know what, I begin to feel warm and protected. It's as if he's encircling me with a special aura. It's something I don't really understand. Do you think I might be a bit psychic?" Bethany asked as casually as she could, but her mother's fixed gaze seemed to come as a warning: *'Don't even go there,'* it said. "So come on, what do you think, about Elizabeth, I mean?" Mrs. Mallinson paused. Bethany waited and waited. Then, with a determined sigh, she slipped out of the room for a moment.

"I was saving this to show you," she said, handing Bethany a dog eared envelope, "but you won't rest until…well, you're just like your father, not a drop of patience!" Bethany felt a rush of adrenalin.

"What is it, mum?" she said, unfolding and spreading the document out on the bed.

"See for yourself."

Bethany's eyes flitted back and forth over the page. "I can't take it all in, mum!" she said, ringing her hands with frustration.

The Mallinson Family tree

Jessica Marsh (m) John Hardy
(Childless couple adopted Eliza in 1793)

Eliza Hardy (m) Peter Radcliffe

Robert   **Adeliza**   James   Matthew

Adeliza Radcliffe (m) Richard Moore

Henry   John   **Lisbet**

Lisbet Moore (m) Samuel Oates

Samuel   Frederick   **Betty**   Jack

Betty Oates (m) Peter Cadman

Peter   **Beth**   Thomas   Phillip

Beth Cadman (m) Frank Cooper

Bess   Lionel   Harold

Bess Cooper (m) Samuel Albert Dale

David   **Elizabeth**   Michael

Elizabeth Dale (m) Geoffrey Abel

Kenneth   **Lisa**   Barbara

Lisa Abel (m) Paul Mallinson

Bethany (Bn 1993)   **Bethany (Bn 1995)**

"I know. Just for now, concentrate on the last and first entry. Believe me, they'll give you enough to think about!"

"See here." Her mother pointed to her daughter's entry.

"But...but...there are two Bethany's here, mum." Mrs. Mallinson toyed with her handkerchief, folding it and refolding it.

"Yes," she said, "you had an older sister, Bethany....older by two years. She was only a few hours old when she died."

For a fleeting moment Bethany thought of Albert and of the child he had lost and spoken about so poignantly. Leaning over she put her arm around her mother and for a little while they stayed together silently absorbing a shared moment.

"And you named me after her." Bethany said.

"Not really. We thought about it a lot, afraid you might think we wouldn't see you as your own person; afraid that you might think we were harbouring a loss...not wanting to let go. But no. You'll notice that every first born daughter has a version of Elizabeth. It was for her sake that we decided to stay with the tradition...it was to Elizabeth's memory that we named you Bethany." Bethany sat back allowing the bean bag to enclose her.

"Oh, look! Eliza's at the beginning! She was adopted – so is that the Eliza scratched on the wall? But...but...that would make her our ancester!" Bethany paused, her frown deepening, "so...so we are all related to Rossitor!" she said, her voice rising in disbelief.

"Yes dear," her mother said. A conspiring and engaging smile crossed her face. "Rightly or wrongly, we've kept it quiet for generations...it was an unspoken understanding that we should keep it secret. But which ever way you look at it, Bethany, it was tragic. Elizabeth...the poor lass never did get to Penhill, never did test the kindness of the fisher folk. It was the cliff fall: one minute she was waving to the men in their boats and the next, well, you can see from the castle land slide that she wouldn't have stood a chance. Put it this way, she was never heard of or seen again." At Bethany's sudden intake of breath her mother paused. "I know, lass. Just thinking about it makes your blood run cold," she said, the fingers of her left hand spreading out around the lump growing in her throat.

"So there's no record of her death, no mark of remembrance. Maybe that's why she's always -." Realising that she was voicing her thoughts, Bethany stopped short.

"She *is* always? She *is* always, nothing!" her mother said in the no nonsense tone Bethany hated. "She died! She died suffocating under tons of earth and she's still there whatever some folks -"

"- might say, mum?" Bethany's words seemed to hang in the air. Mrs. Mallinson got up. She paced the floor. Bethany waited.

"Yes…anyway…"

"Hang on, mum!" Bethany held her mother's gaze. "Come on. Say it!" Embarrassed by her earlier outburst Mrs. Mallinson's tone softened. She sighed. "They say they've seen her up on the cliff. You know how stories get about," she said with a dismissive wave of her hand. "The thing is they hadn't the machinery to shift all that rubble in those days so…well, better to be entombed for all eternity than to disturb the poor lass! As for the bairn. Of course the fisher folk knew about her and rushed up there. They found the open barrel with the letter lying in the crib beside the little soul." Mrs. Mallinson stared out at the dark, brooding sky…"Yes," she said. "It was a sorry business and an upsetting one, which is perhaps why some Pandora's boxes should be kept under lock and key. But not ours, not ours…not any more," she said, patting Bethany's knee.

Chapter 37

"Not a good night I take it," her mother said when Bethany appeared for breakfast the next morning. With a hang dog look peeping out from a mop of unruly hair, she sank into a chair. "You look as if you've been pulled through a hedge backwards!"

"An understatement, mum. It was horrendous. I seemed to be dreaming the whole night long."

"Well, I did give you a lot to think about!"

"I'll say, but it was more about Robert. It was such a cruel way to die," Bethany said, rubbing her eyes free of the gravel that always seemed to build up after a restless night.

"Hm…horrible, but don't take on now," her mother said when she heard her daughter's voice crack.

"But my dream was so real. He was scratching his name on the rock face. I only saw his profile but he was so thin and the skin was stretched over his face. It was ashen. He was a broken man, mum."

"Oh, Bethany, when are you going to let this go?" she said, putting a comforting hand on her shoulder. "You'll be making yourself ill, girl. And there's nothing you can do about it. Tearing yourself apart won't change anything. What's done is done."

"I know. I do try. I just can't get the image of him crouching there out of my mind. It was such a tiny space, a cold, damp tomb. And the stench! His own waste was spilling over his bare feet and I had to get out, get out to breathe in the salt sea air. I staggered down the cliff face. I had to get down and escape but the gorse bushes kept holding me back like in a fairy tale. In the end I wrenched myself free and ended up in The Bolts. But there he was again…Robert bent low in the gloom of the alleyway, sweating and retching…"

"Come on now, that's enough," her mother said, stroking her hair but Bethany hadn't finished. She pulled away.

"Yes, but don't you see," she said with a plea that tore at her mother's heart. "I reached out to him, mum. I touched his arm. He turned then, but it was Daniel's eyes that I saw, Daniel's huge, terrified eyes set in a sunken face. They were appealing to me and…and…and -"

"Yes, yes, Bethany, but come on now," she said, holding her even closer. This time Bethany stayed there until there were no more tears to cry.

"Now look at you," her mother said. "I don't know what that boyfriend of yours will say when he sees you all red-eyed and woe-be-gone!"

"It's OK. I'm not seeing him till tomorrow."

"Ah…" Mrs. Mallinson delved into her apron pocket for a hanky and wiped her daughter's eyes. "He called," she said. "I didn't want to wake you."

"Really? So what did he say, what did he want? Come on, tell me, mum!"

"Well," her mother said, nibbling on a piece of cold toast, "he…I…oh lawks…down the wrong way!" she said, between bursts of wheezing and coughing. Bethany began to pat her back "Harder, Bethany!" she said between gasps…"It 'll… it'll pass!" And pass it did, but it was a full five minutes before her mother's rasping voice eased.

"Well?" Bethany said, impatience etched on her face.

"Well what? Oh, good gracious, girl. Give me a minute!" Bethany sighed. She waited and waited some more.

"Ah, that's better," her mother said, worrying the end of her nose with her handkerchief.

"OK. So - what - did - you - say?" Bethany said, slowly enunciating each word.

"There's no need to make out I'm an imbecile!" her mother said. "Just wait till you have something go down the wrong way, then you'll know about it, my lass. And let's hope it won't be tonight because I've invited him to supper and I don't want you spluttering and choking and blotting your copy book! He suggested a walk, said something about wanting to experience heaven again," she said with a knowing smile.

"Oh, mum," Embarrassed and winded by Bethany's enthusiastic bear hug, her mother had to catch her breath.

"Yes, well...that's all right then! I just thought it was time I got to know the young man!"

"Daniel!" Bethany said, catching her mother's eye.

"Yes, dear! Daniel it is!" she replied, cupping her hands around her daughter's cheeks.

Using the living room mirror, Bethany scrunched her hair. Then, "Have I made the right choice?" she said, smoothing her hands down the front of her Levis.

"You'll do," but her mother adjusted the straps on Bethany's lemon, camisole top just the same. "Still, I'm pleased to see you're going to pop a cardi over your shoulders. It might be summer, but it can get a bit chilly when the sun goes down. There's a breeze and -"

"Mum, stop fussing!" but her hyena grin deflected any real hurt her mother might have felt. "Whoops! He's here!" she said, peering out of the window and rushing to the door. "Hya!" Daniel's smile had set her heart racing.

"Long time no see! Is your ankle OK?" he said, grinning and warming his face on her blush.

"Fine- and stop that!"

"Hello Mrs, Mallinson," he said, giving her a conspiratorial wink.

"So you've both got it all worked out. It's a walk I take it?" Bethany said.

"Yes, I thought we might wander down to the harbour. The tide's out. We could paddle."

"That would do your ankle the world of good Bethany. It's nature's way!"

"Then I thought we could have a drink at The Jolly Tar. Will you join us later, Mrs. Mallinson? I could pop back and walk you down."

"Gracious me, no, but it's good of you to ask, Daniel," she said, throwing a knowing smile to Bethany. "Besides, I've got a lot to do. You'll be as hungry as hunters when you get back after all that sea air. So off you go now but watch that ankle on the cobbled ways! Oh and say hello to Walter for me!"

"I think we've moved on!" Daniel said, catching and returning Mrs. Mallinson's wave.

"Yeah, she's been great, ever since...Oh, I've got such a lot to tell you... but first tell me quickly, what's been happening at school?" A sudden, uninvited thought crossed her mind.

"Well, no! The rumour hasn't quite gone away," he said, picking up on her anxiety. "But don't worry, that's only because I've been wandering around with a permanent grin on my face!"

"Oh, Daniel! I wish you'd be serious."

"OK, misery!" Bethany floored him with a look. "Right, well, it wasn't even going to be a nine day wonder. Not after I'd finished with Smithard."

"You didn't -?"

"Biff him? Well, he's still whole and, if at all possible, even a bit more wholesome! It's as Ron said, he fancies you like crazy, has done for years! I think our snogging session on the beach was more than the nerd could cope with. Mind you, who'd blame him!" Daniel teased. "I mean, it's not every day a guy gets to -"

"Yeah, yeah, stop fantasizing and get on with it!"

"Yes boss, OK. No sweat. Shall I say we came to an understanding!"

"Really?"

Daniel paused, let go of her hand and wandered over to the other side of the cobbled way that led to the sea front.

"What...what's up now?" Bethany said in tone that bore more than a trace of suspicion. "What have you done!"

"Not a lot. I just told him he'd better back track- undo all the damage he'd done, that's all."

"And he agreed? Just like that?"

"Yep, but only after I'd promised him he could pick you up when I ditched you!"

"Daniel Foster! You b -!" she mouthed.

"Whoa! Be careful, Freckles." Daniel sauntered back. "I'll have none of that there bad language!" he said putting an arm around her. "Well, come on, I couldn't leave the poor chap without any hope at all, could I?" he said as they headed for the beach.

"Hm…some sort of a jerk you turned out to be! So how long do you intend to stay around, Casanova?"

"Well now, how long is a piece of string, Freckles?"

"Is that your clichéd way of saying you'll be there for me forever...love me, I mean?" Bethany asked, slipping off her shoes and slurring her toes into the warm sand. "Well...answer me!"

"I've told you before, Freckles. Forever is a long, long time! The point is, are you up for it?"

"Oh I suppose I could give it a whirl," she said, looking up at him with a coquettish smile, "besides..." Bethany glanced over to the horizon, "I think we're bound by a stronger force." Daniel gave her a searching look. It was enough. The time was right. "Last night I dreamt, well, it was weird. Awesome really. Robert was in the dungeon in that tiny space and I was there with him. It was disgusting, the smell and everything. I had to get out and stumbled down the castle slopes into The Bolts just like we did that day, remember? Robert was there, naked from the waist up and retching. He'd been whipped, Daniel. His back was scoured and when I touched his shoulder, he shot round like a wounded animal, snarling with anger and yet, subservient, like a dog that's been ill treated. I wanted so much to see his face, but when he turned round, it was you!"

"Strange. Down there in The Bolts that time, well, I've never felt so bad, not ill exactly but wretched, drained and trapped, as if my world had come to an end and all the time a deep sense of loss." For a moment or two Daniel was silent, thoughtful. "So we know what happened to Robert, the poor blighter," he said, wrapping his

arm around her "but Elizabeth? I wonder where she got to."
Bethany paused. Daniel followed her gaze.

"Up up there, Daniel," she said, nodding toward the coastline.
Elizabeth died up there in Little Penhill. It was that cliff fall, you
know, the one your dad told us about. But they never did find her
body so I guess she's still there, buried deep in the cliff face...oh
God...just think Daniel, where we spent the night. But the baby,
Eliza, survived!"

"Hold on, Bethany. Who said anything about a baby and how
do you know?"

"Mum knew all along. She got the family tree out and guess
what? We're related to Elizabeth!"

"What? Elizabeth Rossitor?"

"The very same. It's true. I'll show you when we get back. And
that's why mum's been so funny about everything. And I had a
sister, another Bethany, but she died and -"

"Another sister? Hang on! You're going to have to slow down,
Freckles. You're losing me again."

"Yeah...yeah, I know," she said with an indulgent sigh but just
let me tell you about the barrel!"

"Go on then. What of it?"

"It opens. Mum opened it for me and it all fits, don't you see?"
she said, squeezing his arm.

Bewildered, Daniel scratched his head. "Well," he said, feeling
the strength of her conviction, "I'm trying!"

Bethany paused to catch the lump in her throat. "It's strange,
Daniel, and so sad," she said at last. "There was a letter.
Apparently, Elizabeth fell pregnant but when the baby was born
Robert agreed to go back to the castle and tell Lord Rossitor he had
a grandchild. And that's another thing," she said, interrupting the
flow. "When you left me on the moors I was desperate not to let
you go, remember? I was so worried, but my thoughts about you
maybe being lost on the moors were all mixed up with Robert. I
kept on having kind of flash backs. I saw him...saw him chained up,
even heard his leg irons jangling. It was really weird..." Bethany's

words tailed off. Snuggling into Daniel's shoulder, she fought off the tears. "God, why am I so paranoid? It's ridiculous…it happened such a long time ago."

"Know what…I can't believe I'm going to say this! Sure you want to know what I think?" he said, leading her to the sea wall.

"Try me," she said between sniffles.

As if to hide his unease, Daniel pulled on his lower lip. "Well…I think…I think Elizabeth loved Robert as I hope you love me. I know he loved her as much as I do you. It's as if -" His pause was palpable. Bethany waited "as if Elizabeth was looking for someone to sort of fit the bill, a couple who would, you know, understand and empathize, a couple who'd be receptive to the paranormal…to your ghost maybe…and you definitely were. I mean. I've always known you were two people, sort of. The Bethany of this world is a tomboy, reactionary, always confronting things. The other Bethany has been like a lost soul, anxiously searching for something. Think of it this way. All this time you've been living two, even three lives. Elizabeth couldn't rest. You couldn't. All this time you've been wrestling with what you saw as reality. And she appeared to you…only you."

"So you think we were sort of chosen…and you really believe that?"

"I'm beginning to!"

"Oh, Daniel! At last…at last!" she said, linking arms "It's been such a long, lonely journey with no one to understand…no one to share it with."

"Have you told your mum about it?"

"No. She's not into the spirit world. It'll take time, but I will." Bethany looked at the play of light and shadow on the water and upward to the coastline…to the pale pink sky smudged dove grey. "Oh my God!" Bethany ducked. In a flurry of soft white down a seagull squawked and flapped its wings above her head. Waving her arms she warded it off. "That was close," she said, blowing down her nose to rid herself of the wisps of fine feathers. "Some of the locals want the council to organize a cull. For some reason they're becoming bolder."

"Oh I don't know." Surprised by Daniel's quiet tone of voice, Bethany followed his gaze. In a playful exhibition of flashing, white underbelly, two seagulls swooped and dived, flirting outrageously. "They're just looking for attention, a bit like you do!" he said with a grin.

"Hm...maybe." With a sigh and a Mona Lisa smile Bethany nestled closer. "Know what though...somehow I think there might be two seagulls on my sill tonight or maybe even none! Still, let's not go down that road at the moment. Let's talk about you and your dad instead. Why can't you get along? What's -?" Daniel put his finger to her lips.

"Another time, Bethany," he said, presenting her with a feather from her tangled red hair. "Another time!"